THE PURSUIT OF A DUCHESS

THE LADIES OF THE ARISTOCRACY

LINDA RAE SANDE

Twisted Teacup
PUBLISHING

ALSO BY LINDA RAE SANDE

The Daughters of the Aristocracy

The Kiss of a Viscount

The Grace of a Duke

The Seduction of an Earl

The Sons of the Aristocracy

Tuesday Nights

The Widowed Countess

My Fair Groom

The Sisters of the Aristocracy

The Story of a Baron

The Passion of a Marquess

The Desire of a Lady

The Brothers of the Aristocracy

The Love of a Rake

The Caress of a Commander

The Epiphany of an Explorer

The Widows of the Aristocracy

The Gossip of an Earl

The Enigma of a Widow

The Secrets of a Viscount

The Widowers of the Aristocracy

The Dream of a Duchess

The Vision of a Viscountess

The Conundrum of a Clerk

The Charity of a Viscount

The Cousins of the Aristocracy

The Promise of a Gentleman

The Pride of a Gentleman

The Holidays of the Aristocracy

The Christmas of a Countess

The Knot of a Knight

The Holiday of a Marquess

The Snow Angel of a Duke

The Heirs of the Aristocracy

The Angel of an Astronomer

The Puzzle of a Bastard

The Choice of a Cavalier

The Bargain of a Baroness

The Jewel of an Earl's Heir

The Vixen of a Viscount

The Honor of an Heir

The Rose of a Sultan's Son

The Ladies of the Aristocracy

The Lady of a Grump

The Lady of a Sultan

The Wager of a Wallflower

Beyond the Aristocracy

The Pleasure of a Pirate

The Making of a Mistress

The Bride of a Baronet

The Caton of a Captain

Puss and Pots

The Betrothal of a Baron

Stella of Akrotiri

Origins

Deminon

Diana

The Lyon's Den (Dragonblade Publishing)

The Courage of a Lyon

The Lady of a Lyon

Note: Translations of select titles are available in German, Italian, Spanish and Portuguese.

PROLOGUE

ay 1814, Mayfair, Woodleigh House

M A sense of dread had been building in Michael, Lord Crawford, from the moment he entered the huge mansion owned by the Woodleigh dukedom. Although he was sure he wasn't late, his chronometer had stopped at exactly one o'clock, and no matter what he tried, the timepiece would not restart.

"His Grace, the Duke of Woodleigh, will see you now," the portly butler said when he reappeared from wherever he had gone more than ten minutes earlier. With his pocket watch out of commission, Michael couldn't be sure that much time had passed, but it certainly felt far longer.

He followed the servant past several closed doors to one that stood open to reveal a dark paneled study. With its coffered ceiling above and Turkish carpeting below, it reminded Michael of his banker's office—stuffy, pretentious, and smelling of cheroot smoke. The man sitting behind the gigantic ebony desk even looked as if he could be a banker.

"You must be Crawford?"

"I am, Your Grace," he acknowledged, bowing deeply.

"My butler tells me we had an appointment." Bertram, Duke of Woodleigh, waved to a wooden chair in front of his desk. "Have a seat."

The manner in which the words were spoken had Michael on alert. The footman tasked with sending word of his desire for a meeting had said the duke would see him.

Had the servant been mistaken?

"I sent a request earlier this morning, Your Grace. The reply said you could meet me at two o'clock."

The older man waved a hand, not bothering to look up from whatever had his attention. "Yes, yes. What's this about?"

His hands pressed onto the tops of his doeskin-encased thighs, Michael said, "Your daughter, Your Grace. I'd like your permission to court her."

Woodleigh raised his head for the first time since Michael had entered the study and regarded him with a curious expression. "Are you speaking of Lady Helena?"

"I am, my lord."

Settling back into his leather chair, the duke let out a huff of breath. "That's not going to be possible," he stated.

"Your Grace?" Michael swallowed.

"You're too late. She's already been promised to someone else," Woodleigh stated.

For a moment, Michael was sure his heart had stopped beating. His vision grayed at the edges. "Does... does *she* know that, Your Grace?"

One of Woodleigh's graying brows arched up. "Well, I should hope so. She was present when the papers were signed," he replied. The brow dropped when he seemed to reconsider his comment. "Although she was rather young at the time." He chuckled softly. "It's been fifteen years or so since I signed that contract."

"So... an arranged marriage then?" Michael asked in a small voice. His heart had begun beating again, the pounding so loud he feared the older man could hear it from across the desk.

"Well, of course. Have you already spoken to her about courtship?" the duke asked suddenly.

"I... I have, Your Grace. From her comments on the matter, I don't believe she's aware she is betrothed."

Woodleigh's eyes narrowed with suspicion. "Did you already propose marriage?"

Knowing his pained expression gave him away, Michael merely nodded. "We have been acquaintances for many years, my lord. My regard for her—"

"Matters not." The duke set aside his pen. "Have you two been playing house?"

Michael's eyes rounded. "Of course not, Your Grace. I would never. Not without your permission to marry her."

"Well, that's a relief," Woodleigh remarked, waving his hand as if in dismissal. His gaze turned to the papers on his desk.

Not about to give up, Michael blurted, "If she

married me, she would one day be the Marchioness of Fenwick." Lifting his chin in defiance, he added, "I love her."

The duke rolled his eyes. "She's going to be the Duchess of Weston," he countered. "She is betrothed to Weston's oldest whelp." His attention darted to the side for a moment. "Hugh… Herbert…

"Lord Harcourt?" Michael stated in disbelief, a rock falling into his stomach at the thought of his Helena with Harcourt Sheppard.

"Harcourt, yes. That's his name," Woodleigh said, a pudgy forefinger waving about. "There's a provision in the contract which releases her from the obligation in the event he dies before they wed, but I'm quite certain he'll be taking my daughter to wife before the end of this decade."

Michael swallowed. For a moment, he wondered if an accident could be arranged. One in which Harcourt Sheppard met his untimely death by the hand of a highwayman or a deranged horse. Perhaps an especially hard punch during a bare knuckle match. A stray bullet from a hunting foray. A perfectly placed stab from a fencing foil with a missing blossom.

Mayhap he would be required to challenge the arse to a duel in Wimbledon Common. Having never shot a pistol, he was as likely to shoot himself as he was Harcourt, though.

"I assure you, Your Grace, I hold Lady Helena in the highest regard. I would never do anything to hurt her."

From the way the duke narrowed his eyes, Michael

thought for a moment he had succeeded in changing Woodleigh's mind. When the man scoffed and then chuckled, he realized he hadn't.

"Go home, Lord Crawford. Find another young lady with whom to play house. God knows there must be a dozen diamonds of the first water who would suit the Fenwick marquessate," Woodleigh said on a sigh. "Helena is marrying Harcourt Sheppard, heir to the Weston dukedom."

Not about to give up so easily, Michael puffed out his chest. "And if she doesn't?" Stunned at hearing the challenge in his own voice, he quickly added, "Your Grace?"

"I'll send her to a nunnery," the duke announced. "Now off with you." Woodleigh returned his attention to whatever he had been reading when Michael arrived.

Finally rising from his chair, Michael bowed deeply and backed out of the study. When he turned to head for the front door, he stopped short and blinked.

Lady Helena stood before him, tears streaming down her face. Dressed in a white gown with mahogany ringlets framing her oval face, she would have appeared positively angelic but for her reddened nose and puffy eyes.

"My lady," he said softly.

"Oh, Michael," she whispered before a sob robbed her of breath. "I'm so sorry. I have no memory of a betrothal. Especially not to *him*," she added as more tears fell. "I love *you*."

Michael pulled a handkerchief from his waistcoat pocket and held it against one of her cheeks. He stared at her for several seconds, memorizing everything about her. "I share your sentiments, I assure you, my love. Best of luck," he said in a quiet voice.

He took her hand to his lips, kissing it in the manner of how he wished he could kiss her on the lips. When he let go, he straightened and strode towards the front door. Even when he heard her keening cries and sobs, he took his leave of Woodleigh House without so much as a backward glance.

CHAPTER 1
THE END IS A BEGINNING

Thirty-years later, Weston Hall, Mayfair

Giving her lady's maid a grin of satisfaction, Helena, Duchess of Weston, watched as two footmen removed an old wooden trunk from the mistress suite and headed for the attic.

"Good riddance," she murmured on a sigh.

A year's worth of widow's weeds were stuffed into that trunk. Clothes she had no intention of ever wearing again. She might have asked that they be burned, but she feared if they were, someone else in the family would die and she would have to have her modiste make new ones.

"I'll see to airing out your other gowns, Your Grace," Stapleton said, dipping a curtsy before she headed to the dressing room. "Have you an entertainment you plan to attend in the next day or so?"

Helena shook her head. "I've absolutely no idea," she replied. "But it better not involve playing cards. I have had my fill of playing cards this past year." Ever since her son, Alfred, Duke of Weston, had returned from his Grand Tour, correspondence addressed to both of them hadn't made it out of the study. Despite a talk with the butler, Pritchard, asking that social correspondence be directed to her instead of Alfred, the only letters delivered to her upstairs salon were those addressed specifically to her.

"But the Season has begun, has it not?" Stapleton asked.

"Indeed," Helena replied. "It seems invitations are being delivered, but... not to me."

For a moment, she imagined Alfred withholding them as a sort of punishment. He was angry with her, but for what, she had no clue. She couldn't help that his father, Harcourt, had died whilst Alfred was in Greece. She couldn't help that none of her letters bearing the news reached him despite having been sent to the hotels where his itinerary said he would be.

Nor could she help the sense of relief she had felt when Harcourt had died. His illness, although not chronic, had lasted less than a fortnight. For a man who claimed he would live forever, he refused to believe his end was near until the very last day.

"You'll have to help him, Helena," he had said, wheezing between every third or fourth word.

"I will," she had assured him.

"I never taught him what he needs to know to—"

"I know," she had interrupted in an attempt to make him save his breath.

"I am sorry I doubted you."

Those words had her reacting in shock, for Harcourt Sheppard, seventh Duke of Weston, had rarely apologized for anything.

Perhaps he misread her expression, for he added, "You were never unfaithful, were you? Never played me for the fool?"

She had inhaled sharply, her dark brows rising. "Of course not," she replied, her shock turning to anger. "How could you think such a thing?"

He answered with a fit of coughing, and when he finally regained his breath, he had said, "I know you always loved another."

Helena remembered straightening, her spine rigid as she considered how he would know such a thing. She had never spoken of her first love. Her only love. She had never put her thoughts of Michael into writing—to him or to anyone else.

"Really?" was all she could think to say. What else could she say? She had no intention of confirming his suspicion if that's all it was, especially if he later recovered from his illness.

"It bothered me after a time," he said, his voice raspy. "Which is why..." He swallowed and seemed to struggle for breath. "Why I haven't bedded you for several years. Why I didn't get another child on you."

Not sure how to respond, Helena merely stared at her husband of seven-and-twenty years in disbelief.

The cur.

How different her life would have been if Michael *had* been allowed to marry her. Michael had loved her. Kissed her with passion. Touched her in ways Harcourt had never attempted. Pleasured her until she had to beg him to stop.

Made her fall in love with him.

If she had been allowed to marry Michael, she might have had far more than just two children. They might have raised a boisterous brood in a home filled with laughter and love.

Considering what might have been, annoyance with her husband had her overcoming her silence. "And here I thought it was because you hired a mistress."

He visibly winced. "We had a contract."

"We *have* a contract, which I have not broken," she stated. "I'm not to take a lover until I have delivered an heir *and* a spare." The first she had managed within a year of their marriage. The second... impossible to have accomplished since Harcourt hadn't seen fit to keeping up his end of the bargain.

"I am sorry," he had said in a whisper.

A moment later, it was apparent he had taken his last breath.

Their only daughter, Amelia, had been standing in the doorway, thankfully unable to hear their last words. Helena was sure she would never forget the girl's mournful wails at realizing her father had died.

Eighteen years old and only a month into her first Season, Amelia was relegated to mourning when she should have been attending balls and *soirées*, garden parties and the theatre.

With Alfred away on his Grand Tour and no man of

business to see to the dukedom, Helena had simply stepped into her late husband's study and did what she could to see to it invoices were paid and household accounts were maintained. She handled correspondence and kept in contact with the foremen of the farms and the mines.

Six months after Weston's death, when life at Weston Hall had settled into a new routine, Alfred returned from the Mediterranean.

At first, Helena had felt sorry for her son. Harcourt had done nothing to prepare him for the job of running a dukedom. Had done nothing to apprise him of the political requirements of the position. Had done nothing when it came to documenting banking information or informing him of existing contracts.

Despite her offers to help, Alfred sequestered himself in the study, as if he was hiding from the world. Insisting she could see to some of the business on his behalf, Helena was stunned when he not only rebuffed her offers, but his manner towards her abruptly changed. He would accept no offers of help. No recommendations and certainly no advice.

Especially from her.

Helena was forced to allow him to find out on his own what it would take to be the Duke of Weston.

Now that she had endured his cold manner and days on end of little or no conversation, his words always terse, she had decided enough was enough. Alfred could not be allowed to continue to treat her as he had been doing.

. . .

Her patience at an end, Helena, Duchess of Weston, stood on the threshold of the Weston Hall study and cleared her throat.

Loudly.

Alfred lifted his head and regarded her as if he hadn't known she had been standing there for several minutes. "What is it, Mother?" he asked.

She crossed her arms and scoffed. "You tell me. Pritchard said you wished to see me."

His dark brows furrowing for a moment, Alfred appeared momentarily flummoxed. "There was something," he murmured before finally shaking his head. "I can't remember what it was, though."

Helena narrowed her eyes. "Can't remember? Or won't?" She allowed her anger to sound in her words.

The way he looked at her had her giving a start. She was sure she saw tears collecting in the corners of his eyes.

Inhaling softly, she blinked and then hurried to join him behind the desk. She took his head between her hands and kissed the top of his head. "I do not know what is wrong between us, but it must end," she whispered.

She hoped she might feel the tenseness in his body lessen. The rigidness of his spine give way to a slump. Instead, he merely knocked one of her hands away. "Leave me be, Mother. I have work to do," he said.

Given his cold response, Helena stepped back.

Although she was tempted to scold him, she instead took her leave of the study and slowly climbed the stairs to the parlor.

Her cup of tea had long ago grown cold, but it certainly wasn't as cold as her son had become since his return from his Grand Tour. She poured a new cup and settled into a chair near the fireplace.

"What do you suppose happened to Alfred?"

Unaware her daughter had come into the parlor behind her, Helena nearly spilled her tea. "I wish I knew," she replied. "Will you join me?"

Amelia shook her head. "I wish to go to Hatchard's this afternoon to shop for another book or two," she replied. Although she would have preferred shopping at the Temple of the Muses, the older bookshop had burned down three years prior. "I was headed upstairs to change clothes, but I couldn't help but overhear Alfred's last remark to you. He's become so cross."

"Indeed," Helena replied. "And I've absolutely no idea why. He won't tell me what's wrong."

"Do you think it has something to do with Father? With the dukedom?"

Helena gave her daughter an assessing glance. As much as she was worried about her son, she had concerns about Amelia as well. The girl was frequently off to the bookshop or her new friend's house. She was always accompanied by her lady's maid, of course, but her absences from Weston Hall were becoming more frequent of late. She had a thought Amelia might have discovered gambling. It would be easy for her to place a friendly wager over a hand of cards.

"Are you going to play cards?"

Amelia gave a start. "At the bookshop? No, of course not," she replied. "Today is the day of the week the new books are put out for sale."

Helena nodded, remembering it was Tuesday. "Very good. Do be careful, and have the groom join you in the shop. You could be kidnapped—"

"Mother."

"—and your brother doesn't need another problem on his plate right now."

At hearing this last, Amelia swallowed another word of protest. "Yes, Mother."

The young lady hurried from the parlor, Helena sighing when she was once again alone.

This would be her last day spending an afternoon alone in Weston Hall, though. Now that she was out of mourning, she would be paying calls starting the very next day.

And attending an entertainment or two if any invitations made it past her son.

CHAPTER 2
AN ASSIGNATION AT THE BOOKSHOP

few minutes later, upstairs in Weston Hall

Impatience had Amelia sighing as her lady's maid placed yet another pin into her top knot. "Really, Trimble, must you take so long? I'm only going to the bookshop."

The lady's maid dropped the pin she had picked up from the dressing table and stepped back. "Oh, pardon, my lady. I quite forgot you're in a hurry."

Amelia had to swallow her initial response. Although Trimble was a gifted stylist and fastidious with her clothes, the lady's maid always seemed as if she was dicked in the knob. Any hint of displeasure or comments of a critical nature had her bawling her eyes out, but she didn't take compliments well, either. "I'll need you to accompany me to Hatchard's," Amelia said. "The newest books should be on the shelves by now."

"Of course, my lady. I'll just fetch my shawl and be right down." The servant took her leave of Amelia's bedchamber, dipping a quick curtsy before she disappeared.

Amelia allowed a sigh of relief. If they left in five minutes, they could make it to the bookshop in time for her assignation with Philip, the Earl of Crawford.

Third floor, second reading room on the right.

Her heart immediately racing at the thought of seeing the young man again, Amelia pulled on a spencer and matching bonnet. Short white gloves followed before she captured the handle of her favorite reticule and stood before the cheval mirror in the corner.

She grimaced. Why did bonnets have to make their wearer look so idiotic? Even the most outrageous hat didn't youthen a young lady back to her days in the schoolroom like a bonnet did.

Plucking the bonnet from her head and then wincing when she disturbed Trimble's creative top knot, she tossed the offending headwear aside and searched in her dressing room for a small hat.

Once she had the small-brimmed felted bowler in place, she hurried down to the front door.

"Your carriage awaits, my lady," Pritchard said from where he stood holding the door.

"I've spoken with Mother, so she knows I'm off to my favorite bookseller," she said as she breezed past the servant.

"Very good, my lady."

Pritchard was about to close the door when Trimble, breathless, stepped around him and darted out to follow her mistress to the carriage.

"I'll be going to the third floor," Amelia stated when they were settled in the velvet squabs. "You're certainly welcome to shop on whichever floor you'd like, and we can simply meet one another after an hour."

Trimble glanced out the window. "If you don't mind, I'll go up to the top floor. Where the least expensive books are located. I have some money with me, so I'd like to buy a book."

Amelia blinked. "I didn't know you could read."

Trimble dipped her head. "Not well. Not yet. But I'm learning with Mrs. Pritchard's help," she explained, referring to the housekeeper.

"So... what sorts of books are you looking to buy?"

The lady's maid furrowed a brow. "Primers, I believe they're called," she replied. "Did you ever use one when you were in the schoolroom?"

Chuckling softly, Amelia nodded. "I had a governess until I was fourteen," she replied. "So, yes, I had to use a different primer every year." She gave a start. "Which has me wondering if they aren't somewhere in the house. Probably in the library. I'll speak with Mother. See if I can't get her approval to let you use them."

Trimble's eyes widened. "That would be terribly generous."

Amelia shrugged. "They're not being used now, nor will they until..." She stopped speaking and stared at the servant.

"What is it, my lady?"

Giving her head a shake, Amelia said, "I was thinking

they wouldn't be used again until my brother had children."

Trimble's eyes rounded. "Is he courting someone?" Her query sounded innocent enough, but Amelia knew any answer she provided would be shared with the other servants of Weston Hall.

"Not that I'm aware," Amelia commented. "But I'm sure Mother will be making some recommendations in that regard very soon."

She had a passing thought that if Alfred made more of an effort at the balls they were to attend this Season, he might actually discover a young lady suitable enough to be his duchess. Amelia personally knew several candidates, of course, but she wasn't sure she wanted any of them to be her sister by marriage.

There was one she had become fast friends with, though—Lady Violet Cummings, daughter of a marquess and sister of the man she was about to meet on the third story of Hatchard's.

Perhaps an introduction would be in order at the next ball.

Except...

Did she really wish to subject her new best friend to the less-than-amiable Alfred, Duke of Weston? Her brother had become rather cranky of late. Full of himself. And far too proud.

She had no idea what had happened to change him so much from the friendly boy he had been when they were younger. Attending boarding school hadn't been the reason—he returned from Eton significantly taller but no different in his behavior—other than he seemed to know how to play pranks on unsuspecting victims.

Mayhap the several years at Cambridge University had been the reason, or perhaps something had happened on his Grand Tour.

Had he been played by a card sharp? Robbed at knife point? Had his advances been rebuffed by an aristocrat's daughter?

Or was his behavior simply due to the death of their father? Taking on the role of the Duke of Weston seemed almost too much for him to bear.

Perhaps it was.

"Is something wrong, my lady?"

Pulled from her reverie, Amelia regarded her lady's maid with surprise. "Not at all. I was merely considering what sort of books I'd like to purchase today," she said.

The coach stuttered to a halt in front of the five-story bookshop, and the two stepped down to the pavement with the help of the driver, Simmons. "We'll be an hour," she told him, tamping down the excitement she felt when she recognized Philip's phaeton parked at the curb. A young street urchin held the reins as he casually leaned against a post. "Mother has asked if you might guard the door."

"Very good, my lady," Simmons said, his gaze briefly following hers before he hurried to the bookseller's door. He opened it for her and the maid and waited until they were inside before taking up a position near the door to wait.

Leading her lady's maid up the stairs to the third

floor, Violet paused to wish Trimble good luck in finding a primer and then turned her attention to the shelves featuring the newest books.

When she was sure the servant was on her way up the rest of the stairs, she ducked into the second reading room and stopped short near the entrance.

Philip was there to meet her, but there were others sitting about, their heads bent whilst they read books they might or might not buy.

"I was beginning to worry," Philip said as he took her gloved hand to his lips.

"I apologize. My lady's maid took longer than usual," she murmured, nervously glancing about to be sure she didn't recognize anyone.

"I think I found the perfect book for you, my lady," he said a bit louder. "I believe it arrived today." He offered an arm and led her out of the reading room to the opposite side of the third floor, where another reading room was located. More of an alcove with a chair and a side table, the room was empty.

He shut the door and quickly took her into his arms. "I have looked forward to playing house with you all day," he whispered.

"Not as much as I have," she countered. She stood on tiptoe and placed a hand on his shoulder, inviting the quick kiss he bestowed on her.

"Speaking of playing house, I have something I'd like us to discuss," he said, which had her stepping back in surprise. The last time they had met like this, they had spent most of their time in an embrace, kissing one another and sharing their secrets in soft murmurs.

"You sound terribly serious," she accused.

"That's because… well, it is. The thing of it is, I would like you to be my wife. My eventual marchioness," he whispered.

Given their behavior since their initial interaction during a ball, Philip's words might have been expected. The two had been meeting in the bookshop for months, playfully flirting with one another until the flirting led to playful kisses and finally to passionate kissing and fondling.

His words still had Amelia grinning in delight, though.

"I would love to be your wife," she replied. "To play house for real. I think I can manage the duties of a marchioness. Especially if they're anything like that of a duchess."

He nodded. "It's a relief to hear you say the words," he murmured. "There's only the matter of gaining Weston's permission to wed you."

Amelia inhaled softly. "Perhaps asking permission to court me would be better. For appearances' sake," she replied.

Philip seemed to think on her suggestion before he nodded. "Agreed."

They stared at one another for a moment before Philip audibly sighed. "There is one potential problem. I'm hoping it won't be an issue, but—"

"What is it?" Worry sounded in her voice, and one of

her hands gripped the lapel of his top coat, as if she needed it for support.

"Your brother."

Amelia blinked. "Weston?" Usually she would have referred to him as Alfred, but given the six months he had spent in the role of a duke, his serious manner and pompous attitude had her calling him by his title.

"Yes. I'm afraid that although we used to be the best of friends when we were younger, something happened whilst we were at Cambridge," Philip explained. "I'm not exactly sure what I did to offend him—"

"Probably nothing," she said in a whisper.

"I was thinking, perhaps if I paid a call on your mother first—"

"That's an excellent idea," Amelia said with excitement. "She'll be thrilled at the idea of me marrying. She can be the one to let Weston know there is someone interested so that when you do meet with him, he'll already be expecting the question."

Although he agreed with her assessment—to a point—Philip didn't seem happy with the plan. "We could try that, yes," he said, although there wasn't any conviction behind his words.

"Or?" she prompted.

"We could be the scandal of the Season by eloping. Take the Fenwick traveling coach up to Gretna Green and be married there."

Amelia blinked several times before she took a step back. "Oh, Philip. You're playing me. For a moment, I thought you might be serious," she accused, a huge grin brightening her face.

Philip's happy expression faltered before he chuckled softly. "It seemed far more reasonable when I was merely thinking about it," he said with a shrug. "You must know I would do most anything to ensure we can be together."

Staring up at him, her chocolate brown eyes rounding in awe, Amelia said, "You always put voice to the most romantic thoughts."

His lip quirked. "I have them all the time when it comes to you." He pulled her back into his arms and kissed her quite thoroughly. When he finally came up for air, he pressed his lips to her forehead and then to the side of her head not covered by the hat.

"You think about me that much?" she asked quietly, her face heating with a blush.

He nodded. "I know why, too. Now that I've decided I want you as my wife, I'm reminded I'm of an age when I must marry. I need to start my nursery. Do my duty," he explained.

Amelia winced at hearing the word 'duty,' and she knew he saw it. "I do hope you're not reminded only of duty when you think about me."

Chuckling again, he shook his head. "It will not seem like a duty with you," he assured her. "With you, fathering a child will be something I look forward to doing. Often, if possible." He arched a brow, as if he wanted to gauge her reaction.

Sure he was testing her, Amelia said, "Philip Cummings, if you're referring to..." She lowered her voice to a whisper. "Making love, then you should know that I know... well, that is to say... I'm aware of what's... *required*... and..." She swallowed.

"Let me guess. You read it in a book?"

She straightened, her shoulders pulled back. "An illustrated book, actually."

His expression suddenly serious, Philip asked, "That didn't scare you off to the idea of making love with me?"

She shook her head. "Not completely."

Smirking, he kissed her once more. "I won't expect you to do the more salacious acts you no doubt saw in some of those illustrations," he whispered. "Unless... unless you want to."

Sure her face was bright red, Amelia allowed a slight shrug. "I suppose it will depend on how much wine I've had with dinner."

Philip dropped his forehead to hers and grinned. "You are the most delightful creature," he murmured.

She lifted herself on tiptoes and kissed him once more. "I can hardly wait to be yours."

Kissing her lips and then the back of her hand, Philip sighed. "I shouldn't stay any longer. I would hate for you to be a source of gossip because I have kept you in a..." He glanced around. "A closet. I'll take my leave now. Have a seat and wait for a few minutes before you depart," he instructed.

"Understood. When will I see you again?"

He paused before turning the door handle. "Tomorrow night. Will you be at the Everly *soirée*?"

She nodded. "I'll be there."

"Save me the waltzes, if there are any," he said before he slipped out the door.

Amelia crossed her arms and hugged herself as she smiled. Falling into the chair, she opened the book Philip had given her and was well into reading the first chapter when she remembered she wasn't where she was supposed to be.

Trimble was probably already waiting for her.

Pretending interest in the book she was reading, Amelia opened the door and slipped out of the small reading room.

She nearly collided with her lady's maid.

"Oh, pardon, my lady," the maid said as she stepped back in surprise.

"Why, Trimble. I found what I was looking for," she said as she held up the book Philip had given her. "Did you find a primer?"

The lady's maid held two books, one in each hand. She paused a moment before she said, "I'm not sure. There was a very handsome young man who said they were, but..." She leaned in closer. "I could not be sure if he was playing me or telling me the truth."

Amelia glanced down at the spine of the book she held—*A Guide for the Keeping of a House by a Lady*. She rolled her eyes before glancing at Trimble's books. Both had pasteboard covers that made them look as if they had been well-used, but the edges of the pages weren't feathered. "This is a first year primer, and this is a second year primer, so... he did not steer you wrong," she replied. Curious as to who might have helped her lady's maid, she asked, "Would you recognize the young man if you saw him again?"

"Oh, yes, my lady. His name is Crawford, and he had a most happy countenance."

Amelia blinked. "How do you know Lord Crawford?"

"He greeted another gentleman who was climbing the stairs when he was going down the stairs, and that man said his name." When Amelia stepped aside to allow another patron to squeeze by her and enter the alcove, Trimble asked, "Have you two been introduced?"

Indicating they should take their leave, Amelia headed for the stairs. "I have indeed. I've played cards with him at a house party. I've even danced with him several times. He's the son of a marquess." She arched a brow. "I couldn't imagine a better man to be my husband."

They descended the two flights of stairs to the ground floor and made their way to the counter behind which several clerks completed bills of sales for books.

"Ah, Lady Amelia, so good to see you again," Philip said from her right.

Heat suffused her face as she turned to acknowledge the young man who stood in one of the other lines at the counter. "Lord Crawford. Is it true I have you to thank for helping my lady's maid with her choice of books on this fine day?"

Philip grinned, which had a dimple appearing at the base of his left cheek. "It was nothing, my lady," he claimed. "I was happy to help."

Warmth suffused Amelia's cheeks as she lifted the

book he had chosen for her to the countertop. "I came for a new novel or two, but it appears I'll be taking home this," she said, her lip quirking at the same time she arched a brow.

Glancing at the book he had given her—*A Guide for the Keeping of a House by a Lady*—Philip appeared impressed. "It looks as if you'll be in charge of your own house soon," he commented. "Playing wife."

"I do hope so. Sooner rather than later."

His gaze darted about the area around them before he lowered his voice and said, "Then let us hope certain family members can be convinced. I shouldn't want to read in *The Tattler* about how you and your beau were forced to marry in Greta Green."

Amelia's eyes rounded as she quickly glanced around to ensure his comment hadn't been overheard. Satisfied no one was eavesdropping, she whispered, "Then I suppose it's a good idea to keep a trunk packed for such a possibility."

It was Philip's turn to blush, and he did so as a clerk turned to wait on him. "I thank you for the recommendation," he said to Amelia. "I'm sure I'll see you again soon."

"You as well, my lord. Do have a good day."

Amelia was smiling broadly when she and Trimble took their leave of the bookshop.

CHAPTER 3
NEWS AT BREAKFAST

*T*he following day, Fenwick House, Mayfair

Her fork hovering over her breakfast plate whilst she held a letter in her other hand, Violet Cummings gasped softly and looked up to stare at her brother.

Philip, Earl of Crawford, tore his attention from that morning's edition of *The Times* to regard his sister with a curious expression. "What is it?"

"Father," she breathed. "He's coming to London."

Setting aside the newspaper, Philip stared at his sister for a moment before asking, "Does he say when?"

"Well, according to this, he ordered the groom to prepare the traveling coach for the following day. Says he's grown tired of rusticating in the country and wants to join us here at Fenwick House."

For a moment Philip seemed at a loss for words. "He misses you," he finally said.

"He misses *Mother*," Violet countered, dropping the

letter onto the mahogany table. She dipped her fork into coddled eggs and sighed. "Can't say I blame him. They seemed..." She paused as she considered how their parents had behaved with one another. Not as a couple deeply in love, but rather as two people who found one another so amiable, they could have been best friends.

"Friendly," Philip stated. "Which I suppose is the best they could hope for given theirs wasn't a love match."

Violet scoffed softly. "Why do you say it like that?"

For a moment, her brother seemed reluctant to respond, then leaned back in his chair. "Did you ever ask him about Mother? While you were still living there?"

Although Philip had moved to London after finishing university, Violet had remained with their father, Michael, at Fenwick Park in Shropshire, acting as his hostess when he held an occasional dinner party for the local landed gentry or hosted a district ball.

"We talked about Mother frequently," she replied. "Mostly because I wanted to talk about her, though. Not because... not because *he* wanted to." Indeed, for the first year after Barbara Fulton Cummings' death, their father didn't speak of her at all. Not unless Violet mentioned her. Not unless she told him how much she missed her.

Lady Fenwick had been a rather attentive mother. Loving. Determined to see to it her children were worthy of the marquessate into which they had been born.

"Did Father ever tell you how they met?"

Violet lifted a shoulder. "Only that he knew her because her family lived at the Brougham estate during the summers." The neighboring country house frequently hosted visitors from the capital, including the eldest daughter of Charles, Earl of Montaine. Barbara had been expected to wed the son of an earl, but when that young man died of influenza in the winter of 1815, Michael, had asked Charles if he might court her. The earl was happy to give his permission—Barbara would be a marchioness if they married. "I think they knew one another from when they were children," Violet responded. "They used to play together as children."

Philip furrowed a brow. "She died of the same ailment that took the man to whom she was originally betrothed," he remarked. "I wonder if she loved *him*? Or if it was an arranged match?" At Violet's sound of protest, he added, "Aristocrats used to do that, you must know. Arrange marriages for their children. For political reasons, I suppose."

"Father said it was for the money."

Philip winced. "I suppose that could have been the case for some. Certainly not for Father. Not for me, either. I'm going to marry for love."

Helping herself to a toast point, Violet regarded him with a mischievous grin. "I do like the thought of having a sister."

"That's good. Let's hope you two will get along," he countered.

"Oh, we already do," Violet said in a quiet voice.

Philip blinked and then glanced around the breakfast parlor before he said, "How can you possibly know who it is I plan to marry?"

Violet had trouble suppressing an unladylike snort. "Because she and I have already discussed our future as sisters. And I must say, Lady Amelia is a joy to be with. However did you convince her to be your wife?"

The newspaper forgotten, Philip shrugged. "I didn't have to. We've been in love since the first time we danced together. At the beginning of last Season, in fact," he said. "Before she had to go into mourning for her father."

"Love at first sight?" Violet asked, incredulous.

"Not exactly. I mean... we talked for a time. Walked in the gardens. Danced together again." He leaned forward and lowered his voice. "I kissed her goodnight, and ever since... well, I just know I want her to be my marchioness."

"So... love at first sight," Violet accused with a grin. "Have you two already been playing house together?"

"Is that what *she* said?" he asked in a whisper.

"Not exactly. But... she was rather concerned when she fell so hard for you. She feared you would think her fast."

He scoffed. "I never once thought that," he claimed. "In fact, for a time, I feared she might be playing me, that she didn't return my affection."

It was Violet's turn to scoff. "She did from the moment she met you." She sighed with contentment and then suddenly sobered. "I wonder if it will be like that for me?"

Philip winced. "You've only been to two balls so far," he remarked. "I take it no one has yet caught your eye?"

Not about to tell her brother there had been someone

she thought rather handsome, Violet merely shook her head. "Not yet." She hadn't even been introduced to the aristocrat, but given his relationship to Amelia, she supposed it might be soon.

"Well, don't give up hope," he said absently, his gaze on an article in the paper. "Judging from the pile of invitations Browning delivered to my study this morning, we'll have an entertainment to attend just about every night for the next eight weeks."

"I'll collect them and write responses later today," she replied. Violet resumed eating her breakfast, her attention going back to the letter from her father.

For a moment, she felt guilt at having left the marquess alone at Fenwick Park. She might have continued to live there, but at the age of eighteen, she had asked him if she could be allowed to have a Season in London.

There wasn't a single bachelor in Shropshire who appealed to her, nor was there an aristocrat under the age of forty her father could recommend.

As a result, Michael, Marquess of Fenwick, arranged for his aunt, Katherine, Duchess of Pendleton, to be Violet's sponsor for the Season. A fortnight later, and Violet had joined her older brother at Fenwick House in Mayfair. Aunt Katherine had obviously informed everyone she knew of Violet's arrival, for invitations to entertainments began arriving at Fenwick House the same day she did.

Now that her father was on his way to join them in

London, Violet wondered if he would be amenable to attending some of those same events.

If so, she supposed a visit to Aunt Katherine might be in order for the day.

She was fairly sure her father hadn't sent a letter to his aunt informing her of his impending arrival, and she knew her great aunt would appreciate the advance notice.

Katherine could no doubt use her connections to gain invitations for her father. He was long out of mourning, after all, and it was time he be reintroduced to London society.

CHAPTER 4
HEAVY IS THE HEAD

eanwhile, Weston Hall, Mayfair

Cursing softly when the butler appeared at his study door with a silver salver laden with white envelopes, Alfred, Duke of Weston, waved him in. "I haven't even finished responding to the ones you brought yesterday," he groused.

"If I may, Your Grace. Lady Weston will see to responding to the invitations," Pritchard said. Earlier that morning, the duchess had pulled him aside and practically ordered him to bring her the invitations. Now that she was out of mourning, it was apparent she wanted out of the house, too. "You need only see to the business correspondence, Your Grace."

Alfred regarded the butler with an expression of relief. "Let her have them all, then," he said.

"Indeed. She will also see to it the household calendar is maintained. It is the responsibility of the lady of the house, after all."

Pulling the envelopes containing what he was sure were invoices from the salver, Alfred nodded. "Then see to it these are delivered to her," he said, piling several invitations he had opened from earlier mail deliveries onto the platter.

"Of course, Your Grace. Will there be anything else?" Pritchard lifted the salver from the desk.

Alfred gave him a beseeching glance. "I don't suppose you know where I might find more stationery? It seems I am down to my last sheet."

Pritchard held up a finger. "I can see to it an order is placed with your stationer right away, Your Grace."

"You can do that?"

Hiding an expression of offense, Pritchard nodded. "I can, Your Grace."

Suspicious, Alfred regarded the servant with an arched brow before he asked, "Did you do that for my father?"

"I did, Your Grace," Pritchard acknowledged, managing to maintain his patience. "Many times."

Apparently satisfied with the response, Alfred said, "Then do so. Oh, and could you send for the duchess? I need a word with her."

"Yes, Your Grace." Pritchard left the study, pulling the door shut behind him. He had to resist the urge to roll his eyes as he made his way to the stairs.

How much longer would it take for his young master to learn his responsibilities? To learn how a dukedom was to be run? And why wasn't the Duchess of Weston helping her only son?

Pritchard was about to climb the stairs but stopped short at seeing the lady of the house descending them. "Your Grace," he said, giving a slight bow.

"Pritchard," Helena acknowledged. Her eyes widened slightly. "Were you bringing those to me?" she asked, reaching for one of the envelopes on the salver.

"Indeed. His Grace asked that you respond to social invitations. And he wishes to see you when you've a moment."

Helena scoffed before displaying a wan grin. "Finally," she murmured.

"Your Grace?"

She rolled her eyes. "I fear my son has not been amenable to my... suggestions. About running the dukedom," she remarked. "He never learned much from his father—I'm quite sure Weston thought he would live forever—so now he's having to learn the hard way." She glanced back at the salver. "Did you...?"

"I told him you would respond to the invitations and keep the calendar. He seemed most relieved."

"Oh, thank you. I discovered I missed a *soiree* last week, and I only learned of it yesterday when Lady Norwick sent a note saying how sorry Lady Torrington was that I was not in attendance," she said, "I'm quite sure Adele feels offended." Although she had still been in mourning—the year since Harcourt's death wasn't quite over—she would have made an exception to attend the *soirée*.

"I'll put these in your salon, Your Grace."

"Very good. Oh, I'll probably need more stationery."

"I'll order yours right away. I'm about to do the same for His Grace," Pritchard said, arching a graying brow as if he had scored some sort of victory.

"I would say I don't know from where he gets his stubbornness, but that would be a lie," she said. "You didn't hear that from me, Pritchard," she quickly added.

"Of course not, Your Grace." He bowed and hurried up the stairs.

*H*elena watched him go, wincing when she remembered her last words to the servant. In his role as butler of Weston Hall, Pritchard had probably endured more stubbornness than most.

Her late husband, Harcourt Sheppard, had been the most stubborn man she had ever dealt with in her entire life. Well, except for *her* father, Bertram. Although it might have served them both well in the House of Lords, it did nothing to endear them to anyone, including family and those that should have been their friends.

Apparently the apple—Harcourt's only son and hers, Alfred—hadn't fallen far from the tree.

She winced at the thought of how he had behaved at the last ball. He had held his nose so high in the air, she had been tempted to pour an entire glass of champagne on him just to see him sputter to keep from drowning.

What an awful mother I am, she thought suddenly. Alfred merely required guidance. A teacher who knew what was expected of him. Someone who wouldn't be afraid to argue with him. Set him straight when he was wrong.

Someone to play the role his father should have.

Thank God their daughter didn't display the same tendencies. At least, not usually. Now that Amelia had been out since the beginning of the last Season and was beginning her second, she made friends easily. She was comfortable in the company of both young men and women. She was considered amiable. Playful. Best of all, Amelia was a diamond of the first water.

Indeed, it was possible that this would be the year Amelia Sheppard, only daughter of Harcourt and sister of Alfred, Duke of Weston, would land a husband.

Grandchildren wouldn't be far behind.

Straightening to her full five-foot, seven-inch height, Helena strode into the study, not bothering to knock.

"Mother," Alfred said, jerking at her sudden entrance. His brows furrowed and he made a sound of protest as a drop of ink fell from a quill onto his last sheet of stationery. "Dammit."

Helena crossed her arms. "You'll apologize at once for cursing in my presence," she stated.

Alfred's eyes widened. "I'm sorry," he said. "I... I didn't mean to—"

Surprised to hear his apology but determined to make her point, she said, "You never do, and yet it happens nearly every time Amelia and I are in the same room with you."

He let out an audible sigh and tossed the quill onto the desk. "I do apologize. It seems I have inherited too much of Father's manner."

Angling her head to one side, Helena regarded him with an expression that changed from annoyance to one of sadness. "Do you miss him?" She moved to the chair opposite his desk and sat.

Alfred shook his head. "Only because I wish he was doing all of this instead of me," he said, waving a hand over the desk.

"What's giving you trouble?"

He leaned back in the chair and crossed his arms. "They don't teach any of this at Cambridge," he said. "At least, if they do, I missed it."

"Are you referring to the ledgers, because if you are—"

"That's the one thing I *can* do," he interrupted. "It's simple arithmetic. It's all this other... *business*. All these questions that need answers." He picked up a letter. "Did you know we have coal mines in York?"

"Three of them, yes," she replied, arching an elegant brow. "Along with two gypsum mines in Sussex and a copper mine somewhere on the west coast."

Alfred's eyes widened. "We have a copper mine?"

Helena gave him a quelling glance. "Quite a profitable one, yes. Because your father employed a very good foreman there, so be sure you don't do anything to offend the man."

Alfred huffed. "What if he offends me?"

The query was met by silence, although Helena's arched brow had him backing down.

"I'll do my best not to offend him."

Helena allowed a wan grin. "Pritchard said you wanted to see me."

Alfred's eyes widened. "Oh. Yes. Is it true you'll see to the social correspondence?"

"Yes, of course. The calendar as well. You needn't give it a second thought," she replied.

"All right. That's good." He nodded, his hands clasped together at his middle, fingers tapping his waist-coat buttons. He had obviously picked up the mannerism from his father, for Harcourt had done it whenever he was perplexed.

"What is it, darling?" she asked gently.

"I need… I need help," he whispered.

Helena blinked. "Help from a man of business, perhaps? Or a secretary? Or mayhap a clerk?"

He seemed about to pounce on her first suggestion, but glanced to the side, as if he couldn't meet her gaze. "All of them?" He straightened. "There are times I feel as if I'm being played. As if everyone knows I am new at this, so they're trying to pull the wool over my eyes."

Scoffing softly, she leaned back in her chair. "Who-ever you hire will need to be taught how you want things run. Which is why your father didn't employ anyone other than foremen for the mines and farms. He thought it would take more effort to train someone on how he wished things to be done than to simply do it himself."

"That's because he was stubborn," Alfred countered.

Helena couldn't help the grin that lightened her face. "Look who's calling the kettle black."

"Mother," he complained.

She paused a moment before putting forth her next suggestion. "Have you considered you might require help of a different sort?"

Alfred displayed an expression of suspicion. "What do you mean?"

"A duchess, perhaps."

His eyes narrowing, he shook his head. "Are you suggesting I take a *wife*?"

"You're seven-and-twenty," she stated. "The same age Weston was when he married me."

"You honestly think I have time to court someone?" he countered, his annoyance once again apparent.

Helena winced, well aware he had a good point. The young man spent his days from breakfast until nearly dinner in the study, attempting to complete all the business of the Weston dukedom. He rarely went out at night. Even now that the Season was underway, he only made short appearances at balls and *soirées*. He hadn't even attended Lady Morganfield's garden party, and that had at one time been his favorite spring entertainment.

"How long did Father court you before you married?" Alfred asked.

Blinking several times, Helena considered how to respond. "He... he didn't."

It was Alfred's turn to blink. "What?"

Helena sighed. "Ours was an arranged marriage.

Which I was only told about a few months before the wedding."

He frowned. "Was that even legal?"

She gave him a quelling glance. "Apparently it was, since we were both present for the signing of the contract. Not that I remember having been there."

He stared at her for several seconds before he said, "And if it hadn't been arranged? Would you still have married Father?"

Helena swallowed. "I don't see how," she admitted. "I barely knew who he was." She dipped her head. "But I did marry him, and that's all that counts."

"So, duty first," Alfred said with contempt. Although he seemed bothered by the idea of a forced marriage, something else simmered below the surface. His attitude towards her the day before seemed about to return.

"Indeed," Helena replied before her eyes rounded. "But that doesn't mean *you* have to marry someone for whom you don't feel affection. Nothing has been arranged on your behalf. You're free to marry a young lady of your choosing."

"Thank God," he murmured. He seemed to stew for a moment before asking, "What about you?"

Helena blinked. "What about me?"

"Are you going to remarry? Now that you're free to do so?" The sound of annoyance was clear in his tone of voice.

Giving a start, she seemed at a loss for words. "I... I hadn't given it any thought."

Alfred let out a snort. "Liar," he accused.

"Weston," she scolded. "It's only been a year." The longest year of her life given she'd had to play the grieving widow. She hadn't been able to attend any Society events. Worse were the widow's weeds she'd had to wear, even around the house. "I'd rather see to it you and your sister are settled before I consider what I will do for the rest of my life." When her son didn't say anything in response, she asked, "So... is there someone who might have caught your eye?"

"I don't seem to attract the attention of the young ladies at balls," Alfred blurted.

About to say he couldn't when his nose was so high in the air, Helena pretended sympathy. "Perhaps if you make yourself more... *approachable*. Take on a friendly countenance," she suggested. "Maybe ask a young lady to dance instead of your sister and me."

Alfred's face reddened. "Perhaps I shall try," he managed. He glanced about his desk and leaned forward. "About that administrative help?" he hinted.

"I'll have Pritchard contact an agency to have a secretary sent over. Save you from having to write the letters," she offered.

"Pritchard?" he repeated. "What can he do?"

"He's been a butler here since before you were born. He knows everything there is to know about running a household and a whole lot more. Trust him, darling, and let him help you where he can."

Alfred finally nodded. "All right," he responded.

"In the meantime, I have responses to write to all those invitations," Helena said, rising from the chair.

"And a calendar to complete. I'm determined we shan't miss another event."

Alfred stood and gave her a nod as she took her leave.

Once she was out in the hall, the study door closed behind her, Helena let out a long sigh.

Perhaps there was hope for her son after all.

CHAPTER 5
TAKING TEA WITH AN AUNT

*M*eanwhile, at Fenwick House

"The footman has returned, my lady," the butler said from where he stood outside Violet's bedchamber door.

She looked up from the book she was reading. Although *A Lady's Guide to Arranging Entertainments* included a few nuggets of useful information, most of what she had read had been common sense. "Did he bring back an answer?" After breakfast was finished, she had requested a footman be dispatched to Whyte House asking if she might be allowed to join Katherine, Duchess of Pendleton, for tea.

"You are welcome in her parlor at half-past three o'clock. I have ordered the town coach be made ready for you, and I have sent word to your lady's maid to join you momentarily," Browning explained.

Violet's attention darted to the ormolu clock on the fireplace mantel. "Oh, dear," she said, dropping the book on the upholstered chair in which she had been seated. "It appears I have but a half-hour to dress before we must depart."

Browning disappeared at the same moment her lady's maid hurried into the room. "I've a gown ready," Dearing said, shutting the door behind her. "Along with the matching pelisse and bonnet."

Pleased her lady's maid had taken the initiative to prepare something for her to wear that afternoon—the young girl had only been in her employ the few weeks she had been in London—Violet turned to allow the servant to undo the buttons at her back. "Tell me, Dearing. Do you like being a lady's maid?" she asked.

"Oh, yes, my lady. Much better than being a housemaid, I should think," Dearing said. "It seems as if you've settled in here at Fenwick House. As if you've been here your entire life. Do you like it here?"

"Of course," she replied, pulling on the new gown. "But I can't help but think I should be the one to come up with the dinner menus." Ever since her mother had died, she had done them at Fenwick Park. "I've been meaning to speak with Mrs. Browning about it since it is my responsibility."

Dearing did up the buttons on the back of the dress. "I'm sure she would welcome your help, my lady. Lord Crawford doesn't seem to care what's served. She claims he eats whatever is put in front of him."

"That's because he does," Violet said with a giggle. She retrieved the bonnet and her reticule from the bed.

"Come. Let's be off. I don't want my aunt waiting for me when I'm the one who invited myself."

"Very good, my lady. I left my shawl with Browning so you wouldn't have to wait for me."

"You'll be a right proper lady's maid in no time," Violet remarked as they made their way down the stairs.

The coach was already waiting at the curb. Violet stepped in with the assistance of the driver, and the trip to Whyte House was quick.

When she entered the townhouse in Grosvenor Square, Violet took a moment simply to stand and gaze at all the statuary and marbles that lined the hall.

"I'll escort you to Her Grace's parlor," the butler said. "A footman will see to it your lady's maid is delivered to the servants' hall."

Violet nodded her understanding. Having only been to Whyte House once before—Katherine had paid calls at Fenwick House several times since Violet's arrival in London—Violet didn't yet know her way around the townhouse.

The first floor parlor proved as elegant as the hall, its rose-colored fabrics and Aubusson carpeting accentuating rosewood furnishings. A marble fireplace might have provided some of the room's heat, but most of it was coming from the gas lights in the huge overhead chandelier illuminating the room. Violet was glad it wasn't yet summer.

"You've timed your arrival perfectly," Katherine said from where she was seated on a settee. Three other matrons had paid calls and were ensconced in upholstered chairs clustered about the fireplace. "Lady Violet Cummings, may I introduce you to Constance, Marchioness of Reading, Clarinda, Countess of Norwick, and Adele, Countess of Torrington?" She smiled with pride. "Violet is Fenwick's only daughter, come to London for the Season."

Violet dipped a curtsy. "It's very good to meet you all," she said, moving to join her aunt on the settee when Katherine patted the cushion next to her. Violet chided herself for thinking her time with Katherine would be private.

The women murmured their greetings while Katherine poured tea. "We're all quite curious as to why you wished to see me today," Katherine said, handing a cup of tea to her niece.

Knowing her face was reddening—she hadn't expected to be the center of attention—Violet dipped her head. "I received word from my father that he will be joining my brother and me here in London. Perhaps as soon as tomorrow," she said.

Katherine's eyes rounded. "I can hardly believe it. Fenwick hasn't been to Town for... what? Thirty years or more?"

"I don't recall ever meeting Lord Fenwick," Constance said, her brows furrowing before her eyes suddenly widened. "But I wasn't in London at the time."

"I danced with him at a ball the year of my come-out," Clarinda, said with a grin. "At least once. He was quite a handsome buck back then."

"Why, when I first met Lord Crawford, I thought I

had been transported back in time. He is Fenwick's spitting image," Adele claimed. "Which will serve him well when he decides to choose a wife. Why, she'll eventually be a marchioness," she added, making eye contact with each of the ladies in attendance.

The other ladies tittered as Violet's cheeks seemed to burst into flame. These women had known her father when he was her age!

"We'll all have to be sure Lord Fenwick is added to the invitation lists for this Season's entertainments," Katherine said, "Which is no doubt why you wished to speak with me today rather than wait until tonight's *soirée*."

"Indeed, you have the right of it, Aunt Katherine."

The duchess seemed pleased. "He was left a widower..." She paused to turn her attention to the other ladies. "Why, Barbara died over two years ago."

"Influenza, was it not?" Clarinda put in.

Violet nodded. "Yes, my lady."

"But Fenwick is certainly out of mourning now, wouldn't you say, Violet?"

Despite once again being the center of attention, Violet realized she had to rise to the occasion and speak on behalf of her father or none of the countesses in the room would believe her capable of taking on the role of an aristocrat's wife. "He is, of course, but I don't believe he's ready to seek a new wife just yet," she said. He hadn't said anything to her about finding a new marchioness. "If that's what you were thinking."

Katherine seemed to straighten on the settee. "I

hadn't been thinking that at all," she claimed, although her barely suppressed grin belied her words.

Titters sounded from the other ladies, and Violet relaxed. "Although I do want him to attend as many entertainments as he has invitations, I fear he may send his regrets more often than not."

"Oh?" Adele responded. "Why do you say that?"

Violet gave a one-shouldered shrug. "He's been away from London a very long time, my lady. There isn't much in the way of Society near our home in Shropshire, you see," she explained, "and although I have arranged dinner parties with the local land owners and helped him host a district ball or two... I expect he'll ease himself into the Season rather slowly."

Katherine huffed. "Not if *I* have anything to say about it."

Stunned her great aunt would attempt to counter her father's wishes, Violet was unsure of how to respond. She was saved from doing so when Adele said, "We won't introduce him to *every* available widow right away."

"Not that there are that many here in Town right now," Clarinda chimed in.

"You would have been perfect for him if you hadn't married Norwick," Katherine commented.

Clarinda gasped softly. "I rather doubt Norwick would agree." Her second husband had courted and loved her far longer than her first husband had. They might have been identical twins, but the two couldn't have been more different in their philosophies.

Clarinda was finding life with Daniel far more enjoyable.

"Perhaps we should keep him a secret until he can be introduced at a ball," Adele suggested. "A surprise, so to speak."

"Once he's made an appearance at White's, the entire *ton* will know he's in Town," Constance countered. "Everyone knows men are the best gossips."

"A mention in *The Tattler*, and all of London will know," Katherine chimed in.

Violet glanced at the clock, remembering the rule she wasn't to stay for longer than a half-hour. "Oh, dear. I did not mean to overstay my welcome," she said, moving to stand.

"The half-hour rule doesn't apply to you or my friends, Violet," Katherine countered, one of her hands covering her niece's. "Besides, we haven't yet had refills on our tea. Or more biscuits."

Settling back onto the settee, Violet said, "Thank you, Aunt."

Katherine held out the plate of biscuits to everyone. "It's a long time until dinner," she said when all but Violet deferred. The three helped themselves to the lemon confections.

"You do have the best cook when it comes to biscuits," Clarinda commented. "But I do wish I wasn't looking as if I was eating too many of them."

"I intend to take my cook with me when I go to the country house after the Season," Katherine replied, "So, no, you can't hire her away from here."

Adele tittered softly, and they all glanced at her with expressions of curiosity. "My son's wife, Anne, is always on the lookout for a new cook for Worthington House, especially since we took the cook with us when we moved to Torrington Park. Milton has decided we shall remain at Torrington Park for most of the year," the older matron explained.

"I feared you two wouldn't return for the Season," Clarinda remarked. "We hadn't seen you back in Town for some time."

Adele shrugged. "He misses life in London too much to give it up completely," she replied, referring to her second husband, Milton Grandby, Earl of Torrington. Godfather to over a dozen goddaughters and godsons, Grandby, as he was usually called by his friends and family, had apparently informed every other unmarried man to stay away from Adele when she was widowed. He squired her about Town and was her escort for every ball of the Season prior to proposing marriage in 1816. Although most in the *ton* seemed surprised, anyone who knew him personally knew he had finally come to terms with doing his duty as it related to the Torrington earldom.

Adele delivered twins, an heir and a daughter, the following year.

Clarinda beat her to it, bearing a set of twin girls followed a couple of years later by a set of twin boys. The girls were both married to the twin sons of Adam and Diana, Earl and Countess of Mayfield. Clarinda's boys weren't yet of an age to consider marriage.

"How long will you stay at Whyte Hall Park?" Violet asked.

Katherine made an odd sound in her throat. "Depends on Pendleton, I suppose," she replied, referring to her second husband, Thomas. There were those who claimed she married another duke so she could rid herself of the 'dowager' label she had taken on when her oldest son's wife gave birth to a boy. At the time, she had been left newly widowed by the Duke of Whyte.

In reality, she had married the man to whom she had originally been betrothed before duty unexpectedly took him to the Continent. Circumstance required she marry someone else as quickly as possible, though.

Thomas had not only left her at the altar, but left her with child. She wouldn't have accepted Whyte's offer of marriage if she hadn't been with child.

"I never thought Thomas would prefer Bath to London, but he does," Katherine commented, pulled from her brief reverie by Violet's inquisitive gaze. "Claims playing in the waters are what keep him spry in his old age."

"Spry?" Constance questioned in a teasing voice. "Pendleton must be, what? Eighty years of age?"

Katherine seemed to blush before she said, "He's nine-and-seventy, and he'll probably outlive me. You'll see soon enough. He's due to join me here when Jonathan and Sarah return from their anniversary trip." Jonathan might have been the Duke of Whyte, but he was also Thomas' oldest son, a secret which Katherine and Thomas vowed to keep until their dying days.

Now Jonathan's oldest child, John, was grown up and had taken on some of the responsibilities of the dukedom. In fact, he was currently with his new wife, Theodosia, on their wedding trip somewhere in the Kingdom of the Two Sicilies.

"The only new man in *my* life is my latest grandson," Katherine announced. "My second son, James, has sent word that he and his wife are due to arrive back in London in a fortnight. They're bringing him to meet me."

Violet gasped. "I have another cousin," she gushed. "Does he have a name?"

"As it happens, they've named him Michael. After your father, of course," Katherine said.

"Where is your youngest son living these days?" Adele asked.

"In the Cotswolds. Beatrice prefers the country for the children, and I can't say I blame her. James sees to the Whyte dukedom's farmlands near the river, so it works out to everyone's advantage."

The women nodded their understanding and were quiet for a moment before Clarinda turned to Violet and asked, "Have you made many friends here in Town?"

Surprised to have the conversation turned back to her, Violet said, "Oh, yes. One in particular. Lady Amelia has been most amiable."

"Weston's sister?" Constance guessed.

"Indeed." Wrinkled noses followed her confirmation. "Is... is there a reason I shouldn't be friends with her?" she asked meekly.

"Oh, Lady Amelia is perfectly suitable," Katherine assured her. "It's Weston we're not particularly fond of."

About to defend the young duke, Violet realized she didn't know him well enough to form an opinion. Amelia had tried to introduce him at a ball, and although he had acknowledged her with a bow and had brushed his lips over her silk-clad knuckles, Amelia hadn't said more than her name when he had excused himself with word that he needed to return to Weston Hall.

"I've only met him once, and it was quite brief," she said.

"This is all his late father's fault," Adele stated. "Weston never taught him what he needs to know, and he's not been the least bit humbled by his inexperience."

"It's as if he's play-acting as a duke," Constance murmured.

"He is rather high on his horse," Clarinda remarked. "But then, his father always was."

"Poor Helena," Constance murmured. "How she stayed with that despicable man, I'll never know."

"I expect she's trying to set her son straight," Katherine offered. "If Jonathan had been in the same situation, I certainly would. Thank goodness Whyte was so good about seeing to it both his sons could run a dukedom in his absence."

"Helena should be out of mourning by now," Adele commented. "Perhaps she'll seek out the help of another aristocrat on his behalf."

"Everyone knows the boy doesn't have any friends, after what happened..." Clarinda stopped speaking, her attention suddenly on Violet. "Well, after that breeze was raised at university."

"Breeze?" Violet repeated, sure she didn't know what the countess meant. "Do you mean… a fight?"

Katherine placed a hand on Violet's. "Words and… perhaps a bare knuckle or two… were exchanged in anger, is all," she said, waving her other hand as if it was a small matter.

"It was much more than a breeze," Constance stated. "I was told Weston started it and Lord Crawford did everything he could to prevent…" She stopped speaking, her gaze going to Violet. "Further violence," she added lamely.

Violet stared at the countess. "Did my brother strike him?" she asked in a whisper.

"Only after Weston hit him. Twice, I heard. Lord Crawford's fist was apparently more effective, for he only had to hit back once to knock out Alfred," Constance explained. "Got him hard on the nose. Blood everywhere. Your brother was in the right."

"Whatever were they arguing about?" Violet asked, once again turning her attention on her aunt.

"No one is saying, and anyway, it's none of our concern," Katherine replied. "Water under the bridge, as they say."

"It sounds as if His Grace was publicly humiliated," Violet murmured, vowing she would bring up the matter with her brother during that night's dinner.

"He had it coming," Clarinda said, "but it did nothing to temper his prideful airs. His nose is still held so high, it's a wonder there's enough air for him to breathe."

"It's no wonder he behaves with false bravado," Violet murmured.

Four sets of eyes rounded in response. "What are you saying?" Katherine asked.

"He's a man—"

"Barely—"

"Who has had his ego bruised in public," Violet continued. "In my experience, and this is strictly based only on those men whom I know from our area of Shropshire—"

"The country folk," Clarinda whispered.

"–Half would react with humility and apologize for their transgression while the other half would react by acting even worse, sure they are in the right and determined to prove their point, even if it should cost them friends and family."

Katherine blinked before she bowed her head in an exaggerated manner. "Such wise words from one so young."

"Why you sound as if you've already been married twice," Adele commented with a grin.

Violet dipped her head. "I've a father and a brother," she said quietly.

"Who I thought got along swimmingly," Katherine remarked.

"Oh, they do," Violet assured them. "It's all the other members of their sex who seem to misbehave."

Titters erupted from the other women, but they

quickly quieted when the clock on the mantel chimed half-past-four.

"Oh, I must be going," Clarinda said, rising from her chair. "We've a *soirée* to attend this evening."

"Indeed," Constance and Adele chimed in. "So good of you to host us this afternoon, Your Grace," Adele said. "I think it's my turn on the morrow."

"I'll see you at half-past-three," Katherine replied, rising to escort her guests down the stairs and to the front door.

About to follow the older women out the door, Violet paused to kiss her aunt on the cheek. "Thank you for allowing me to join you."

"It was my pleasure," Katherine replied. "You brought good news and held your own with some rather gifted gossipers," she added with a wink. She sobered somewhat. "Do take care should you become acquainted with Weston."

Violet furrowed a brow. "Understood," she replied. Dipping a curtsy, she took her leave of Whyte House and made her way to the Fenwick town coach.

She had until dinner to sort how she would bring up the matter of Weston with her brother.

Someone was at fault for something, and she was determined to learn who it was.

CHAPTER 6
HOW THE BREEZE BLEW

*L*ater *that night, Fenwick House*

Philip was already seated at the table when Violet entered the dining room at seven o'clock. His glass of wine was half drunk, and several papers were splayed out to the side of his dinner plate.

"Here you are," she said. "I've been waiting for you in the parlor."

Philip looked up and displayed a grimace. "Apologies. I was hoping to get through these contracts earlier today, but they're far more complicated than I'm used to," he said.

"Father will probably arrive tomorrow," she said. "Perhaps he can be of help?"

"He'll have to," Philip replied, pushing aside the papers to stand and hold her chair for her. "Browning said you were at Aunt Katherine's today. How is she?"

Violet took her seat. "She was hosting a marchioness and two countesses when I arrived," she replied as Philip retook his seat at the head of the table. "They're going to see to it Father has invitations to all the entertainments."

Philips scoffed. "I rather doubt he intends to attend all of them."

"I warned Katherine, for I think the same, but she seems determined he be reintroduced to Society."

Philip chuckled as a footman poured more wine and another appeared with the soup course. "Are you going to the Everly *soirée* tonight?"

"I am. Aren't you? I sent a reply saying we'd both attend."

He seemed to think on it. "I suppose," he replied.

"I'm looking forward to seeing Lady Amelia there," Violet continued.

Philip's manner changed instantly. "I nearly forgot. *She's* going to be there," he stated.

Giggling, Violet lifted her soup spoon. "Indeed."

"I'll go. I..." He swallowed the rest of what he was about to say, realizing he shouldn't admit he had seen Amelia only the day before at the bookshop.

They sat in companionable silence for a time before Violet said, "A matter was brought up at tea today, and I wondered if you might fill me in on what actually happened?"

Philip paused his soup spoon in mid-air. "What matter?"

She swallowed. "The one involving you and the Duke of Weston. Apparently some words of anger and fists were involved?"

Straightening in his chair, Philip stared at her with wide eyes. "Did Aunt Katherine speak of it?"

She shook her head. "One of the other ladies did. But they all seemed to know something about it. Far more than I, so you can imagine how I felt learning you'd been involved in some sort of row with a duke—"

"He wasn't a duke at the time."

"—And now said duke behaves in a poor manner—"

"Not my fault he doesn't know how to behave."

"—Because he was humiliated."

Philip furrowed a brow and scoffed. "He brought it on himself, Vi."

"Explain to me what happened."

He set down his spoon and slumped back in his chair. "It's been years. Happened before he went on his Grand Tour," he said with a scoff.

"Apparently it's still quite a fresh humiliation for him," she countered. "What else could be causing him to act so high and mighty? So proud?"

He rolled his eyes. "Because he takes after his father?" he asked rhetorically. He sighed. "He was in the wrong—"

"About what?"

"Our father."

Violet inhaled softly. "What about our father?"

Philip displayed a grimace. "Alfred claimed our father was once betrothed to his mother, but that she chose Weston over him because Weston was a duke, and she wished to be a duchess, but not before—"

"That's a lie," Violet whispered, her hackles immediately rising in defense of her father.

"That's what I said," Philip replied. "I told him to take it back. He refused. I threatened to punch him and he got me here..." he paused to point to the base of one cheek, "and here..." he indicated his shoulder, "and I punched him in the nose. Broke it. There was blood everywhere."

"Eww," Violet said in disgust.

"Do not take his side in this," he warned.

"I wasn't going to," she countered. "I just wanted to know what the breeze was all about."

"Breeze?" he repeated.

"The ladies said a breeze was raised."

He seemed to ponder what to say in response, taking another spoonful of soup in the process. "We were both called into the dean's office to explain ourselves, and he changed the story completely. Said I'd cheated by copying one of his papers. I felt as if I'd been played."

"Did the dean believe him?"

Philip shook his head. "No, because I always had the better marks in all my classes. Alfred was rot in school. Except for mathematics. He's crack with numbers, but anything else..." He shook his head and sighed. "He'll have the Weston dukedom run into the ground before he admits he doesn't know what he's doing because he's too damn proud to ask for help."

Violet winced at hearing the curse. Winced again when she saw how upset her brother had become while telling the tale. "Why do you suppose it's so important to him?"

"What do you mean?"

"About Father. About Her Grace and him supposedly being betrothed to one another."

Philip shrugged, pushing his soup bowl to the side so he could lean his elbows on the table. "Because Weston wouldn't exist if our father had married Helena." He seemed about to say something else but merely shrugged.

Violet blinked. She blinked again and scoffed at the same time. "Do you think it's true then? That Father—?"

"Yes, I think it's true that at one time, he wanted to marry Helena Styles-Hyatt," he said in a hoarse whisper.

Her eyes widening in shock, Violet slammed her back against her chair so hard, she nearly knocked the breath from her lungs. "The Duke of Woodleigh's daughter?" she asked in confusion, sure Amelia had mentioned her grandfather's title at some point. "How do you know?"

Philip audibly sighed. "He told me one night. After Mother died. I found him in the library, deep in his cups and talking to himself. When he realized I was there, he started telling me all about what it was like when he was my age."

"If he was drunk, he probably didn't know what he was saying," she countered.

"He knew, Vi. He knew, because he started crying, claiming he married Mother out of friendship rather than love. Because Helena had to marry Weston due to some marriage contract that had been signed when she was still very young."

"Are those still legal?" she asked in dismay.

"Apparently they were back then," he replied. "We are talking... *thirty years* ago," he added in a voice making it sound as if it had been three centuries ago.

"But he *loved* Mother," she insisted.

"He did, but not at first."

Violet took a deep breath, glad when a footman appeared to take away their dishes while another set the second course before them.

"I think I know why Father is coming to London," she said in a quiet voice.

Philip winced. "It's not what you think."

"Duchess Helena is a widow now. Father is a widower," she countered, excitement sounding in her voice. "If he really did love Helena—"

"That's not the reason," he warned.

She gave a start. "Then... then why?"

He used a fork to pick at his fish. "I mentioned in my last letter that I wished to marry Lady Amelia."

Violet shrugged and then her eyes rounded. "You're afraid Weston won't give his permission."

"Because he won't," Philip stated.

"Have you asked?"

"He won't," he repeated. "It will be like grandfather, like son. Both denying we Fenwicks our desire to marry their women."

About to put voice to a protest, Violet settled back into her chair. "So... why exactly is Father coming?"

Philip displayed another grimace. "I think he's going to pay a call on Weston. On my behalf," he said in a hoarse whisper.

"Don't you want him to?"

He rolled his eyes. "I would prefer to handle it myself. Work something out, or... or elope." He immediately held up a hand. "Do not repeat what I just said," he warned. "Not even to Amelia."

"I wouldn't," she assured him. "Besides, the scandal would be... untenable."

His chin lifted. "It wouldn't be that bad," he argued.

She gave him a quelling glance. "Perhaps... perhaps the situation could be smoothed over," she suggested.

"I'm not going to apologize, and neither is he," Philip stated.

Remembering her conversation with her aunt and the countesses earlier that afternoon, Violet realized she had spoken the truth about prideful men. "Perhaps you won't, and perhaps he won't," she replied. "But there has to be another way to secure his permission."

He gave her a glance filled with suspicion. "Eat your dinner. We have to leave for the *soirée* soon," he reminded her.

"Indeed," she replied, tucking into her food as she plotted what she would do that evening.

Perhaps it was time she take up play-acting.

CHAPTER 7
A SOIRÉE SETS THE STAGE

*L*ater that night

Wishing she could have worn a gown in a brighter color, Amelia regarded her reflection in the cheval mirror with a sigh. The pale jonquil silk she held up in front of her was perfectly suitable for that night's *soirée*, but just once, she wished she could wear something darker. Bolder in color.

She caught Trimble's reflection in the mirror. "Have you spoken with Mrs. Pritchard about the primers you bought?" She handed the garment to the lady's maid.

"Oh, yes. We've already spent some time this morning going through the first lesson. I've learned several words," the servant gushed.

"That's wonderful," Amelia said, stepping into the gown as Trimble held it open for her. "I do hope the two of you can continue the lessons every day."

"She says she'll keep a half-hour for me in the mornings whilst you have your breakfast," Trimble said, doing up the buttons at the back of the gown.

"Are you ready?"

Amelia turned to discover her brother at the door. She dared one more glance in the cheval mirror before saying, "I am." Sensing his impatience, she hurried to join him. "You look like a blade... and you look tired. What's wrong?"

Alfred winced. "I couldn't sleep last night. I doubt I'll stay long tonight, but... it's fine if you do."

"How will I get home?"

"Mother sent word she was detained at her modiste's shop. She'll be along in her own coach in an hour or so," he explained

Amelia's eyes widened. "I am not bringing Trimble with me tonight," she countered, thinking she would require a chaperone until their mother was in attendance.

"Fine," he said, apparently not of a mind to argue with her. "I'll play at being your chaperone."

Making their way down the stairs, Amelia glanced over at him several times. "Alfred, what's wrong?"

He huffed. "Nothing. I'm just tired is all."

"That's not it," she accused.

"Amelia," he said in a warning voice.

"Tell me in the coach," she said, turning to allow Pritchard to help her with her mantle.

He offered his arm and the two made their way to the Weston town coach. Amelia stepped up, surprised to discover their mother was already inside. "I thought you were going to be detained," she said, taking the seat opposite.

"My modiste finished my gown for tomorrow night and had this one ready..." Helena opened her mantle to show off a gown in a bright blue silk. "So there was no need to change clothes," she said, watching her son take the seat next to his sister. "Thought I may as well wear it tonight." She turned her attention on Alfred. "Pritchard mentioned you had some applicants for that position we talked about. Were there any you liked?"

He seemed uncomfortable for a moment. "Three, I think. I cannot decide, though. Do I choose the one who writes fast, the one who has the most experience but who writes more slowly than honey drips, or the one who used to be the man of business for the Earl of Montaine?" he asked rhetorically.

"Depends. Why is the one who was the man of business for the Earl of Montaine no longer employed by Montaine?"

"He died, Mother," Amelia said. "His heir has no need of a man of business as he's quite capable of doing it himself. Or so he says."

Both Alfred and Helena turned to regard her with surprise. "How do you know this?"

"We were talking about it at the last ball," she replied. "I danced with him."

Helena arched a brow. "Sounds as if Montaine's former man of business might be your best choice," she said, turning her attention back to her son.

"I'll let Pritchard know when I return," Alfred replied, giving his sister a beseeching glance. "You might have told me."

She scoffed. "I would have told you if you had mentioned you were in the market for a man of business," she countered. "What else do you need?"

He rolled his eyes, but the gesture went unseen in the darkened coach. "Oh, let's see. A duchess?" he said, sarcasm evident in his voice.

Helena inhaled softly, but Amelia wasn't about to be cowed by his behavior. "I'll introduce you to my new friend again," she said in a whisper. "Despite her age, she has plenty of experience hosting events and is quite amiable." Before he could ask, she added, "She's quite comely, too. Blonde hair, blue eyes, and she has a nice figure."

"Why haven't you introduced her to me before?" he asked, annoyance sounding in his voice.

"I did. You barely acknowledged her existence, which makes me think that I shouldn't introduce you again," she countered with a huff. "I hear Lord Daniel is in the market for a wife—"

"I'll acknowledge her existence," Alfred said in a hoarse whisper. "I'll even sit next to her should there be any chairs."

"There will be chairs, there will be a card parlor, and there will be dancing," their mother said from her side of the coach. "Lady Everly apprised us of the details during yesterday's tea."

"You say that as if there was some doubt as to

whether or not she could host such an event," Amelia commented.

"It never ceases to amaze me that just because she was born to a Greek woman, my contemporaries believe Stella incapable of being a good hostess," Helena remarked. "Poor woman has proven over and over again she's a competent hostess and capable of doing her duty. The fact that she gave birth to a spare heir at her age is proof enough as far as I'm concerned."

"Wasn't her father a duke?" Alfred asked.

"Indeed. Westhaven. He was an archaeologist," Helena said. "I expect tonight's event will be the envy of many hostesses this Season."

"If we introduce you to your eventual wife, it will be," Amelia said, nudging Alfred with an elbow.

Alfred moaned as if in pain.

The talk of marriage had Amelia pondering her future with Philip.

Once she was married, she would be moving into her husband's home, bringing with her some trunks filled with clothes and a few personal items. If she agreed to stay on as her lady's maid, Trimble would be moving to Fenwick House as well, which meant she wouldn't be able to continue her lessons with the housekeeper. Hopefully, there would be someone at Fenwick House who could see to continuing her reading lessons.

The coach stuttered to a halt in front of Rosemount House, and thoughts of Trimble were quickly replaced by thoughts of Philip.

. . .

"*N*ow, don't get into any trouble," Philip said when he helped Violet out of her mantle and handed it to a footman in the vestibule of Rosemount House.

"I should be the one telling *you* that," she said, looking about for their hostess. "Come. Introduce me," she ordered.

Having developed a fast friendship with Alexander, heir to the Everly earldom, over their shared interest in metallurgy and jewels, Philip had met the young man's parents on more than one occasion since his arrival in London. "She's the one at the bottom of the stairs."

Violet inhaled sharply. "She's gorgeous," she whispered.

"It's a pity the daughter isn't as pretty, but she's barely had her come-out," he said. "A few more years..."

"You'll already be wed by then," Violet said with a smirk.

"Let's hope."

When Stella, Countess of Everly, acknowledged them, Philip introduced his sister.

"It's so good of you to join us this evening," the countess gushed. "Do enjoy yourselves."

Violet curtsied and allowed her brother to lead her into another room where a four-piece orchestra was playing. The Turkish rug had been rolled up and removed, leaving a bare floor suitable for dancing. In the next room, a table filled with finger foods sat adjacent to a table set with a huge punchbowl. Footmen scurried about with trays of champagne and hors d'oeuvres. Passing through yet another set of open doors, they entered a library featuring a huge glass tank filled with water and colorful fish.

"Oh!" Violet said as she paused to admire the aquatic display. "I could watch these creatures for an hour," she claimed.

"Good, because this is where I'm leaving you," her brother remarked, his attention on the doorway.

"I take it Amelia has arrived?" she asked rhetorically, never taking her eyes off the colorful fish. "Are you two going to play house?"

When he didn't answer, she glanced around and realized she was alone in the library. Shrugging, she turned her attention back to the fish, not taking her eyes from a bright blue one that darted about from one side of the tank to the other.

Apparently he wasn't used to being seen by someone other than whoever fed him.

When she moved to one end of the tank, her gaze through the water and two layers of glass brought a rather oddly distorted image into focus, and she stepped back in surprise.

"Your Grace," she said, belatedly dipping a curtsy.

Alfred blinked and stared at her for a moment before he reached for her hand. "Forgive me. You look familiar, but I don't believe we've met," he said, his statement becoming a query at the last moment.

Violet glanced around, hoping to discover someone

she knew who could do the introduction. When she realized they were alone, she said, "Violet, Your Grace. I'm a friend of your sister's."

He took her hand to his lips and brushed them over the back of her glove. "Amelia seems to be friends with everyone," he remarked. "You may call me Weston."

Violet's eyes widened. To be allowed the courtesy to call him by his title surprised her. "I am honored, Your Grace."

"If Amelia learned otherwise, she would scold me quite thoroughly," he replied. His attention went back to the fish. "Have you seen these creatures before?"

"I have not. They are fascinating to watch, though," she replied, her gaze going to a brightly striped fish.

"I understand Everly brought back a number of them from a trip to the tropics many years ago. Before Alexander was born," Alfred explained, referring to the Earl of Everly's oldest son.

"They must have long lives."

"Or he's been successful with some sort of breeding program," the young duke remarked, at the same moment miniature versions of the striped fish swam by.

Violet giggled. "It's as if they have decided they wish to put on a show for us," she said, turning back to discover Alfred staring at her. "Is something wrong?"

He gave a start. "No. Nothing's wrong. I was merely wondering how it is I don't recall seeing you before this evening."

Lifting a shoulder, she said, "I've only been in Town

for a month at most. I doubt we've been at more than one or two of the entertainments at the same time."

"I'm sure I would have remembered," he said, dipping his head.

"You've no doubt been otherwise occupied," she countered.

He pulled his head back as if he'd been punched in the jaw. "What... what do you mean?"

Violet realized she might have offended the duke. "I only meant that with the death of your father, you've been having to run the Weston dukedom all by yourself," she said, reaching out to touch his forearm with her gloved hand. "You can hardly be expected to trouble yourself with such trivial matters as attending balls and *soirées*," she added. "So I'm very glad to see you this evening."

"You are?" He seemed surprised by her comment.

"Well, of course. There are rarely enough intriguing young men at these events."

He blinked. "Do you think there will be dancing this evening?"

"Oh, yes. Lady Everly has had the carpet rolled up in the room next door," she replied, indicating the adjacent parlor. "An orchestra is in there playing now."

Alfred seemed to listen for a moment before he said, "You're right. I'm not sure how I didn't notice the music before."

"Well, it is hard to hear over this device that's making all the bubbles in the water," Violet remarked, a finger pointing to a strange machine located beneath the tank.

"Must be powered by gas," Alfred guessed, bending down to inspect a contraption with hoses snaking out of it.

"It is indeed," Harold Tennison, Earl of Everly, stated, joining them to examine the machine in question. "Provides heat and air for these critters."

"Lord Everly," Violet said, dipping a curtsy.

"Everly," Alfred said. "So good of you to invite me."

"It's good of you to come," Everly countered. He turned to Violet. "You're a friend of Lady Amelia's, are you not?"

Violet beamed in delight. "I am, my lord. I am Violet—"

"There you are, young lady," Katherine said, joining them from the parlor. She turned her attention on the gentlemen. "Your Grace, Lord Everly," she said, curtsying to their bows.

"Your Grace," Everly said, a moment before Alfred afforded her the same courtesy.

"Aunt Katherine, Weston and I have been admiring Lord Everly's aquatic kingdom," Violet said, giving the duke a shy grin.

Everly scoffed. "It is a kingdom of sorts, and every one of these creatures acts as if they own the place," he said. "They play about all day and provide absolutely nothing in return, but they expect to be fed, kept warm, and provided air to breathe."

"They provide entertainment," Violet argued.

"They are rather relaxing to watch," Alfred chimed in. "Almost makes me forget how much I must do when I return to Weston Hall this evening."

Violet gave him a beseeching glance. "It is a pity you're not able to enjoy the *soirée*, Your Grace."

"I should enjoy it more if you afford me a dance, Lady Violet."

"Of course I shall dance with you," she said, well aware her aunt seemed less than pleased by the plan.

Katherine and Everly exchanged quick glances before Everly said, "Pardon me, but I believe I am being summoned. My countess is waving at me."

Violet curtsied as the earl hurried toward the parlor.

"I'm off to the card parlor," Katherine said, her gaze darting between Alfred and Violet. "Do behave."

"Yes, Your Grace," the two said in unison. When the older woman took her leave, Alfred and Violet faced one another and chuckled softly. "I'm not exactly sure what she thinks we might try," Violet commented.

Alfred didn't say anything in response, and when she arched an eyebrow as if that might urge him to agree, he inhaled suddenly. "So, you're not going to play cards with her?"

"Oh, mayhap later. Probably when Amelia is ready to do so," she replied.

The comment seemed to please him. "Although I enjoy an occasional game of cards, I'm afraid I haven't the interest. Perhaps because I'm not much of a gambler."

"My aunt said something about them that gave me an appreciation for them," Violet responded.

"Oh?"

"It's silly, really," she said with a shrug. "But she explained there are fifty-two cards in a deck, and those represent the fifty-two weeks in a year. The two colors are for day and night. There are four suits for the four seasons, and thirteen weeks per season."

Alfred's eyes widened. "I suppose the twelve court cards represent twelve months?"

"Exactly," she replied. "And there's something about the value of the cards? Their numbers adding up to something?"

He angled his head to one side. "Let's see. If you add up each of the cards in a deck," he went on, "Ace counts as one plus two plus three plus..." He paused, his fingers splaying out as his brows furrowed. "Jacks count as eleven, queens as twelve, and kings as thirteen..." He seemed to think for a moment. "Then you have ninety-one for each suit and a total three-hundred-and-sixty-four, which is equal to the number of days in a year."

Violet blinked. "Did you do that addition in your head?" she asked, obviously impressed.

He chuckled softly. "I did. The one thing I am good at is numbers," he commented. His brow suddenly furrowed. "So... why do you suppose there are jokers in a deck of cards?"

"For use in a leap year," she replied, grinning in delight.

Alfred rolled his eyes. "Of course. Like this year is," he

remarked. "I shall remember this information when I next play cards."

"It has made it more interesting for me," she admitted. When he didn't respond but merely stared at her, she nervously glanced around the study.

"Oh, uh, will you dance with me?" he suddenly asked.

Violet grinned. "I would be honored."

The two made their way into the parlor, where a longways dance was already in progress. They joined the end of the line, merging in with the other dancers.

Keeping her eye out for her brother—she had expected him to be dancing with Amelia—she realized he wasn't in the parlor.

"Who are you looking for?" Alfred asked, when they were joined together for a moment.

"Lady Amelia, of course."

He seemed surprised by her response. "She makes friends so easily," he commented before they were separated by the dance and a new set of partners.

When the two came together again, Violet said, "Indeed she does. Makes friends easily, I mean. She has an ease about her that has me quite envious."

"You needn't be, Lady Violet. You share the trait, I assure you," he said.

Violet felt her face heat with a blush that wasn't due to the exertions of the dance. "Thank you, Your Grace. It's very kind of you to say."

Alfred seemed to lose his place in the dance, but

before he attempted to resume the steps, the music ended.

He bowed, and Violet curtsied.

"Will you take a turn about the room with me?" he asked, offering his arm.

Violet placed her hand on his arm and said, "I will if you're on your way to the refreshments," she replied.

"Something to drink, yes," he said.

*M*eanwhile, in another room "Where are they now?" Philip asked, his back pressed to the wall adjacent to a door. He had been careful to ensure he wasn't in the same room or visible from wherever Alfred, Duke of Weston, was in the Everly household.

"They've left the parlor. Looks like they're off to the refreshment table," Amelia said with a happy sigh. "It's terribly sporting of your sister to keep my brother occupied like this." She gave him an expectant glance.

He shook his head. "I didn't ask her to, if that's what you're thinking," Philip claimed.

She lifted a brow. "Neither did I," she whispered. "I certainly didn't expect he would still be here.. He usually leaves after he's made a round or two."

Philip pulled her into his arms and kissed her. "I'll never tire of doing that," he whispered.

Grinning up at him, Amelia said, "I shall never tire of being kissed, but we're about to be discovered by the lady of the house."

Philip immediately offered his arm and escorted her out of the library, nodding as they passed by Stella, Countess of Everly. "You've a beautiful house, my lady," Philip remarked.

Stella beamed in delight. "I'm happy to share it for these sorts of occasions," she replied. Turning to Amelia, she added, "I wasn't aware your brother was such an admirer of tropical fish."

Amelia blinked. "Neither was I."

"Well, if Everly should ever have too many for the tank, perhaps Weston would be willing to start his own fishdom."

"Perhaps," Amelia agreed.

Philip and she watched the countess move onto another cluster of aristocrats before turning to regard one another in surprise. "Fish?" he whispered.

"I'll show you," she said, pulling him in the direction of the library. They ducked into the room at the same moment Alfred and Violet returned to the parlor and the dancing.

"I can't stay hidden from him all night," Philip said in a quiet voice.

"Nor should you," Amelia replied. "But I've been invited to play cards, so... here is where I'll leave you."

He looked about to be sure no one could see them from where they stood on the other side of the fish tank before he leaned down and stole a quick kiss. "I love you," he whispered. "Oh, and I nearly forgot to tell you. When I next see you, I may be in the company of my father. He's due in London any day now."

Inhaling softly, Amelia said, "I thought he didn't like London."

"He doesn't, but I think he's grown bored of the country since Mother's passing. And Violet isn't there to keep him company."

"I look forward to meeting him."

"I'm sure he's looking forward to meeting you," he replied, a finger brushing over her bare arm above her glove.

"Me?" Amelia's eyes narrowed.

"I told him about us. That I wish to marry you. I hope that was all right," Phillip whispered.

Amelia straightened and regarded him with a curious expression before she said, "Of course it was. I'll see you at the ball night after next." She dipped a quick curtsy before she headed off in the direction of the card parlor.

His attention going to the fish, Philip watched their chaotic movements for some time before deciding he'd had enough of avoiding Weston for the night. Ducking into the card parlor, he said his farewells to his aunt and took his leave of Rosemount House.

*M*eanwhile, in the study

"Is it really midnight?" Alfred asked, his attention on his chronometer. From another room, the sound of a clock's chimes could be heard.

"Indeed. Must you go so soon?" Violet made sure her query sounded of disappointment.

Alfred blinked. "Oh, I've stayed far longer than I

planned," he replied. "I still have a letter I must complete this evening as well as a ledger to update."

She angled her head to one side. "Do you ever take time away from your study?"

Lifting a shoulder, he seemed to think on her question for a time before saying, "These days, rarely."

"Not even to ride your horse? Or to go for a walk?"

He scoffed softly. "I haven't been riding since I was on my Grand Tour," he said, the sound of lament evident in his voice. "And certainly not since my return to England."

Violet gave a start. "But you have a horse?"

His eyes rounded. "Oh, yes. An Irish walker, perfect for the park," he claimed.

Violet angled her head to one side as she displayed a smile. "I have one as well," she said happily. "I've had two opportunities to ride him since my arrival. I plan to go again the morning after next. I like to ride the day of balls. Helps put color in my cheeks," she said, waggling her brows in a teasing manner.

"As if all the dancing you'll do won't be enough?" he countered.

She tittered. "I'm still too new to have a full dance card," she said with a shrug. "Or anyone to ride with. At least one of the grooms comes along."

"What about Amelia...?"

Violet shook her head. "She has something on her calendar. A fitting for her gown, I think?" Her eyes rounded. "Perhaps you might join me? Surely you can take an hour out of your day to enjoy some fresh air.

Give your walker some exercise. That is, if it's not raining."

Alfred stared at her for a moment before his brows furrowed. "Maybe for a half-hour? Which gate will you use to go into the park?"

"The Grosvenor Gate. I expect about ten o'clock," she replied.

After hesitating for a moment, he finally said, "I've an appointment with my solicitor at half-past eight that morning. In Oxford Street. So if I'm not there..." He winced. "Please don't take offense."

Violet displayed a smirk. "I wouldn't, of course. But if you can join me, I look forward to it."

Color suffused his face. "Thank you for dancing with me."

"Oh, it was my pleasure, Weston," she said, hoping her words sounded heartfelt. In reality, they were more close to the truth than she dared to admit to herself. "Will I see you at the ball night after next?"

Alfred seemed surprised by the query. "I'll make an appearance, of course," he replied. "I'm not sure how long I'll stay, though."

Feeling emboldened, Violet asked, "Shall I reserve a dance for you?"

He nodded. "Please do. I would be honored," he replied. He lifted her hand to his lips. "I should leave you in the company of the Duchess of Pendleton, should I not?"

"She's in the card parlor. I'll make my way there now," Violet said. "What of your sister and Her Grace?"

He blinked. "Oh, uh, our mother is still around here somewhere, I think. I'll send the carriage back 'round for them."

Violet nodded her understanding. "Well, then good night, Your Grace." She dipped a curtsy.

"Good night, my lady." He bowed deeply, brushing his lips over the back of her hand.

Violet watched him go, suppressing the urge to give him a teasing grin when she noted how he seemed to take one last look at her before a footman helped him with his greatcoat and hat.

A moment later, and he was gone.

Stunned at the odd sensation she felt just then, Violet remained where she was for a moment longer than necessary.

"You didn't have to afford my brother so much of your time this evening," Amelia said from her left. "It appears you played him perfectly."

Violet turned and gave a start. "Where have you been?" she asked in surprise. She leaned over and kissed her friend on the cheek. "Your gown is gorgeous," she added, stepping back to admire the bell skirt.

"Thank you. And I was anywhere *he* wasn't," Amelia said, arching a dark brow.

"Amelia," Violet gently scolded. "Weston was very pleasant. He's far easier to talk to than I was expecting."

"That's because he didn't feel threatened by someone else," she said, her eyes rolling in disgust.

"You're far too harsh on your own brother." They stood watching the dancers for a moment before Violet added, "Speaking of brothers, what have you done with mine?"

Amelia tittered. "He took his leave a few minutes ago. He didn't want a scene should Alfred catch sight of him."

Violet scoffed. "Well, we shall just have to enjoy the rest of the evening without them," she said, hooking her elbow around Amelia's. "Cards? Or more champagne?"

Giggling in delight, Amelia said, "More champagne first, of course. Then let's play cards."

The two hurried off to the refreshment room.

CHAPTER 8
A MARQUESS RETURNS TO LONDON

The next day

Jerked awake when the Fenwick traveling coach hit a hole in the cobbles, Michael, Marquess of Fenwick, sat up straight and pushed aside the curtains covering the window to his right.

He had no idea of how long it had been since his departure from the coaching inn near Basingstoke that morning. As he had the day before when they departed Fenwick Park, he had succumbed to the rolling motion of the coach and the rhythmic sound of the hoofbeats of the four horses pulling the coach and had fallen fast asleep.

A quick glance out the window showed they had made it to a city. When he knocked on the trap door above, it was a moment before the groom's pimply face appeared.

"Where are we?"

"Almost to Park Lane, my Lord." He disappeared a moment before returning to add, "We're in Kensington."

"Very good," Michael said, waving a hand to indicate the groom could close the trap door. He used the same hand to scrub the side of his face, wincing at feeling the stubble of a late afternoon beard.

"There should be time for a shave before dinner, my Lord."

Michael directed his attention on his valet. Thaddeus had been with him for over a decade, and although he usually rode in a separate coach with the luggage, Michael had decided they need only take one vehicle to London.

He wasn't yet sure how long he would stay in the capital. He wasn't even sure what had possessed him to make the trip in the first place.

Well, he had an inkling. Two, really. The most recent letter from his daughter, Violet, contained a nugget of information he found most intriguing.

She had made friends with Lady Amelia, a young lady whose father, a duke, had died a year ago.

Surely the girl's father was the Duke of Weston, for no other duke was reported to have died at the time. And if he was indeed the Duke of Weston, then that meant the Duchess of Weston was a widow recently out of mourning.

Helena.

Michael couldn't help the curiosity he had felt when he had finished reading Violet's missive.

Was his one and only true love free of a commitment not of her making?

He had experienced a moment of guilt when

Barbara's face came to mind. She had been a good friend, a saving grace, really, especially when she agreed to marry him knowing he might never feel for her what she felt for him.

Barbara had loved him. She had been free with her words of adoration. Free with her kisses on his cheek and forehead in the mornings and at night. Free with her body when he was in need of her.

Their friendship had bloomed into something more after the birth of Philip. Perhaps even a loving relationship when Violet was placed into his hands, her tiny body squirming despite the swaddling cloth in which she was wrapped.

He had grown to love Barbara. Even if he had never experienced the thrill and excitement he had felt for his first love, he did love her.

As for the second reason he had decided to make the trip to London, there had been the letter from his son lamenting something that had happened several years ago, an unfortunate incident that was now putting his possible future happiness at risk.

Philip, heir to the Fenwick marquessate, wanted to marry, and Michael was fairly sure the victim of the unfortunate incident was related to Philip's choice for a bride.

He knew one thing for certain. He was not going to allow his son to suffer as he did because of a stubborn father or brother or whoever it was who needed to grant permission for the girl to marry.

If permission wasn't forthcoming, he would see to it

the couple made it to Scotland—even if he had to drive the coach himself.

"My lord?"

Pulled from his reverie, Michael directed his gaze on Thaddeus before realizing the valet held out a handkerchief.

"What is it?" he asked, gingerly taking the square of linen.

"You... you have tears on your face, I think," Thaddeus said. He glanced toward the window. "Perhaps you have something in your eye?"

Michael blinked several times, then wiped his face with the handkerchief. "I hadn't noticed," he replied at the same moment the coach came to a halt. "Ah, we're here," he announced, barely recognizing the townhouse he had called home three decades earlier. "The trees are certainly taller than I remember."

The coach door opened, and he was quick to step out. Late afternoon sunshine had him squinting before he turned around to stare at Fenwick House. His assessing gaze went from the bright blue painted front door to the row of windows framed by black shutters at the top, and he soon realized it looked as if it had been built only the year before.

"Appears as if Fenwick House has been well maintained, my lord," Thaddeus offered.

"Philip is a stickler for that sort of thing," Michael acknowledged. "Better about it than I am."

If anyone at Fenwick Park had questioned his decision to send Philip to London to run most of the marquessate from there, they didn't now. Ever since Barbara had died, Michael hadn't been as driven to do his duty. Hadn't been as interested in the business of running the marquessate, choosing instead to concentrate on the tenant farms and those who worked his lands.

He supposed some thought him mad for choosing the country over the capital. For choosing the company of farmers over aristocrats. For choosing to socialize with landed gentry rather than royalty.

Perhaps he was.

If Violet hadn't taken on her late mother's duties as a hostess, he might never have hosted another social event at Fenwick Park. Might never have met the new families who had moved into the nearby village of Ludgershall or enjoyed a sour ale with the new parson whose living he provided.

"Father!"

His gaze darted to Violet, who was smiling broadly as she ran in his direction. He was nearly bowled over when she collided with him, wrapping her arms around his neck before kissing him on the cheek.

"Your timing is perfection," she gushed. "Dinner is to be served in an hour, so you have plenty of time for a shave," she teased as she rubbed a forefinger over his blonde stubble.

"You haven't yet adapted to a later dinner time?" he asked, offering his arm. "Now that you're in London?"

"Not now," she replied, placing a hand on his arm. "There are entertainments nearly every night of the week. In fact, Aunt Katherine is due here at eight o'clock to take me to a card party."

"Is she now?" He hadn't considered he would be seeing his aunt so soon.

"She has me scheduled for two balls this week and three next week," Violet went on. "As well as a *soirée*, and we've been invited to tea at several houses."

He was about to respond when Philip appeared framed in the open doorway, his right hand held out in anticipation of shaking his father's. Michael pushed it aside and pulled his son into a quick embrace. "Town seems to agree with *you*," he said with a huge grin.

"It does. Well, except for all the soot that seems to rain down all the time, I rather like London."

Michael gestured to the house. "You'd never know the soot fell around here."

"That's because I arranged to have it cleaned off the house and pavement last week," Violet stated, stepping into the house.

Michael and Philip exchanged knowing glances. "You realize when she marries, you're going to have to find a wife," Michael warned with a grin.

Philip's happy expression faltered for a moment. "I am well aware," he replied.

The butler bowed. "The master suite has been made ready for you, my lord."

Michael aimed a curious glance in his son's direction.

"Oh, I never moved into it," Philip explained. "I took the one I stayed in when I last visited London. Before university."

"The mistress suite is empty as well," Violet remarked, leading them to the stairs once Thaddeus and a pair of footmen had passed them carrying trunks.

"I don't know how long I'm staying," Michael warned.

"Aunt Katherine is already seeing to it you'll receive invitations, probably as soon as tomorrow night's ball," Violet said, grinning when she saw him wince. "Oh, don't be like that," she scolded. "Everyone will be curious about you, so you can play at being as mysterious as you'd like."

Michael scoffed at hearing her assessment, but he knew she was right.

He would be the curiosity, at least for a fortnight. Beyond that, he wasn't sure what to expect. By then, he would at least know if he had a future with a certain duchess.

And hopefully his son would have his future marchioness.

CHAPTER 9
DINNER REVEALS A DIFFERENCE IN A DUKE

*a*n hour later, at Weston Hall

Helena entered the dining room on the arm of her son, Amelia following behind.

"I didn't see much of you last night," she said, directing her attention on Alfred. "I do appreciate you sending the coach back for us."

He chuckled. "I spent most of the evening admiring tropical fish," he replied, holding her chair for her. Once she was seated, he moved to hold Amelia's chair for her.

Stunned by his act of courtesy, Amelia didn't immediately sit down. "Thank you," she said, almost making it a question.

"Did you two enjoy playing cards last night?" he asked.

Both Helena and Amelia regarded him with looks of shock. "Yes," they said in unison.

"Your sister more than me, I imagine," Helena added,

nodding to a footman who was waiting with a bottle of wine.

Alfred directed his gaze on his sister. "Why is that?"

Turning her attention to her mother, Amelia frowned. "I'm not sure what you mean. I only played a few hands," she argued. "Until Violet had to leave with the Duchess of Pendleton, and I certainly didn't win any hands."

Helena displayed an odd expression. "I hardly noticed. I always seem to end up playing with the same old biddies," she complained. "Although I enjoy a bit of gossip as much as anyone, I find it tiring after a time. There's never anything new."

"Actually, there is," Alfred countered. "My new man of business will start work on the morrow," he announced, lifting his glass of wine as if in a toast.

Helena regarded him with an expression of surprise, now realizing why he was in a much better mood than usual. "Why, that's wonderful."

"Did you choose the one who used to work for the Earl of Montaine?" Amelia asked.

"Indeed. Name's Nelson. Seems competent and eager to see to the business," he replied. "I'll keep the ledgers and pay the bills while he sees to the correspondence. With my input, of course." This last was said with a hint of arrogance.

"That's to be expected," Helena said. "What of the last of your father's affairs?" When she noticed how he stiffened, she immediately regretted the query.

"I'm paying a call on the solicitor in the morning to

finalize the matters of estate," he replied. "As long as there are no surprises in father's will, I expect that will be the end of it."

Helena dared a glance at Amelia. Although the solicitor had informed her of the arrangements Harcourt had made on their behalf, Mr. Barton had warned her the last will and testament was signed before their daughter had been born. Why Harcourt had thought he was immortal, she could never say, but his refusal to see to an updated will greatly bothered her. "I do hope he has a dowry set aside for Amelia is all," she murmured, hoping to convince him she wasn't concerned on her own behalf.

Having just taken a sip of her wine, Amelia nearly choked on it. "He said he was going to see to it. Last year. Before the Season started," she said.

"If he didn't, *I'll* see to it," Alfred said between spoonfuls of soup, returning to his usual sullen manner.

"Another morning or two, and I shall have all the social correspondence caught up," Helena said brightly. "It seems as if we've been invited to *everything*."

Alfred's momentary funk seemed to clear. "Perhaps I'll be able to attend a few events. Enjoy playing a card game or two."

"Did you dance last night?" Amelia asked.

Glancing up from her soup, Helena shook her head. "No one asked me," she said, darting a glance at her son. "But then most of those who were dancing were much younger."

"I danced once," Alfred remarked proudly. "I feared I'd forgotten how, but the steps came easily enough."

When he didn't offer more on the matter, Helena asked, "Who had the honor of being your partner?"

Alfred visibly reddened. "Amelia's friend. Lady Violet," he replied. "Thought it best I make her acquaintance since she was apparently introduced to me at another event," he added, a quelling glance directed in his sister's direction.

Helena furrowed a brow. "She's rather new to Town, is she not?"

"She's from Shropshire," Amelia replied. "Hasn't even been in Town for a month."

"She must come from a good family if her aunt is the Duchess of Pendleton," Helena remarked.

"Indeed," Amelia replied. Determined not to mention Violet's relationship to Philip, she was about to change the subject when the footmen appeared with the next course. "Oh, Mother, you've outdone yourself with tonight's dinner," she said.

Helena regarded her daughter as if she'd grown another head. "Thank you?" she replied, directing a glance in Alfred's direction.

He wasn't paying attention to either of them, though, his gaze apparently on his mind's eye. Deciding it best she let him continue his reverie—from his expression, it seemed he was enjoying himself—Helena merely concentrated on her dinner.

There was something different about Alfred on this night, and she hoped it was a sign he was changing.

For the better.

If he hadn't—or didn't very soon—she had already

begun devising a scheme whereby she could leave London to go on a holiday. With Katherine, Duchess of Pendleton, already seeing to sponsoring a young lady for the Season, Helena was sure she could convince the woman to take on another in her stead.

Helena suppressed the stab of guilt she felt at the thought of leaving her children. Perhaps she could make it through the rest of the Season without a change of venue. Perhaps she could endure a few more months of entertainments, but after that, she would leave London.

Now that she was out of mourning, she was determined to live the rest of her life free of a man's control.

CHAPTER 10
A PLAN IS MADE

*M*eanwhile, *in the Fenwick House dining room*

"I'll leave you two to your brandy," Violet said when the dessert course was finished. "Aunt Katherine should be here at any moment to collect me for the card party."

Her father and brother both stood as she took her leave of the dining room, Philip watching closely until he was sure she was out of earshot.

"What's going on?" Michael asked, his suspicion evident.

Philip managed a look of contrition. "She has become fast friends with Lady Amelia," he replied. "So I don't want her to hear what I have to say."

Michael furrowed a brow. "But she's aware of your fondness for the girl?"

His son nodded, but he grimaced at hearing his father's choice of words. He was more than fond of Amelia Sheppard. "Oh, yes. I had to admit it to her because, well, I'm sure they've talked about me," he murmured. He winced. "And because Violet would have sorted it of her own accord. She's terribly clever."

Chuckling softly, Michael nodded. "She is at that. She'll make a fine wife for someone who will appreciate it, so I do hope she doesn't end up with some bounder with half a brain."

"A man with half a brain would need her though," Philip remarked.

A footman appeared with a decanter of brandy and two crystal glasses. Once Michael acknowledged him, the servant poured the drinks and hurried off. When the door to the butler's pantry closed, Michael held up his glass. "A toast to your impending nuptials?"

Chuckling softly, Philip held up his glass. "Let us hope."

They sipped the dark amber liquid at the same time and returned their glasses to the table before Michael leaned back. "When will you ask Weston for permission?"

Inhaling softly, Philip said, "I thought to pay a call on him in the morning."

"Will you send a footman ahead? To set a time?"

Philip shook his head. "I thought about it, but I think it's best if he doesn't have a chance to... to deny me before I can even ask."

"Will you apologize?"

Jerking in surprise, Philip stared at his father. "I hadn't thought to—"

"Do so. Whatever you must to set things right," he

stated. At hearing Philip's scoff, he added, "He's a *duke,* son. He can make things very uncomfortable for you for the rest of your life if you don't," Michael warned.

Philip dipped his head. "Oh, all right. And if he still doesn't give me permission?"

"I'll have a word with him," Michael said. "I... I should pay him a call anyway. Introduce myself. If he's like his father, then I believe we're of the same political leanings, so that should help." He paused a moment. "There's something you should know which may or may not complicate the situation."

A look of worry crossed Philip's face. "Go on."

Michael cleared his throat. "His grandfather, the Duke of Woodleigh, denied me permission to marry his mother."

Philip blinked. "You're... you're speaking of Her Grace, the Duchess of Weston?" he asked carefully, the memory of his father's drunken musings coming to the forefront.

"Helena, yes," Michael responded. "I loved her, and I wanted her to be my wife. But... when I paid a call on Woodleigh to ask his permission—"

"He said no," Philip remembered.

"Said she was betrothed to Weston. A marriage contract had been arranged when she was but a young girl."

"Damn," Phillip whispered, pretending he didn't already know the tale.

Michael inhaled and let the breath out in a *whoosh.* "I

recall a moment of feeling as if I'd been played, but it was evident from her reaction she knew nothing of the betrothal."

Philip dipped his head. "So... she wanted to marry you?"

"Indeed."

"Were you two... playing house?" he asked, trying hard to suppress a smirk.

"That's none of your concern," Michael replied. He arched a brow. "Have you been playing house with Lady Amelia?"

Philip's face bloomed with color. "We enjoy kissing, he admitted. "I've not taken her virtue, if that's what you're asking."

His father seemed satisfied with his answer. "What I'm about to say... please don't take it wrong."

Shaking his head, Philip displayed a look of confusion. "All right."

"I loved Helena. I always have. Until I see her again... until I have a chance to speak with her... I still love her," he stammered.

Philip gave a start. "Do you write letters to one another?" he asked. "Did you... while you and Mother——?"

"No," he responded firmly. "Never. I left London to lick my wounds and live in the country. And that's what I've done for thirty years," he replied, a grimace marring his features.

"But you married Mother."

He nodded. "I married your mother because I needed an heir, and because... well, I knew her from when we were younger—"

"Because she was a neighbor," Philip stated. "You played together as children."

"That's right. She was always very pleasant. Very amiable."

"But... you didn't love her," Philip guessed.

Michael shook his head. "I did after a time. After you two were born, I grew to love her. The longer we were married, the more regard I had for her."

"She loved *you*," Philip accused.

Michael dipped his head. "She did. With all her heart and more," he acknowledged. "So please know that I don't wish to seem heartless when I tell you that given Weston's death, I intend to renew my acquaintance with Helena."

Philip leaned back in his chair and crossed his arms. "All right," he finally said. "So... what's your plan?"

"I'll wait until you return tomorrow and then pay a call on the duke. Introduce myself. Plead on your behalf if I must—"

"To beg on my behalf, don't you mean?"

"I'll warn him what's to happen if he doesn't give his permission—"

"Which is?" Alarm sounded in Philip's voice.

"A trip to Gretna Green for you and Lady Amelia."

Philip's eyes rounded. "You're *condoning* it? I...I know I've threatened it in my letter to you, but I never really thought I would—"

"I will not have what happened to me happen to you," Michael stated, stabbing a forefinger onto the tabletop. "He'll probably deny you the dowry, so we shall see to it funds are set aside for her and your children."

Settling back into his chair, Philip drew his brows together. "If you hadn't married Mother—"

"I know. You and your sister would not exist," Michael acknowledged. "But I don't want you to suffer as I did. I don't want you to become bitter—"

"Were you? You never seemed bitter."

Michael winced and inhaled deeply. "Then I did a damned good job of hiding it."

Philip finally nodded. "If I have to take Amelia to Scotland, there will be a scandal."

"Indeed," he agreed. "Which is why we need to do what we must to secure Weston's permission. There is strength in numbers. If he turns you down, I'll ask on my behalf. Explain that I want Lady Amelia as a daughter."

"You haven't even met her."

Michael gave him a quelling glance. "And yet I feel as if I already know her. I've been reading your letters about her for several months, and Violet's letters about her the last two weeks," he said.

"And if Weston denies *you*?"

Dipping his head, Michael said, "I'll ask if Helena might be available to see me." He shrugged. "Once I explain the situation, surely she'll agree to have a word with her son. She may have some sway with him."

Philip nodded. "Perhaps Amelia can help as well," he murmured. "As a last resort, of course."

"Strength in numbers," Michael said with a wan grin. "And if that doesn't work, then… it's off to Scotland."

Chuckling softly, Philip finally nodded. "Oh, all right."

Michael lifted his glass. "Here's to a plan."

Grinning, Philip lifted his glass and said, "To a plan."

CHAPTER 11
AN AUNT'S ADVICE AND COUNSEL

eanwhile, just outside the Fenwick House dining room Violet listened intently to the conversation taking place between her father and brother, not at all surprised to hear her father's confession. The two had talked at length about how duty and devotion sometimes clashed with one another.

That her father and brother had devised a four-pronged plan that didn't include her wasn't the least bit surprising, but she couldn't help but feel left out.

Neither one knew she had deliberately spent time with Weston the night before, attempting to curry favor with the young duke. She had mentioned to Weston she would be riding in the park on the morrow. If he actually showed up to join her, she would tolerate his presence as best she could. Pretend an interest in him. Compliment him on his riding skills. Do whatever she must to gain his trust.

Play him.

She was halfway up the stairs and on her way to the parlor when a commotion at the front door had her turning around.

Aunt Katherine had arrived.

Violet quickly descended the stairs. "Aunt Katherine, so good of you to have come into the house," she said, dipping a quick curtsy. "I would have met you out in the coach if I'd known it had arrived."

"Why, I had every intention of coming in," the older woman claimed, handing her mantle to Browning before removing her gloves. "He's here, is he not?"

Grinning, Violet waved a hand toward the dining room. "He is," she acknowledged. "He'll be happy to see you."

The sound of their voices had Katherine's nephew and grand nephew joining them in the hall.

"Aunt Katherine," Michael said, pulling her into an embrace. "Time away from your husband obviously agrees with you," he added, referring to Thomas, Duke of Pendleton.

She slapped his arm. "I actually miss the old coot, I'll have you know. He keeps me warm at night when the fire goes out."

Both Violet and Philip struggled to hide their grins of embarrassment, but Michael didn't bother. "I'm happy for you both. He feels terribly blessed to have had you as his duchess these past few decades." He grinned at seeing one of her eyebrows arched in a scold at the mention of how much time had passed since her second marriage had begun. "Is he coming to London for any of the Season?"

Katherine shrugged. "Possibly. He's in Bath at the moment. Hosting some event or the other," she replied as Michael stepped back to regard her with a grin.

"Isn't he eighty years old?" Michael asked in disbelief.

"He's nine-and-seventy, and he doesn't look a day over sixty," Katherine replied on a huff. "Now, how is it *you* still look the same after so many years?" she asked in disbelief. She raised a hand to the side of Michael's face and angled hers first to one side and then to the other.

"Country living, Kate. It looks as if it's done the same wonders for you."

She acknowledged his comment with a grin. "I like life in Wiltshire," she agreed. "But it's nice to be in London once in a while. My boys are here—"

"As are the grandchildren?" he guessed.

"Indeed. And your children. Violet's been the perfect young lady. No trouble at all with her come-out," she said, giving Violet a nod. "This one...," she indicated Philip with a wave of her hand, "Could have his choice of any young lady in the *ton* and be married on the morrow if he wished."

Michael scoffed softly. "Given he'll be paying a call on a certain young lady's brother on the morrow..." He paused. "Let's hope your words are true."

Katherine's eyes widened. She turned her attention on Philip and sobered. "So... it's to be Lady Amelia, is it?" she guessed.

Philip's expression faltered. "Yes. How... how did you know?"

She gave him a quelling glance. "I might be old, but I'm not blind, young man."

For a moment, Philip displayed an expression of guilt. "I was sure we were discreet," he claimed.

She shrugged. "Well, it's not as if I've heard you were playing house clandestinely," she replied. Her eyes suddenly rounded. "Were you?"

Violet tittered, quickly raising a hand to cover her mouth when Katherine directed her gaze on her.

"Out with it, young lady."

"I cannot say, Aunt Katherine. I promised Amelia."

"Oh, you're no fun," Katherine teased. She turned to Michael. "I'm taking Violet to a card party. There won't be gambling at this one, of course."

"Well, I should hope not," he replied in alarm.

"And I won't keep her out beyond... oh, let's say one o'clock—?"

"In the morning?" Michael finished, his voice rising. "Isn't that terribly late?"

"Well, it's early for a card party, actually." At seeing his expression didn't change, she said, "You're back in the city, Fenwick." When he still didn't capitulate, she said, "Oh, then midnight, if you insist. Come, Violet. Let's let these two drink their brandy and play a game of billiards."

"Yes, Aunt Katherine." Violet hurried to the vestibule to allow Browning to help her with her redingote while Katherine pulled on her gloves.

"I want a report just as soon as you've secured Weston's permission to court Lady Amelia," Katherine stated, her gaze squarely on her nephew.

"Yes, Aunt Katherine," Philip replied.

Once Violet and Katherine had left Fenwick House, Michael turned to regard his son with a grin. "It seems we have yet another among our numbers," he said, arching a brow.

Philip nodded. "If I didn't dislike him so intensely, I might almost feel sorry for Weston. He's about to be played, I think."

Michael chuckled as the two made their way to the study for another glass of brandy.

CHAPTER 12
CALLING ON A DUKE

The following morning

When he halted his single-horse phaeton in front of Weston Hall at precisely ten o'clock in the morning, Philip glanced about in search of a street urchin who might see to holding the reins. Finding none, he secured them to the post and offered the horse a carrot.

Although he had expected the groom might give him an apple, the servant explained the other groom had taken off with the last of the fruits. "You just missed your sister, my lord," he had said. "She went riding this morning."

Philip thought it odd she hadn't said anything about it over breakfast, but then he had been preoccupied with rehearsing what he would say to Weston when he was finally in the duke's presence. Making a mental note to ask her about it later that day, he made his way to the front door.

When the Weston Hall butler appeared, Philip handed him a calling card. "Lord Crawford to see His Grace." He paused when he remembered Amelia saying the servant's name. "You're Pritchard, are you not?"

The butler's eyes rounded slightly. "I am." He examined the white pasteboard before saying, "The duke is not in residence, my lord."

Philip gave a start. "Not at home? Or... or not receiving callers?" He immediately wondered if Alfred had warned the servant about him. Perhaps Weston had told them he wasn't to be admitted.

"He has left for an appointment, my lord. Would you like to wait?" Pritchard offered. "I cannot say how long he will be. He so rarely leaves the house, my lord."

Surprised by the comment, Philip was also relieved to hear he could stay if he wished. He shook his head. "Uh, I can come back. Is ten o'clock in the morning too early for His Grace?"

The butler shook his head. "His Grace is an early riser, my lord. Should I let him know you'll return on the morrow?"

Having already decided it best Weston not have any advance notice, Philip said, "No. In fact, it would be better if he didn't know. Could you maybe *not* mention I was here?"

Shrugging, Pritchard said, "Of course, sir." He handed back the calling card.

"Much obliged," Philip said, tucking the pasteboard into his waistcoat pocket.

Feeling a combination of relief and dread, he turned and made his way back to the phaeton.

There was always tomorrow.

CHAPTER 13
A RIDE IN THE PARK PUTS A PLAN IN MOTION

*M*eanwhile, at the Cumberland Gate, *northeast corner of Hyde Park off Oxford Street*

His chronometer not yet showing ten o'clock, Alfred was relieved when the Weston town coach reached the end of Oxford Street. There it turned into St. George's Row, and next to the Cumberland Gate entrance, one of his grooms stood holding the reins of his Irish walker as well as another horse from the Weston stable.

More importantly, at least from his perspective, was the horse and rider approaching the same gate from the south in Park Lane.

Wearing a bright blue riding habit and a hat adorned with a short peacock feather, Lady Violet had her mount in a trot that was neither hurried nor slow. When a smile appeared to brighten her face, he realized it was because she had spotted his coach.

The oddest sensation had him anxious to greet her as

he exchanged his top coat with a riding jacket. To alleviate the need to return to Weston Hall to change his clothes, he had worn riding breeches and a pair of Hessians to his appointment. He pulled on his shorter top hat and bounded from the coach when the driver opened the door.

"Lady Violet!" Alfred called out, giving her an exaggerated bow before he hurried to mount his gray walker. He took the reins from the groom. "Your timing is impeccable."

Violet slowed her walker until it was abreast of his and then pulled back on the reins. "As is yours, Your Grace. What a beautiful horse you have."

Alfred felt a moment of pride. He had spotted the mare at an auction at Tattersall's several years earlier and paid what his father claimed was far too much for the three-year-old. The walker was fully broken, though, and an easy ride. "This is Mouse," he said by way of introduction. He gave the walker a gentle kick, and she made her way toward the gate. At the same moment, Violet urged her mount into motion, and the two horses passed beneath the gate.

Giggling, Violet said, "Because of the color of her coat?"

"Because she is as quiet as a mouse," he replied. "She never complains. At least, she hasn't in my company." He nodded to her walker. "And who have we here?"

Leaning forward to smooth a kid leather-gloved hand along her bay-colored mount's neck, Violet turned her attention entirely on the horse and said, "George, may I have the honor of introducing you to His Grace, Duke of Weston?"

Alfred chuckled. "I was afraid you were going to say his name was Thunder or Lightning or Zeus or Aries," he replied, his brows waggling.

"I think those names were already taken by the other horses in my father's stable," she said with a grin. She sighed contentedly. "We could not have asked for fairer weather today."

Alfred dared a glance up and around them. "Agreed. When I saw the rain this morning, I feared we would have to cancel our plans." He looked behind them to discover her groom riding at a respectable distance.

"Let's hope it stays this nice for tonight's ball," she commented. "My aunt claims it will be a crush, so I expect many will wish to escape the ballroom to the gardens."

He chuckled softly. "My mother said the same thing this morning," he claimed. Although it had taken a few minutes to become reaccustomed to his horse, he was glad when he felt comfortable enough to simply let the horse set the pace and follow the crushed granite path that led straight west. "I think all the duchesses must discuss these things during some secret meetings."

"Over tea, I'm sure," Violet said. "In their parlors."

"With cakes and biscuits," he murmured. "Or scones with clotted cream."

She tittered. "Oh, dear. You sound as if you haven't had your breakfast yet this morning," she said, concern sounding in her voice.

"You have the right of it," he said, surprised she would notice. His mother always seemed to know, as if he went about with a sign on his chest with the words, *haven't yet had breakfast* painted on it.

"Would you like an apple?" Violet held out the round fruit in his direction. "I'm not sure how good it is, given it's from last September's harvest."

He leaned over and took it. "You're a lifesaver, my lady. Thank you. How is it you...?"

She patted the pocket of her riding habit, where a slight bulge indicated there was at least one other apple. "George has come to expect a treat at the end of a ride," she explained. "It's always best to bring two."

Glancing back, he was almost disappointed to discover her groom still followed them. He absently rubbed the apple on his thigh before he took a bite. "I'm hoping my groom saw fit to bring something for Mouse. I came here straight from my solicitor's office, and I fear the last thing I would have thought to bring was a treat for Mouse." He took another bite of the apple and chewed, sure Violet was watching him.

For a moment, he wondered if she found his form acceptable. He hadn't ridden in over a year, but he was sure he was seated properly. Mouse seemed fine with how he casually held the reins in one gloved hand.

Perhaps she enjoyed seeing his profile—a nose reminiscent of Ancient Romans on a face featuring high cheekbones, a wide forehead, and a square jaw.

He couldn't claim he had inherited any of his appearance from his father, but the cheekbones and eyes were definitely from his mother.

Did she find him handsome? He was almost tempted to ask. Before these past few days, he hadn't given his appearance a second thought. His valet shaved him every morning and took a scissors to his hair once a month. He saw to the maintenance of his clothes. Chose conservative waistcoats for the day and more elaborate ones for the evening. As far as Alfred knew, his valet was doing his best to ensure he cut a fine figure without looking like a dandy.

"I trust your appointment went well?"

Pulled from his brief reverie, Alfred chuckled. "As well as can be expected, I suppose. It was with my father's solicitor. He has simply continued in his duties since his death, which has worked well for me. Thought it best I meet him in person, though." She gasped, and he turned to regard her with a questioning glance.

"You hadn't met him before this morning?" she asked in disbelief.

He shrugged. "I've exchanged a number of letters with him, of course, but when I discovered how close his office is to Park Lane, I thought it would be quicker to simply speak with him. I needed to ensure my sister's dowry has been arranged, which it has." At hearing her sudden intake of breath, he glanced over at her. "She doesn't now, but it's possible she'll have a suitor this Season."

"Oh, of course," Violet responded. "Was your solicitor what you expected?"

Alfred shrugged. "I suppose. Perhaps younger than I thought," he admitted, remembering how he had assumed Andrew Barton, Esquire, would be gray, balding, fat, and at least fifty years of age. He was none of those. "His father had been seeing to the dukedom's affairs since before my father inherited," Alfred continued. "And now the son has simply taken up the reins and continues to run the office."

"I should think continuity is important in the affairs of a dukedom," she remarked.

Coming upon an intersection, Alfred directed his horse to take a path that led to the southeast. "Agreed," he commented, once their mounts were one again abreast of one another. "I might be doing things a bit differently from my father, but I've kept the same foremen. The same solicitor."

"The same man of business?" she prompted.

He made a groaning sound in his throat and wasn't surprised when she regarded him with curiosity. "My father never employed one. After these past six months, I've come to realize why it is I always seem to have so much to do when he did not."

Her blonde brows furrowed. "Are you saying he wasn't doing everything required? To run the dukedom?"

Although he was impressed with her conclusion, Alfred winced. "Something like that. I've hired a secretary to see to the letter writing. That should help. I've finally caught up the ledgers. That took..." He audibly sighed. "Well, far longer than it should have."

"Were they not being done, either?"

He hesitated to respond. "I think my father might have been more ill than he let on at the end. Mother always said he thought he would live forever, but even when his mortality was staring at him in the face, he wouldn't allow anyone else to touch the books."

"I'm so sorry," she replied. "And here I thought it rather odd that my father would already have my brother looking after his affairs. Learning everything he needs to know to run a marquessate."

The reference to a marquessate had Alfred giving a start. For some reason, he had assumed Violet was merely the daughter of an earl or viscount. "Your father is obviously a very wise man," he remarked. He turned to stare at her. "Is he here? In London?"

Violet grinned. "He arrived yesterday afternoon from our country house in Shropshire," she replied. "My Aunt Katherine has already ensured invitations are being delivered to the house, although I think Father would be happy to skip most of the entertainments."

"Your aunt... she is the Duchess of Pendleton, is she not?"

"Indeed," Violet replied. "She was the Duchess of Whyte—a long time ago—but I think she likes Pendleton far more than she did Whyte." Her eyes rounded. "And she enjoys living near Bath better than living in London, but you didn't hear that from me," she quickly added.

Alfred chuckled, angling his horse to follow a path that led back toward the Cumberland Gate. "I had the impression she was enjoying herself at the *soirée* the other night."

"Oh, she was. She loves playing cards. In fact, we were at a card party last night that seemed to go on for hours. I didn't realize so many women in the *ton* like to play card games."

"Cards?" he repeated. "Do they play for... for blunt?"

Violet giggled. "She did place wagers on most of the hands, and she did win," she admitted. "Far more than she bet."

"And you?"

Her eyes rounding, Violet shook her head. "Oh, no. I merely play for the fun of it. Whist, mostly."

"Ah," he replied, relieved to hear she wasn't a gambler.

"I hate to bring this up," she said. "But... should we mayhap hurry the horses along? You said you could only afford a half-hour, and I'm quite sure it's been at least that since we started."

Alfred struggled to hide his disappointment at hearing her words. Was she trying to end their ride early? Or was she merely reminding him of his own words from the night at the *soirée*? "It's fine, my lady. You were right, you must know."

Violet turned to stare at him. "Right about what, Your Grace?"

"The good it would do me to get some fresh air," he replied, pulling his chronometer from his waistcoat pocket. "It's not even half-past eleven o'clock."

Her eyes widening, Violet said, "Oh, my. We've been here in the park for over an hour!"

"Indeed. And I have enjoyed every moment of it," he said. When he noted she displayed a look of consternation, his good mood faltered. "What... what is it?"

Rolling her eyes, Violet said, "Your sister is due to pay a call on me at any moment. I do hope she doesn't mind waiting."

Relieved to hear the reason for her concern, Alfred chuckled. "Will you be telling her why you're late?"

"Would you prefer I didn't?"

He thought about her query for a time before saying, "If you tell her, I'll be sure to suffer a round of teasing when I return to Weston Hall," he said. "If you do not, then I will be left in peace to accomplish what I must before I can leave for the ball this evening."

"Then I shall not tell her," Violet said with a smirk.

Alfred felt a twinge in his chest, and his breath caught. "You would keep this secret betwixt the two of us?"

She blinked. "If you wish me to, of course. It will be *our* secret."

He glanced back, not surprised to see the groom still following them.

"What is it?" she asked, looking behind her.

He shrugged. "Just ensuring we hadn't lost him, is all," he said, arching a brow.

For a moment, he considered offering the groom a coin in exchange for him to ignore what he wanted to do, but the reminder of the ball had him reconsidering.

He wanted to steal a kiss, but there might be a better opportunity to do so later that night.

"Do have good day, Your Grace, and thank you for joining me today," Violet said when they were back at the Cumberland Gate.

"I will have a good day because of this ride with you, my lady. And don't forget... you promised me a dance."

"I shall save two for you, Your Grace," Violet said, dipping her head in his direction. She grinned before she aimed her horse in the direction of Park Lane and set off at a run, the groom right behind her.

Before he dismounted, Alfred watched her go until she was out of sight. Rather pleased by what he had to look forward to that evening, he bounded into the coach and sat back with a sigh of satisfaction.

CHAPTER 14
CALLING ON A DUCHESS

half-hour earlier, Weston Hall

Michael regarded the front of Weston Hall through the window of the Fenwick town coach and sighed. His heart was racing with anticipation, and he couldn't decide if it was due to the thought of a possible verbal spar with Alfred, Duke of Weston, or of seeing the love of his life for the first time in three decades.

Probably a bit of both.

The front door opened even before he had a chance to use the boar's head knocker. "Michael, Marquess of Fenwick, to see His Grace." He handed the butler his calling card, but the servant didn't even glance at it.

"His Grace is not in residence this morning, my lord. Would you like to wait inside?"

Michael sighed. "Was he in residence an hour ago?"

The butler shook his head. "He was not, my lord."

Feeling a combination of disappointment and relief on behalf of his son—if the duke wasn't in at Weston

Hall an hour ago, then Philip wouldn't have been able to speak to him.

At least his request hadn't yet been denied.

Michael considered his second mission of the morning. "Is the duchess here?"

His gaze dropping to the calling card, the butler said, "I'll see if she is, my lord. Do come in."

Following the butler, Michael scanned the interior of the vestibule and then the marble-tiled hall before he was led into a reception room with windows facing the street. From the feminine furnishings and rose and green color scheme, he assumed it was Helena's sitting room. He took an experimental sniff but didn't detect a hint of perfume or cologne.

"Tell me, would she see me if she didn't know my identity?" Michael asked of the butler. "If you didn't give her my name?"

Perplexed by the query, the butler seemed to think on it a moment. "She might if I told her you wished to surprise her, my lord."

Michael grinned and nodded. "Yes. That's it exactly."

The butler smirked and bowed before heading for the stairs, and Michael watched him until he disappeared from view.

Moving to the window, he glanced out to discover the trees of Hyde Park lined up beyond his town coach and the patterned bricks making up Park Lane. The last time he'd been in London, the park had been hidden from view by a tall brick wall. He absently wondered when it had been torn down. The park was certainly a better view.

Given the earlier morning rain had stopped some time ago, the clouds were parting to reveal a blue sky and spring sunshine.

"It's a beautiful vantage, is it not?"

Michael whirled around. Although the voice was familiar, the young lady who stood on the threshold of the salon was not—at least, not quite. Her facial features were similar to Helena's, and her hair was the color he remembered—a rich mahogany with hints of gold and red. "It is indeed," he replied before bowing slightly. "Might you be Lady Amelia?"

The young woman's eyes rounded as she straightened from a curtsy. "I am, sir."

Michael stepped forward and took her hand to his lips. "Since there is no one to do the honors, allow me to introduce myself. I am—"

"The Marquess of Fenwick," she breathed, staring at him in wonder. "Why, you look exactly as I expect Lord Crawford will look in twenty years," she said in awe.

Chuckling softly, Michael dipped his head. "Make that closer to thirty years, and you'll have the right of it," he said.

"Oh, that cannot be," she said with a brilliant grin.

He arched a blonde brow. "I think I shall adore having you as a daughter," he commented in a hoarse whisper. "An old man can always appreciate such compliments. As for you..." He paused, wondering how much he could tell her. Had Helena ever told her daughter about him? About their intentions to wed?

Perhaps Helena had forgotten about him. Perhaps his move to the country had kept him out of sight and out of mind. Or perhaps she had merely kept him a secret. A hopefully pleasant memory from half a lifetime ago.

"As for me?" she prompted.

Jerking from his reverie, Michael angled his head to one side. "You look very much like how I remember your mother."

Her eyes rounded again. "Is that... is that a good thing?"

His hearty laugh could probably be heard throughout the entire ground floor of Weston Hall. "Indeed. She was the most gorgeous woman I ever looked upon," he said, his attention turning to a tall woman making her way in their direction across the marble floor. He stepped around Amelia and added, "And she still is."

Amelia turned around, following his line of sight. She was about to thank him for his compliment, but instead stood and stared.

Helena, Duchess of Weston, strode up to the salon's open doorway and said, "My apologies for keeping you waiting, sir. What's this...?"

Michael watched as her eyes widened the same way her daughter's had. Watched when she quickly blinked twice. Watched as the rigid backbone found so frequently in duchesses seemed to give way and become one of jelly. Watched as her head began to fall backwards.

"Helena," he said at the same moment he stepped forward and reached out to keep her from falling to the floor. "Helena?"

"Oh, my goodness," Amelia said from somewhere behind him. "She's... she's *fainted*."

Michael hefted Helena into his arms, making sure the side of her head ended up against his shoulder. Despite the bell skirt of the green day gown she wore, he was able to get an arm behind her knees. "It would seem so," he whispered, never taking his eyes from Helena's face.

The thirty years since he had seen her had apparently been kind to his first love. Although there were faint lines at the edges of her eyes, she still displayed the peaches and cream complexion he remembered. Long, dark lashes rested on the tops of her cheeks, and lips made more red with cosmetics reminded him of their last, desperate kiss.

"My mother has never fainted a day in her entire life," Amelia claimed, motioning Michael toward the salon's Greek chaise lounge beneath the room's only window. "Why, I don't believe she even owns a vinaigrette."

He lowered Helena to the thick cushion and then sat, adjusting her so he cradled her head and shoulders in one arm. "She'll come 'round of her own accord," he said, leaning down to kiss Helena's forehead.

Amelia sighed as she sank into the adjacent uphol-stered chair. "That was so romantic," she said softly.

His attention torn from the duchess, Michael arched a brow. "Her fainting?"

Shaking her head, Amelia said, "Oh, no. The way you caught her. As if you *knew* she would faint." Her eyes widened. "Does that happen often to you? Women fainting upon meeting you, I mean?"

Torn between claiming that it did and allowing another hearty laugh, he simply shook his head. "Never in my experience, actually."

Amelia sighed. "You loved her once, didn't you?" she asked softly.

Michael didn't look up, determined to memorize every new feature he could find on the duchess' face. "I never stopped," he replied absently. He finally glanced in Amelia's direction. "One never forgets their first love." Amused at seeing the blush that colored her face— Amelia looked so much like how Helena had appeared at the same age—he allowed a long sigh.

"Is she why you came today?"

He shook his head. "I actually came to speak with Weston."

"Oh." Amelia straightened in the chair. "He's gone off to meet with his solicitor, I believe. First time he's left the house... well, except for the Everly *soirée*... in nearly a week, I think."

"Has he an aversion to being out of doors?" Michael asked, his brows furrowing. If the young duke rarely left the house, it would certainly explain his poor mood.

"Oh, no," Amelia replied. "Before he went off to university and then his Grand Tour, he used to ride horses every day. Went for walks in the park and to his club."

Michael regarded her with a questioning glance. "What happened to change him?"

She lifted a shoulder. "He inherited a dukedom. A burden that seems rather too heavy for him to bear alone, I think."

"I can imagine," Michael replied. "Surely he has a man of business, or a secretary—"

"He hired a secretary yesterday," Amelia stated. "To help with the correspondence."

"What about an accomptant? A clerk?"

"He's crack at doing the ledgers, so he prefers to do those himself," she explained.

"Foremen for the farms? And the mines?"

She shook her head. "I'm not quite sure. He's never been very forthcoming about his duties with me," she said with a shrug. "May I ask what your business was with him?"

Michael inhaled deeply. "In the event Philip had gained an audience with him in order to ask that he be allowed to court you," he began, an eyebrow arching, "I was prepared to argue his case if he was denied—which is what he expected to happen. I came to see if I couldn't help smooth things over between the two of them."

"Oh!" Amelia breathed. "It's rather sporting of you to try."

"It's that, or you'll find yourself in a coach on your way to Scotland," he stated, his manner serious.

"My lord?" she asked in surprise.

"With me at the reins," he went on, a mischievous

grin finally lighting his face. "Gretna Green for a quick wedding, and scandal be damned. Excuse my French."

Amelia giggled in delight. "Oh, my lord, for a moment, I thought you were *playing me*."

Michael sobered. "I was. I am," he claimed. "My son is in love with you, and I don't want him to suffer as I did." He glanced down at Helena, sure she had awakened at some point and was merely keeping her eyes closed. He leaned down and kissed her forehead again. "Life is too short to be denied the people that matter the most to us." He paused when he looked up and noticed Amelia's look of confusion. "You do love my son, do you not."

"Oh, very much, my lord," she claimed. "But I'm certain I have some influence over my brother. Perhaps I can help smooth things over betwixt the two of them. Save us all from certain scandal."

"You already sound like a marchioness," Michael remarked. He glanced down at Helena to discover her watching him, an expression of bemusement on her face. "Good morning, gorgeous."

"Hello, handsome," she whispered.

Amelia sighed, her hands clasping together as she beamed in delight.

Helena turned her head to regard her daughter with an arched brow. "I thought you were going to pay a call on your new friend. Lady Violet. Isn't that her name?"

Nodding, Amelia stood. "I am. Right now," she said, dipping a curtsy. "Please, do not stand up on my account, my lord," she added, directing her words to Michael.

He chuckled softly. "It was very good to meet you, Lady Amelia."

"And you as well, my lord."

Michael watched her practically run from the salon before turning his attention back to Helena. "I suppose you'll be wanting to sit up now?"

"I don't know why I would," Helena whispered. "It's rather comfortable right here, and you smell delicious."

"God, but I've missed you."

Helena blinked, apparently staving off tears. "I was afraid I would never see you again."

"I stayed away as long as I could, but when I received Philip's letter informing me of his intention to marry your daughter, I sorted the coast was clear."

"It was clear a few days ago when I was done with my mourning period," she said in a scolding voice. She made an attempt to sit up, but Michael tightened his hold on her.

"You fainted," he said.

"Well, it's no wonder. I am starving," she replied.

"It's nearly noon. As I recall, you're an early riser," he said. "Breakfast at nine?"

"If you must know, I've been up since before eight o'clock," she huffed. "I was actually on my way to the breakfast parlor when Pritchard told me I had a surprise caller. Truer words were never spoken."

Michael grinned and stood, turning to help her up. "Then let's get you to the breakfast parlor," he said. He led her out of the sitting room and then walked with her to a brightly lit room featuring a round oak table, an oak sideboard, and two footmen. Michael held a chair for her. "May I fill a plate for you?"

"Have a seat, Fenwick. That's what the footmen are for," she replied, settling into her chair. "Would you like coffee or tea?"

"Coffee, please," he replied, not surprised when both servants were suddenly in motion, one seeing to their food while the other saw to their drinks.

"Something must have been terribly important for you to delay coming downstairs for so long this morning," he remarked, his brows rising upon seeing plates filled with coddled eggs, rashers of bacon, and several toast points placed in front of both of them.

"I've been upstairs in my salon doing correspondence," she explained, lifting a toast point to her lips.

"For nearly four hours?" he questioned.

She nodded. "My stubborn son finally realized he could not handle the social responses with everything else he's supposed to be doing. I knew if I didn't wrest control of something from him, I would miss more entertainments, and I couldn't bear the thought of unintentionally snubbing another hostess." She took a bite of buttered toast and made a sound of appreciation.

Michael furrowed his brows. "Aren't invitations supposed to be handled by the lady of the house?" he asked, before tucking into the eggs. Although he had eaten breakfast a few hours earlier, the smell of the steaming hot bacon had his stomach growling.

She sighed. "You know that, and I know that, but for some reason Alfred seemed to think anything brought to his study on that silver salver of Pritchard's was his responsibility."

"Pritchard is your butler?"

"Yes."

"Hmm. Sounds as if Weston was never taught otherwise."

"He wasn't," she confirmed, a brow arching. "Weston... the late Weston... he thought he was going to live forever," she remarked, her eyes rolling in disgust. "He kept such tight reins on everything that when he died, it took months to determine what needed to be done."

"You offered to help?"

"Of course," she replied, giving him a quelling glance.

"Lady Amelia seems to think he's handling the accounting part of it all right," Michael offered.

"He is." She inhaled softly. "No worries there."

Michael noted her attention was no longer on her food. "What is it?"

She glanced in his direction. "In all my worries about Alfred, I sometimes forget about Amelia. She made her come-out last year, right before Weston died, and then we couldn't be seen attending entertainments once he did. This Season it's as if she's had to start over. And lately..." She grimaced.

"What?"

"I think she may be gambling."

Scoffing in disbelief, Michael had to suppress a chuckle at seeing Helena's serious expression. "Why ever in the world would you think such a thing?"

Helena rolled her eyes. "I don't have any proof, of course. I only have a suspicion."

"Go on."

She sighed and said, "Every week, at the same time, she goes to Hatchard's to shop for books. She's always gone exactly the same amount of time—takes her lady's maid with her, of course—and is always in a very good mood when she returns."

When she didn't offer anything else, Michael asked, "Does she come home with a book or two?"

"Oh, always. Usually a novel, although this latest trip had her bringing home *A Lady's Guide to Keeping a Household*, which is rather odd. And which has me even more suspicious. It's as if she didn't even try to shop for a book. As if she was in one of the reading rooms playing cards for an hour or more and then just grabbed the nearest book she came across on her way to the counter."

Michael leaned back in his chair and crossed his arms. "Anything else?"

Scoffing softly, as if she thought he was teasing her, she said, "There have been card parlors at two of the balls we've attended. I saw her in one, although she wasn't seated. She was standing behind a young man, examining his cards, I think."

"Did she ask for money to play?"

Helena shook her head. "Of course not. She wouldn't need to, though. Alfred gives her an allowance. Pin money, merely, but it's enough to play for a time if her wagers are reasonable." She sighed and added, "She attended a *soirée* at the Everly's a couple of night's ago—"

"Kate took my daughter to that *soirée*," he said. "My aunt is seeing to Violet's come-out," he quickly added, wondering if she would make the connection. Before Amelia had taken her leave of the sitting room, she had said she was on her way to pay a call on Violet. Now Michael wondered if perhaps she was really off to Fenwick House to see Philip.

Was the young lady pretending to play cards while she was really playing her mother by seeing his son in secret?

Helena paused a moment before allowing a shrug. "There was a card room set up at Rosemount House. Lady Everly told me she had to offer one for the older ladies, and I did see Amelia in there later in the evening. With Lady Violet."

"Did she attend last night's card party?" he asked. "Kate took Violet to that one. I believe they intended to play whist all night."

Inhaling to answer, Helena seemed on the verge of tears. "Oh, dear. I expected Amelia to be gone more now that the Season has started simply because we've received so many invitations, but now I think I must insist she stay at home."

Fairly sure Helena had her suspicions misplaced, Michael asked, "Are you aware your daughter is being courted?"

Helena's fork clattered to her plate as she turned to stare at him. "What's this?"

Michael blinked and realized he had some explaining to do. "First, you should know Violet is my daughter."

"I gathered that," she said slowly.

"She and Amelia have become fast friends. Violet only arrived in London a few weeks ago, so I was glad when she wrote to say she had a friend here."

"Amelia is very amiable," Helena agreed. "She makes friends easily."

"They didn't meet at an entertainment, however."

Stiffening in her chair, Helena stared at him. "Then... how were they introduced?"

Wincing, Michael said, "My son, Philip, Earl of Crawford, did the honors."

For a moment, Helena looked as if she might faint again. "Your son is in London?"

"Has been for over a year. He's taken over running the marquessate in my stead. Done rather well, actually, and I'm going to petition for him to receive a writ of acceleration. See if I can't get him into the House of Lords, since I doubt I'll ever attend."

She nodded her understanding. "So, he obviously met Amelia last year. Before Weston died."

"He did," Michael acknowledged. "He, uh... he fell in love with her. He's been courting her in secret for some time, and he hoped he could secure Weston's permission to marry her when he paid a call earlier today." He paused to gauge her reaction.

Helena blinked. "Are you saying she... Amelia *hasn't* been gambling?"

Not expecting the question, Michael chuckled softly. "I'm quite sure she hasn't been gambling."

Helena placed a hand on her chest and let out a breath of air. "This is such a relief," she whispered. "You've no idea what I've been imagining."

"Oh, I can imagine a lot. I have a daughter, too," he reminded her. After a pause, he said, "So... you're not terribly upset that she's been courted by Philip?"

Helena struggled for a moment, as if she was fighting an internal battle. "Like father, like son?" she finally countered. "If he's as charming and handsome as you, however could I blame her?"

He nodded. "The apples did not fall far from our trees," he remarked.

She narrowed her eyes. "When I got to the sitting room, you two were having a conversation."

"I was waiting for you, and she appeared. I introduced myself and told her I was looking forward to having her as my daughter."

Helena inhaled softly. "Now I think I am going to cry," she whispered.

Michael pulled a handkerchief from his waistcoat pocket and held it out for her. "Because you're happy, or because you're sad, or—"

"*Relieved*, of course," she replied with a huff. "Do you realize what this means?"

Glancing to the side, he considered how to respond. "She's not gambling, and you're gaining another son?" he guessed.

"She's going to be *married*," Helena stated, as if she thought him thick.

"Indeed. I expect there might be an heir by this time next year," he said, joining in her joy.

Helena's face fell. "Oh, God," she whispered.

"What?" he asked in alarm.

She rolled her eyes. "If Amelia marries, Alfred won't be far behind, and then he'll have an heir. I'm going to be bestowed with that awful title," she murmured before shoving another toast point into her mouth.

"What awful title?"

She gave him a quelling glance. "*Dowager* Duchess of Weston," she stated, a groaning sound following her proclamation.

Michael glanced around the breakfast parlor and leaned towards her. "Or you could agree to be my wife and become the Marchioness of Fenwick."

Helena stared at him for a long time before she leaned back in her chair and let out the breath she had been holding.

She seemed about to give him an answer when Pritchard appeared at the door and said, "Your Grace, His Grace has returned from his appointment and is asking for you."

Michael managed to keep an impassive expression on his face as he reached over and placed a hand on Helena's. "Will you be at the ball tonight?"

She blinked and nodded. "Yes. Yes, of course."

"Save all the waltzes for me, my love." He stood,

leaned over, and placed a kiss on her forehead before taking his leave of the breakfast parlor and of Weston Hall.

He didn't realize he was being watched once he passed the study.

CHAPTER 15
THE TALE OF A REUNION

*M*eanwhile, at Fenwick House

Lady Amelia Sheppard approached the front door of Fenwick House as she usually did, her lace-trimmed parasol hovering overhead while her lady's maid followed several steps behind.

Browning opened the door before she had even crossed over the area, stepping aside to allow her entry. "Lady Violet hasn't returned from her ride, my lady. Would you like to wait in the parlor?"

Amelia turned to Trimble. "I'm going to wait for Lady Violet upstairs. Go on to the back, and I'll send for you when I'm ready to leave." Her attention going to Browning, she said, "I know the way to the parlor."

The lady's maid nodded her agreement and joined the butler as they made their way toward the back of the house.

When the servants had disappeared, Amelia moved to the study and peeked in. She grinned at seeing

Philip behind the desk, his head bent as he read a letter. "Good afternoon, my lord," she said in a quiet voice.

Philip gave a start and quickly refolded the note. "Amelia!" He waved her into the study as he stood and made his way in her direction. "To what do I owe this honor?" He closed the study door and, rather than kissing the back of her hand, he kissed her cheek and then pulled her into his arms.

"Your sister, of course. She's not yet back from her ride in the park," Amelia replied, purring when she felt his warm hands smooth over her back.

"Do you suppose she has stayed away deliberately?" he asked, suspicious. "Because her best friend asked her to?"

Amelia scoffed. "I had nothing to do with it, I assure you," she claimed, but her subsequent giggle gave her away. "Oh, dear. Now you'll always be suspicious of my motives," she claimed.

"Nevertheless, I'll have to thank her later," he said, finally letting go his hold on her. He led her to a sofa at one end of the study and they sat. "Your color is very high this morning, and although I am flattered at seeing it, I cannot believe it is all due to me," he said, taking her hand to his lips. For a moment, his gaze went to her reticule, and he traced a finger along the intricate stitchery decorating it.

"You and your Father," she said, arching a dark brow.

Philip gave a start. "What are you talking about?"

"He came to Weston Hall this morning. An hour or

so ago," she explained. "I saw him in the downstairs salon and knew right away he was your father. You two—"

"Look alike, I know. Mother used to say it all the time." He displayed a smirk, which brought out a dimple in his lower left cheek.

"I'm going to be the most fortunate wife in all the *ton*," Amelia said on a sigh. "He's so handsome for a man his age."

Philip chuckled softly. "Thank you. I think."

"You could have told me Lord Fenwick knew my mother," she gently scolded.

His brows furrowing, Philip gave her a glance of uncertainty. "Actually, I wasn't certain he did until last night. We spoke of it after dinner."

Amelia scoffed softly. "Mother took one look at him and fainted."

"Fainted?" he repeated, his mouth dropping open in shock. "The Duchess of Weston fainted?"

"That was my thought exactly! Anyway, his lordship caught her before she fell to the floor," Amelia continued, turning on the sofa to face him. "It was so romantic." She reached out a gloved hand and pulled his head down before dropping a kiss on his forehead. She inhaled deeply, then let the breath out at the same time she hummed softly.

Philip arched a brow. "I hardly see how fainting can be romantic," he argued, pulling her onto his lap until she sat on one of his knees.

"Oh, but you should have seen him. The way he

looked at her. Said my mother was more gorgeous than he remembered." She audibly sighed again.

Furrowing his brows, Philip scoffed. "Father said that?" He leaned back in the sofa. "Well, I was reminded last night that he knows your mother from a long time ago," he mused. "Which makes sense, I suppose, since he apparently lived here in the capital until he moved to Shropshire and married my mother."

"Wasn't your mother from London?"

Philip started to answer and then stopped. "Um... actually, her family's country estate is very close to the Fenwick lands in Shropshire. Father met her when her family was staying there during the summers," he explained before scrubbing the side of his face with a hand. His eyes suddenly widened. "So... Father has met *you*?"

She nodded as she smiled. "Indeed. He's so terribly handsome for a man of his age," she repeated. "You should have warned me."

"Father?" Philip rolled his eyes.

"Well, of course I shouldn't be surprised. You're simply a younger version of him in appearance. He must have looked exactly like you when he was your age," she reasoned. "Which means I shall enjoy looking upon you for the rest of my life."

Chuckling, Philip angled his head first one way and then the other. "If you insist," he replied.

She leaned in, making it apparent she wished for them to kiss. Philip didn't hesitate, wrapping his arms around her shoulders to bring her closer. When their lips touched, their eyes closed, and for several seconds, they reveled in the touching of tongues as they tasted one another.

A knock at the door had them both straightening in alarm. "Damnation," Philip said in a whisper as he helped her to stand.

Amelia shook out her skirts and hurried to the chair in front of the desk.

"Come," Philip called out, moving to take his chair behind the desk.

The butler opened the door and gingerly poked his head around the opening. "Pardon, sir, my lady. Lady Violet has returned from her ride and is asking for Lady Amelia."

"Oh, good. I won't have to bother you any longer, my lord," Amelia said, her teasing grin aimed in Philip's direction.

"You're never a bother, my lady," he said, giving her a wink. He leaned forward. "Wait. You never said what happened after your mother fainted."

Amelia paused near the door. "Oh. Well, Mother woke up and she was quite embarrassed, of course, and she told me she needed to speak with Lord Fenwick alone, so I left."

Philip gave a start. "I'll have to ask him what he was doing there," he murmured.

Rolling her eyes, she said, "Why, reacquainting himself with my mother, of course." When he displayed a blank look, she added, "It's quite obvious they were once lovers," she whispered, her brows dancing in delight.

Philip huffed as if he didn't believe her words. "My father and your mother?" he asked. "You're mad," he added, waving a hand as if to shoo her out. "Don't keep Violet waiting any longer, or she'll hound me at dinner."

"I love you," Amelia whispered, barely dipping a curtsy before she ducked out of the study.

Grinning until the door was once again closed, Philip quickly sobered and returned to his desk.

What would Weston do once he learned his mother's long ago lover had returned to London? Somehow, Weston had known about Michael and Helena—it's what had gotten he and Weston into so much trouble at university—and Philip was fairly sure it wasn't because the duchess had admitted anything to her son.

So how had Weston learned of their *affaire*?

More importantly, would Weston be more likely to give his blessing for a marriage to his sister if his mother renewed her relationship with is father?

Or less?

Philip was almost afraid to pay another call on Weston Hall to find out.

*L*ady Violet stood in the middle of the hall, her gloved hands on her hips. She was still dressed in her bright blue riding habit, the feather in the matching hat drooping on one side. "I stayed out as long as I could," she said. If the Duke of Weston had left her in the park any earlier than he did, she would have taken another turn about the grounds to delay her return to Fenwick House.

"It was the perfect length of time," Amelia assured her. "Although I haven't been here very long."

"Oh? I thought you were going to be here at eleven o'clock. What kept you at Weston Hall?"

Amelia hooked her arm into Violet's and led them to the stairs. "Your father, as it happens," she said with a brilliant grin.

Violet's eyes widened. "You've already met him?"

She nodded. "He came to the house."

Stiffening, Violet's expression changed to one of worry. "Oh, dear," she murmured.

"What?"

Indicating they should climb the stairs, Violet kept her voice down as she said, "I think he meant to plead my brother's case with your brother."

Amelia frowned. "Why would he do that?" she asked, pretending she hadn't learned of the reason first hand from the marquess.

Violet lowered her voice to a whisper. "Because your brother told your mother who told her lady's maid who told my aunt's lady's maid who told *my* lady's maid who told me that he has no intention of giving anyone permission to marry you if he learned they didn't hold him in high regard, and everyone knows my brother and your brother didn't get along at school." She took an exaggerated breath. "And I might have mentioned it to Father."

Blinking, Amelia scoffed softly. "He may have encountered an unexpected surprise when he got there."

Violet stopped at the top of the stairs. "What do you mean?"

"My mother," Amelia stated.

Angling her head to one side, Violet stared at her friend for several seconds before she said, "You think Her Grace is trying to protect Alfred from my father?"

Amelia shook her head. "No. After what I witnessed, I rather doubt Lord Fenwick even remembers I have a brother."

Scrunching her face in confusion, Violet opened the door to her bedchamber and waved Amelia into it. "I am confused."

"As am I. What do you know of your father's time in London? Before he married your mother?" she asked, settling into one of the chairs by the fireplace as Violet hurried to change clothes behind a japanned screen in the corner. Although Dearing wasn't in the room, she had left a day gown draped over the screen.

"I don't know that I know anything about that," Violet replied, her words muffled by the yards of fabric she was removing from her body. "He talks of his time at Cambridge once in a while, but I don't recall him speaking of London."

"Well, he obviously lived here at some point. In his younger years," Amelia insisted.

"He did. He had to. He said he attended every session of Parliament before he married Mother."

"But not after?" Amelia asked. She moved to join

Violet behind the screen and did up the buttons at the back of her day gown.

"I don't know. I think when I was younger, he might have gone to Town on occasion," she mused. "Probably for Parliament. But he was back home right away. I don't think he attended balls or *soirées*. He was never much for London Society, and Mother..." She paused and blinked several times. "She was happy to stay with us. I think she was too shy to want a life here in the capital."

Amelia winced, knowing the reminder of Barbara Cummings was always hard for Violet. Losing her mother when she was barely fourteen coincided with when Philip was away at school. Once he completed his studies at Cambridge, he had headed to London to run the Fenwick marquessate while their father, Michael, and Violet remained at the country estate in Shropshire.

"So he never told you that he and my mother were... close? Lovers, perhaps?"

Violet's brows furrowed, and she remembered the conversation she had overheard the night before. "Is this *before* she was a duchess?"

"Indeed. They were in love," Amelia insisted. "You should have seen your father. You should have seen *her* when she saw *him*." She pretended to swoon, which had Violet gasping.

"Your mother *fainted*?" she asked in disbelief. "But... she never faints!"

Amelia nodded. "It was so romantic," she said on a sigh, her hands clasped together and held to her chest as she fluttered her lashes.

A knock sounded at the door.

"That will be Browning with the tea tray," Violet said, feigning relief at being saved from seeing more of her friend's playful antics. "Come!"

The butler entered and set a salver with the tea set on a table near the fireplace. "I'll serve," Violet said, moving to take one of the chairs. Amelia waited until Browning had left the bedchamber and closed the door before she flopped into the adjacent chair. "What aren't you telling me?" she asked, her suspicion evident.

Violet finished pouring tea and offering biscuits before she answered. "I might have eavesdropped on a conversation where my father shared what happened. Before he married Mother. *Why* he married Mother," she admitted, offering Amelia a cup of tea. She poured another for herself before she stared at the embers in the fireplace. The few lumps of coal the maid had left that morning had already burned to ash.

"Go on," Amelia urged, helping herself to a biscuit.

"Two lovers, prevented from marrying because your grandfather claimed there was a marriage contract and a betrothal already in place," she stated.

"*My* grandfather?" Amelia repeated in confusion.

"The Duke of Woodleigh."

Amelia gave an unladylike snort. "That old fart? Doesn't surprise me. He probably *reveled* in telling your father he couldn't have her. Which is what I'm imagining my brother is going to do when Philip finally gains an audience with him."

"Amelia," Violet gently scolded. "You're far too harsh

when it comes to Weston." After that morning's ride, her opinion of the young man had changed considerably. She had thought to simply make friends with him. Soften him up for when Philip finally requested an audience with him.

Now that she had spent time in his company, she understood why he behaved as if he was a curmudgeon. Why it was he had aged so much since taking on the duties of a duke. Why he seemed so unpleasant, when in fact he was simply overwhelmed with all he needed to accomplish on behalf of the Weston dukedom.

That she had already arranged the ride in the park with Alfred for the very same time Philip had intended to meet with him that morning merely meant she now had more time to work on Weston. Ply him with compliments. Play him.

Besides, she didn't know it was Philip's intention to pay a call at Weston Hall at the same time she was to be with the duke.

It was simply a happy coincidence.

Amelia furrowed a dark brow as she regarded Violet with surprise. "He's become a toad," she said on a huff.

"You're never going to gain his permission to marry my brother if he finds out you think he's a toad," Violet warned.

Tittering, Amelia took a sip of tea, then said, "I suppose not." She dared a glance at Violet before adding, "You do realize that if your father and my mother had ended up together thirty years ago, we—"

"We would not exist," Violet finished for her.

"Or we'd be someone else."

"I'd look like you. Like your mother," Violet said.

"Alfred would look like your father. Which would be a *huge* improvement," Amelia remarked. "I absolutely adore that Philip looks so much like Fenwick."

"Amelia," Violet scolded again, deciding a change of topic was in order. "Has your gown for tonight been delivered?"

"Indeed."

"What color?"

"Oh, white, of course," Amelia replied in disgust. "When I'm a married woman, I am never wearing white again," she vowed.

Violet giggled. "My aunt chose the fabric for mine. We picked up the gown yesterday from the modiste, and imagine my shock at seeing it's not a true white."

"What's this?"

"It's not even ivory or cream. It's the palest of blues. I can't tell you how happy I was when I tried it on. Aunt Katherine said I should never wear white, but I didn't expect she meant while I was still in the first year of my come-out," she explained.

"You're so lucky to have her," Amelia remarked. "Even though she and my mother are both duchesses, Katherine seems to flaunt convention whilst my mother clings to it."

Violet chuckled. "I think it's because Katherine is so much older. She doesn't fear reprisals from the *ton* any longer."

"Will you ask if she'll adopt me?" Amelia murmured, her grin the only evidence she was teasing.

Violet helped herself to a biscuit. "You do realize that if your mother and my father end up together, we—"

"We'll be sisters!" Amelia announced, grinning in delight.

"We're were going to be anyway when you and Philip marry," Violet countered.

Amelia's face suddenly fell.

"What is it?"

"Philip and Alfred will be brothers," she whispered. She swallowed. Hard. "It will be awful."

Violet furrowed her brows, understanding her friend's concern. "Let's not get ahead of ourselves, shall we?" she urged. "We're not even sure what Father and your mother have planned for the Season." She glanced at the clock on the fireplace mantel. "Which reminds me, I need to bathe for tonight."

"You do smell of horse," Amelia said with a grin. She stood and huffed. "I'll let myself out and find you later tonight. Oh, and don't forget the flower for your hair," she said, pulling a bloom from her reticule. She offered the silk hibiscus to Violet.

"Are you sure this ball has a tropical theme? I never saw the actual invitation," she said as she accepted the flower.

"Indeed it does. A tropical paradise," she said in a sing-song voice. "Lady Reading has been telling everyone the ball will even feature a buried treasure, whatever that means."

"We'll be sure to have fun," Violet said.

"Indeed, and I must say, I rather like knowing both waltzes have already been claimed by your brother. If I don't have a partner for any of the others, I shall not feel as if I've become a wallflower."

Violet grinned, but she decided it best she not mention who *she* would be dancing with that night.

She was going to save both waltzes for Alfred, Duke of Weston, and she was looking forward to them far more than she had thought possible.

CHAPTER 16
A BALL REVEALS A MOTIVE

ater that night, Reading House

Michael, Marquess of Fenwick, stepped down from the town coach and turned to help his daughter. "Did my aunt happen to mention when she would be arriving this evening?" he asked, stepping aside to allow Philip to exit the equipage once Violet was on the pavement.

"I'm right here, Fenwick," Katherine, Duchess of Pendleton, stated on a huff. "You're late."

"Are we?" he asked, pretending innocence as he took her gloved hand to his lips. "Love the feather," he added, referring to the purple plume hovering over them both.

Although Amelia and Philip had been ready to leave Fenwick House at the appointed time, he had struggled with choosing a waistcoat. After trying on three in various colors, he had finally opted for a gold-on-gold embroidered version for the only reason that it did not enhance the gray in his otherwise blonde hair.

He decided the chandeliers in the Reading House ballroom would do that without any assistance.

Katherine gently slapped his arm at hearing his teasing compliment. "Constance mentioned she had a tropical paradise theme in mind when arranging the decor," she said, referring to their hostess for the evening, the Marchioness of Reading. Katherine regarded Violet from head to toe. "The flower on the side of your coiffure is perfect for this evening," she remarked. "Did you have to order that from a hot house?"

"Oh, no. It's silk. Amelia and I made them for this evening. To coincide with Lady Reading's theme," she explained, gingerly touching the flower meant to look like a large hibiscus bloom.

Turning to her nephew, Katherine allowed an audible sigh. "Fenwick, you should have worn a much brighter waistcoat."

About to argue he didn't know there was a theme involved, Michael held his tongue when she added, "I haven't gone in yet. Thought it best I wait out here."

"Any sign of the Weston coach?" Philip asked nervously, his gaze sweeping the row of coaches and carriages lining Park Lane.

"It's not due for another five minutes or more. I had my groom looking out for it when we passed Weston Hall," she explained. "All three of them are expected to attend this evening, though, so do be on your guard," she added in warning.

"Noted," Philip replied on a sigh.

Meanwhile, Violet felt excitement at the thought she

would be dancing with the Duke of Weston that night. After Amelia's departure that afternoon, she had replayed her earlier conversations with the duke in her head, picturing Weston's expressions to better determine his reactions to her every word. Perhaps she was biased, but she could not detect a hint of avarice in his manner nor a moment when he seemed bothered by her comments.

Indeed, his parting words were proof.

I will have a good day because of this ride with you.

"As for you, young lady," Katherine said, turning her attention on Violet.

Pulled from her brief reverie, Violet's eyes rounded. "Yes?"

"Constance has promised there will be a card parlor, so since your father is with you this evening, I will entrust you to stay close to him and to be on your very best behavior."

"Yes, ma'am." She dared a glance at her father, sure for the briefest moment he winced at hearing his aunt's edict. "If he's otherwise engaged, I'll be sure to stay in Lady Amelia's company."

The comment seemed to appease her father as well as Katherine, but Violet noted Philip's slight grimace. He no doubt had plans to spend time near Amelia, and probably not in the ballroom.

The duchess accepted her nephew's proffered arm. Philip did the same for Violet, and they headed to the front door of Reading House.

"There's an announcer, but no receiving line,"

Katherine explained as they gave their wraps, coats, and hats to two footmen. "Might I walk down the stairs with you?" she asked, her query directed to Michael.

"Of course," he replied, stepping back to admire her purple satin ballgown. A necklace of amethysts and emeralds matched her jeweled earbobs. Despite her age, she had kept her svelte figure and ramrod straight back. "I would hate having to go down by myself," he commented. "How many steps are there?"

"Oh, not many," she replied. "Not like at Weatherstone's manor. Just don't go tripping down them in those," she added, pointing to his shoes. "When was the last time you had a new pair of dance shoes made?"

Violet giggled. "Aunt Katherine," she scolded gently. "Careful, or he'll be taking his leave before we even reach the stairs."

Michael lifted his chin. "She has the right of it, Kate. The shoes fit, and they're comfortable."

For a moment, Katherine seemed as if she might put voice to a protest, but she dipped her head, the feather arcing through the air to create a slight breeze. "Promise me you won't..." She paused to greet Lord and Lady Everly as they passed by.

"What?" Michael prompted. "Promise you what?"

Katherine angled her head to one side, which sent the feather dangerously close to a gas-lit sconce. "You won't go proposing marriage the moment you see her."

Both Philip and Violet inhaled sharply. Their father arched a blonde brow.

"Not that it's any of your concern quite yet, but—"

"Fenwick? Is that you?"

Michael was prevented from admitting he had already made an offer of marriage to Helena when Randall Roderick, Marquess of Reading, stepped up and held out his right hand.

"Reading! Marriage seems to have done you a world of good," Michael said, vigorously shaking their host's hand.

"I saw your name on the guest list, and I could hardly believe it," the marquess said. "Join us in the card room later?" His attention went to another couple, saving Michael from having to answer.

"I'll escort you down," Philip said, offering his arm to Violet. "Then I'll find Amelia when you two are done comparing dance cards."

"All right," she replied, suppressing the urge to snort at hearing his words. She understood his desire to keep a low profile during the ball, although at some point, it would be evident to Weston there was something going on between Philip and Amelia.

The two couldn't help how they behaved in one another's company. Couldn't help how they stared at one another with moon eyes. Couldn't help how at ease they were together. She would have to do what she could to be sure Weston didn't pay witness to them.

She lowered her voice to a whisper. "Do you have any idea who Aunt Katherine meant by her comment?"

Philip winced. "I do, but I'll tell you later." He lifted his arm higher, urging her to join him.

Violet scoffed, hoping he would confirm what she

had overheard outside the dining room the night before and what Amelia had talked about that afternoon. She placed her arm on his, daring a glance behind her to be sure the Duke of Weston hadn't yet arrived. If they hurried, Weston wouldn't hear her name being announced along with her brother's.

She and Philip followed their father and aunt to the top of the stairs leading to the ballroom.

Michael leaned over and spoke in a whisper to the announcer. A moment later, the servant's booming voice called out, "Her Grace The Duchess of Pendleton. The Most Honorable The Marquess of Fenwick. The Right Honorable The Earl of Crawford, and The Lady Violet Cummings."

Although the ballroom wasn't yet a crush, a murmur sounded amongst those in the crowd at the mention of Michael.

"Now *everyone* knows he's in Town," Philip whispered as Violet grinned with excitement.

"At least I'm no longer the new one," she said, her expression brightening when she spotted several young ladies Amelia had introduced her to at prior events. Beyond them, older aristocrats were making their way to the base of the stairs to greet both Katherine and Michael.

In the brief melee that followed, Philip was left standing on the last stair, making him tall enough to admire the colorful ballroom decor.

Besides the potted palm trees lining one end of the room, a long table dressed in bright yellow and orange tablecloths bore arrangements of flowers, pineapples, and tropical greenery. Platters of finger foods and glasses of champagne were set on a layer of fine sand. Instead of an ice sculpture, a giant bird cage was mounted on a pedestal in the middle, its mostly-green inhabitants occasionally squawking loud enough to be heard above the murmuring crowd.

"Are those parrots?" he asked of Lord Everly.

The earl grinned. "They are. Lady Reading asked if I might loan them to her for the evening."

"They certainly fit right in with her idea of a tropical paradise," Philip remarked, helping himself to a glass of champagne. He gave another glass to Everly.

"Indeed. Although I think they might actually like the change of location from my study, I still expect they might occasionally say inappropriate words," Everly warned. "Not that I've taught them any," he added, smirking.

Philip chuckled. He was about say more, but his attention had gone to the top of the stairs.

The Duke and Duchess of Weston were staring out over the crowd. Amelia was standing next to the duke.

"Pardon me."

*T*he sound of music was already in the air when the baritone voice of the announcer called out, "His Grace The Duke of Weston. Her Grace The Duchess of Weston. The Lady Amelia Sheppard."

The three descended the steps, Helena's hand on her son's arm.

"Constance always outdoes herself," Helena remarked, her words intended for Amelia.

"The decorations are marvelous," Alfred said, his face displaying an unusual grin. "I think this tropical island theme is inspired. Do you suppose there's a buried treasure located somewhere?"

Helena nearly tripped on the last step as she aimed an expression of surprise at her son. "How did you know?" she asked. When her gaze swept the ballroom, her attention was immediately drawn to Michael.

Although he was surrounded by several older aristocrats, his gaze was directed at her.

Inhaling softly—how was it the man could still incite such a reaction in her after thirty years?—Helena dipped her head in acknowledgement and displayed a grin of embarrassment.

"Have you already grown overheated, Mother?" Alfred asked with worry in his voice. "Your color is rather high."

She dared a quick glance at him before once again finding Michael in the crush. "Oh, I'm quite sure it's only because I'm wearing red," she replied, referring to the poppy colored satin ballgown she wore. Her lady's maid had adorned her hair with a ring of red silk flowers, and rubies encircled her neck and white-gloved wrist. "I'm fine, Alfie. Do try to enjoy yourself this evening," she said absently, her attention never leaving the marquess.

"I will," he said, his gaze following hers. Although he

couldn't make out exactly who she was staring at—the ballroom was already quite crowded—Alfred noticed one of the gentlemen making his way toward them. A gentleman with blonde hair who looked familiar, but not because he had met him before. "Will you introduce me?" he asked, his dark brows furrowed in curiosity.

Helena finally turned to regard him with uncertainty. "I will, but you must promise me you won't make a scene."

Alfred gave a start. "What? I... I won't, of course," he stammered.

"You're a vision, Helena. As always," the gentleman said before taking her hand to his lips. "The most gorgeous flower in this huge bouquet." He swept his other hand to indicate the other ladies in attendance.

Helena grinned and curtsied. "Bounder," she murmured happily. They stared at one another for a moment until the sound of Alfred clearing his throat had her giving a start. "Oh, Michael, Marquess of Fenwick, may I have the honor of introducing you to my son, Alfred, Duke of Weston?"

Finally sorting how it was the man seemed familiar, Alfred's eyes briefly narrowed. "It's good to meet you, my lord," he said, dipping his head.

Michael bowed from the waist. "Your Grace. It's an honor."

"How... how is it you two are...?" Alfred paused when his attention was captured by a young lady in the crowd.

"We knew one another a long time ago," Michael replied. "Before she wed your father."

He tore his attention from Helena, expecting to see the young duke staring at him with malice in his eyes. Instead, Alfred's gaze, directed at someone else, made the young duke look as if he was a long lost puppy, his owner having returned to claim him.

"Pardon me, Mother. Lord Fenwick," he said, backing away from the older couple.

Helena had inhaled to add to Michael's answer, but she let the breath out in a chuckle as she watched her son disappear into the crowd. "I don't know what's happened, but my son is behaving most strangely today," she murmured.

"They do that. Frequently," Michael said, moving to stand next to her. "Will you take a turn with me about the room? I'm told we're to hunt for buried treasure."

"And here I thought you already found it," she teased, pretending offense.

Michael chuckled. "True, especially given that coronet you're wearing. I fear it puts the Fenwick version to shame," he commented.

"If it's any consolation, this one is terribly heavy and rather uncomfortable," she complained. "And I have reason to believe it's mostly paste."

Chuckling, Michael said, "Ah, then you'll definitely prefer the Fenwick coronet." He paused a moment. "I am told by our host that the treasure we should seek is of a different sort," he said. "Lord Reading claims there's a trunk or two somewhere with prizes inside."

Tittering, Helena said, "It won't be fair for me to

look," she claimed. "Constance already told me what she had in mind."

"Well, then tell me so I can find it," he said with a grin.

Helena indicated which direction they should head. "It's in a trunk, but not the size you're expecting," she said.

"So, larger or smaller?"

"Smaller. Much smaller."

"So, not much of a treasure?"

Her dark brows arched. "Sometimes the very best treasures come in tiny boxes," she countered.

"Ah," he said in understanding. He absently patted his waistcoat pocket to ensure the ring he intended to give to her later that night was still there. "A jewel of some sort?" he guessed.

"The marchioness was inspired when she paid a call at Ewen and Ewen," Helena explained. When she noted his look of confusion, she added, "It's a jewel shop. It's actually owned by the Earl of Everly. His oldest son—"

"Alexander?"

"Yes. He's married now. To a gemologist, and he creates beautiful jewelry. As a hobby of sorts."

Michael allowed a smirk. "So I've been told."

Helena gave him a look of surprise. "Did Lord Crawford tell you about it?"

"Philip did, yes."

"I wasn't aware your son was of an age to be shopping at such an establishment," she said, arching an elegant brow.

"Uh, he may have recently spent some of my blunt in the acquisition of a bauble intended for someone of your acquaintance," he teased.

Her eyes rounding, Helena stopped walking, which had Michael turning to face her. "Is he proposing marriage? To Amelia? Tonight?" For a moment, her widened eyes suggested she might faint.

Michael displayed a grimace. "No," he assured her. "At least, I don't think so. He hasn't yet asked Weston's permission. He intended to ask today, but—"

"Alfred had an appointment with his solicitor this morning," she finished.

"He'll try again another time," Michael said in a low voice. "Is it still a surprise to you? That he favors your daughter?"

Helena shrugged. "I'm not sure. I've only ever seen them dance together," she admitted. "Truth be told, I have never met the man."

"Would you approve of him though? For your daughter?"

Chuckling softly, she aimed a grin in his direction. "Of all the young men who might consider her for marriage, Lord Crawford probably affords her the best future," she hedged.

"He does," Michael affirmed. "Affection as well as the Fenwick coronet. At least... after you're done with it."

Helena inhaled sharply. "As I recall, you haven't yet properly proposed—"

"I know," he said. "We were interrupted before I could do so this morning."

Turning her head so quickly, Helena felt the coronet shift atop her head. "Michael, it's been nearly thirty years—"

"You literally fell for me this morning," he countered with a smirk.

"Bounder," she accused.

They resumed their turn about the ballroom, occasionally stopping to greet others until the dancing music started. "You did save me two dances?" Michael asked.

"You could have them all if it was allowed," she replied. She pointed to a long table dressed in blue where mounds of sand surrounded a series of short potted palms. Small seashells dotted the dunes while tiny rocks arranged in rings around the sand piles kept them from spreading. At the base of the palm, a miniature treasure chest was half-buried in the faux beach.

Michael gingerly approached the display, touching a finger to the top of the trunk. He tapped it. "Does the lid open?" he asked.

"Well, try it and see."

He bent and used his forefinger to lift the brass latch and lid. Inside the felt-lined chest were several jewels.

"Your Grace," he said, stepping back so she could peer inside.

"We have a winner!" a baritone voice called out.

The shout had the nearby conversation ceasing as those nearest them turned to look.

Helena glanced up to see Randall Roderick, Marquess of Reading, applauding.

She pointed to Michael. "He's the one who found it."

The marquess stepped up and removed the treasure chest from the sand. He poured the jewels into his hand and turned to Michael. "Take these to Ewen and Ewen, and Lord Alexander will make them into whatever bauble you'd like," he said, his open palm holding a collection of green and purple gemstones. He poured the jewels back into the chest and handed it to Michael. "There are enough there to make a bracelet and earbobs, perhaps. I'm sure Ewan and Ewan will be happy to sell you more should you require a necklace."

A round of laughter accompanied the marquess' last words, and Michael dipped his head and grinned. "Thank you, Reading. I believe I have the perfect recipient for such a generous prize."

For a moment, Helena looked as if she wanted the floor to open and swallow her whole.

They were saved from further embarrassment when the orchestra began playing the music for the second dance, a longways country dance.

"Have you promised this dance to anyone?" he asked.

She shook her head. "I usually don't dance at all," she replied.

Michael tucked the small chest into his waistcoat pocket. "I want both waltzes," he reminded her.

"You shall have them," she replied. "But first I'll need champagne. Lots of champagne."

Grinning, Michael offered his arm and they made their way in the direction of the refreshments table.

Neither one paid witness to what their children were doing.

CHAPTER 17
A BALL PROVIDES A COVER

*M*eanwhile "I want to kiss you so badly, I fear I shall do so in front of all these people," Philip claimed, his eyes directed on the dancers rather than on the young lady who stood to his right.

Amelia tittered. "I rather doubt my mother will notice I'm missing if you wish to take me to the gardens. She seems to only have eyes for your father," she remarked.

"Don't think I haven't noticed," he said. His mouth dropped open upon hearing their host's proclamation that there was a winner. "Did you hear that?" he asked in disbelief. "I think my father won the treasure," he said.

"Which means my mother will end up with a new bauble," she said happily. "There's nothing wrong with that."

"*I* wanted to win the treasure," Philip countered. "So I could have something made for you."

Amelia regarded him with a look of surprise. "Someday you will," she said in a quiet voice. She was about to say more, but the five-piece orchestra began playing the dancing music, and the sound of the instruments made conversation more difficult.

"Come out to the gardens with me?" Philip asked, his manner making his nervousness apparent. "You haven't promised this dance to anyone, have you?"

She shook her head. "No, of course not. In fact, no one has had a chance to claim any of my dances except you," she reminded him.

"Good." He took her hand in his and led them to the French doors at the back of the ballroom. Once outside, the night air was cool but not brisk.

Following the pavers that led to a path through the garden, Philip slowed his pace. "I was going to do this later," he said, pausing his steps when they reached a clearing surrounded by hedgerows. "But... I cannot wait any longer." He turned to face her. "Amelia, will you do me the honor of becoming my wife?" He held a sapphire-studded ring in her direction.

Amelia's eyes rounded. "Philip!" She swallowed. "It's gorgeous," she said, pulling her glove from her left hand. She held out her bare hand and watched as he slid the ring onto her fourth finger.

Before she could pull it away, Philip had his lips covering it, kissing the base of her knuckles. "Will you marry me?"

She nodded. "Of course. Yes, I'll marry you," she

replied with a giggle. When he straightened, she stepped into his arms and kissed him.

"Even if we have to go to Scotland?" he whispered.

Tittering, Amelia said, "Even if," she agreed.

"Will you be telling your mother?" he asked in a whisper.

Amelia inhaled to answer. "Should I?"

He took her glove from her and held it open. "Maybe not just yet," he murmured, watching as she reluctantly slid her hand into it. With the glove on, it wasn't immediately apparent she wore a ring. "Give me a chance to gain Weston's permission."

"Even if Mother could help talk Alfred into it?" she reasoned.

Philip chuckled softly. "Something tells me your mother might have her own announcement to make."

"Oh?" Her eyes rounded. "So soon? They were only just reunited this morning."

"That was my thought, but he joined me on my trip to Ewen and Ewen today," he said, giving her hand a slight shake. "I received a note saying your ring was ready—I was actually reading it when you arrived this morning—and, uh, he asked if he could come along."

"To shop for a ring?" she guessed.

He nodded. "As well as some other baubles."

Amelia inhaled softly. "Do you suppose he's going to propose tonight?"

"He's wanted to marry your mother for thirty years. I rather doubt he's going to wait a minute longer than necessary to make her his marchioness," he claimed.

"Which can only help our cause," Amelia reasoned. "When they marry, he'll be my..." She stopped speaking, one brow furrowed.

"Stepfather," Philip finished for her.

"And you'll be my... my brother."

"Stepbrother," he corrected her, rolling his eyes. "It won't be like that if we beat them to the altar," he reasoned.

Amelia placed her head against his chest and groaned. "I despise my brother," she whispered.

"Amelia," he gently scolded. "As it happens, your brother may have been right."

She pulled away from him so quickly, he almost didn't catch her in time to prevent her from falling backwards. "Right about what?"

"My father and your mother," he said. "At university..." He paused and swallowed. "Our fight was because Alfred claimed my father was once betrothed to your mother, but that she chose Weston over him because Weston was a duke, and she wished to be a duchess. I took exception and goaded him into hitting me. So that I would have reason to punch him in the nose."

Amelia inhaled softly. "My mother had no say in who she married," she argued. "Her betrothal was arranged when she was a young girl," she insisted, "so my brother was in the wrong. He deserved a broken nose."

"Father said as much when he explained it to me," Philip replied. "So I suppose it's a bit of a relief to hear she didn't choose Weston willingly. Because she wanted to be a duchess."

"Back then, I suppose the promise of a coronet was enough of an incentive for a young lady to marry, but had she the choice, my mother would not have married Weston," Amelia murmured.

"I'm glad she did," Philip whispered. At seeing Amelia's eyes widen with shock, he added, "You wouldn't exist otherwise, and then who would I marry?"

She tittered. "You wouldn't exist, either," she reminded him.

He grinned and pulled her into an embrace, kissing her thoroughly before the sound of a clearing throat had them quickly stepping apart.

"Lord Everly," Philip acknowledged, dipping his head in Harold Tennison's direction.

"Lady Everly," Amelia said, dropping into a curtsy.

"Evening, you two," Harold said. "A bit early to be out in the gardens this evening, is it not?"

"Yes, my lord. I was showing Lady Amelia a particularly beautiful flower—"

"A blue one. A sapphire, in fact," Amelia said, wiggling her left hand despite the glove that hid her ring from view.

"We were... we were just about to head back into the ballroom," Philip stammered. "If you could—"

"Keep our secret, it would be most appreciated," Amelia finished for him.

Stella, Countess of Everly, tittered in delight. "My lips are sealed, but once word is out, I am going to claim *I* was the first to know."

"What about me?" Harold countered.

Giving him a wave, Stella said, "Oh, all right, second," she amended.

"Do have a good evening," Harold said, leading his countess past them and into another part of the gardens.

Amelia glanced up at Philip. "I couldn't help it," she said. "I had to tell someone."

Philip guffawed and offered his arm. "They probably already knew, my sweeting."

She gasped. "How?"

"Alexander made your ring," he replied, referring to the heir to the Everly earldom.

"So?"

"Well, Everly might have been *in* the shop when I picked it up this afternoon."

"Oh," she replied and then inhaled sharply. "So... he knows about your father and my mother."

"No," Philip insisted. "Father never said who his purchases were for."

She gave him a quelling glance. "All they had to do was take one look at your father tonight and they would know," she reasoned.

They were on the last few pavers before reaching the French doors when Philip suddenly changed their direction, moving them across the lawn until they were behind a yew.

"What's going on?" she asked in a whisper.

"Your brother was heading for the doors," Philip said, holding a finger in front of his lips at the sound of footsteps on the pavers. When they retreated until only the music from inside the ballroom could be heard, he led them back to the French doors, and they slipped inside just as another dance was beginning.

"I can't imagine my brother going into the gardens during a ball," Amelia said, "unless it was to leave the premises entirely."

Philip glanced down at her, his brows furrowed. "I don't think he planned to leave," he murmured. He was about to say more, but one of Amelia's friends approached, and she left his side with an apologetic glance.

Thinking he should follow the duke, Philip was prevented from doing so when several of his friends approached, one holding out a glass of champagne in his direction. "Join us in the card parlor? We're about to play a hand or two."

Directing one last glance at the French doors, Philip nodded. "Sure, but only until the first waltz," he warned.

He headed off with the young bucks.

CHAPTER 18
A BALL IS A BEGINNING

A half hour earlier, in the ballroom

Sure someone was watching her, Violet slowly turned her head until she spotted the reason the hairs on the back of her neck had risen.

Alfred, Duke of Weston, was standing near her father and Helena, Duchess of Weston, and his gaze was directed squarely on her.

If he felt any malice toward her father, it certainly didn't show in his eyes, for they reminded her of a long lost puppy. Not sure how to react, she gave him a prim grin and dipped her head. She dared a glance to her left and then right, wondering if she might sneak further into the crowd and disappear from his view. Another look in his direction, and she realized it was too late.

He was already making his way towards her.

Time to pretend again, she thought, remembering how easy it had been to do in Lord Everly's study and during their ride in the park. Surely it wouldn't be difficult in the crowded ballroom.

As he drew closer, the sense of excitement that passed through her surprised her. The music for the second dance hadn't yet begun, which meant he wasn't coming to claim it.

"You're a vision, Lady Violet," he said, reaching for her gloved hand even before she could offer it.

"Your Grace," she replied, dipping a curtsy. "You looked so regal descending the steps," she said with as much enthusiasm as she could muster. "I hardly expected you to notice *me*."

His expression of joy faltered for a moment. "I was searching for you," he claimed. "Are you well?"

She couldn't help how her eyes rounded at hearing his claim. "Very, Your Grace," she replied with a grin that came far too easily. "And you?"

"Very well, now that I've found you."

Violet gave a start, stunned at the fluttering she felt in her stomach. She was sure her face displayed a blush as red as his mother's gown. "Did you have a good day? After our ride?" she asked, placing her arm on his when he offered it. She didn't know where they were going, but the ballroom wasn't that large.

"I did indeed," he said. "We'll have to do it again, sooner rather than later."

"I should like that. Very much," she replied. "As will George of course. He is always happy for the exercise."

"I'll be sure to bring treats for the horses," he said.

She grinned and dipped her head before holding

out her dance card. "No one has claimed any of the dances yet, so you can choose which ever one you'd like."

He helped himself to the tiny pencil dangling from her wrist and wrote *Weston* on two of the lines. "Mayhap you will forego the second dance?" he asked, "So that we might take a turn around the room?"

"Of course, Your Grace—"

"Call me Weston."

Violet inhaled softly. "Weston," she said. "Are you in search of the buried treasure?"

He gave her a look of confusion. "Treasure?"

She tittered. "Lady Reading has apparently hidden a treasure somewhere here in this tropical paradise, and whoever finds it gets to keep it," she explained.

Alfred regarded her with a curious expression. "And here I thought I'd already found it," he mused.

Violet blinked. "Sir?"

He chuckled softly, which had her allowing a tentative grin. "Any clues as to where it might be hidden?" He had them heading in the direction of the refreshment table.

"I doubt it will be in the punchbowl, but I wouldn't object to a glass of punch," she said, deciding holding a glass would mean she wouldn't have to leave her hand on his arm. The strangest sensation of tingles had developed in her fingertips.

"What about champagne?" he asked, helping himself to a glass and offering it to her.

"Oh, thank you," she said, giving up her hold on his

arm to take the glass. The tingling immediately ceased. She took an experimental sip.

He took another glass, and they continued to stroll along the length of the blue cloth-covered tables. They were filled with trays of finger foods separated by a palm trees under which were piles of sand dotted with tiny seashells.

"I think these are supposed to be tropical islands," Violet said when they paused in front of one of the trees. "The tablecloth is meant to be the water, and the sand makes up the island. But what are those?" she asked, pointing to a cluster of round, brown balls at the top of one of the trees.

"Coconuts," he said with a chuckle. "Rather clever."

"Indeed," she said before they moved on to the next display. "Look, there's a small treasure chest next to that palm tree's trunk."

"Do you suppose that's the treasure we're supposed to find?"

"It would have to be an awfully small treasure," she remarked.

"Could be gemstones," he reasoned.

"Could be coins," she countered.

"Could be empty."

She giggled. "We may never know, unless..." She stopped speaking when she spied her father on the other side of the table. He was escorting Alfred's mother from the opposite direction, and it was apparent he was about to touch the small chest.

"Unless?" Alfred prompted.

Violet shrugged. "Let's see if we can find a larger treasure chest," she said, hoping to move him away from the table. "Perhaps there's another, even larger treasure."

"Like what?"

"Well, what other kinds of treasures are there?" she asked. "And what might they be hidden inside of?"

He had paused and was staring at her mouth when their host, Randall Roderick, Marquess of Reading, called out, "We have a winner!"

The noisy ballroom quieted almost immediately, a few shouts punctuating the discovery of the treasure. They both turned, but the crush of bodies moving toward the tables kept them from seeing who Reading referred to in his announcement.

"I think we missed our chance," Violet murmured. "And it's all my fault. I'm so sorry."

Alfred stared at her. "You've no reason to be sorry," he replied, his head bent to hear someone comment on the prize. "It sounds as if it's merely a few emeralds and amethysts."

She angled her head to one side. "So it *was* jewels. You were right."

"Gemstones," he stated with a shrug. "Easy enough to acquire. It was an inspired idea, though. This entire tropical island theme is exquisite," he said, waving a hand to indicate the entire ballroom. "Has me wondering if it continues out in the gardens." He finished his champagne and placed both their glasses on a passing footman's tray.

Violet glanced towards the French doors, fairly sure

her brother and Amelia had gone through them some time ago. "Perhaps we could go out and get some air," she suggested. "See what Lady Reading might have done out there in the way of tropical decor."

Without saying another word, Alfred pulled her hand onto his arm and they headed for the doors. They were almost to them when he suddenly stopped. "What about your... your aunt? The Duchess of Pendleton? Will she... will she wonder where you've gone?" he asked with suspicion in his voice.

"She's in the card parlor," Violet replied, "So I rather doubt it." Her gaze darted to where her father had been, and she confirmed his attentions were entirely on the Duchess of Weston.

He wouldn't be missing her, either, it seemed.

Alfred nodded and continued on, opening one of the doors for her and stepping aside to allow her to exit first.

Violet's gaze swept the garden area illuminated by the ballroom's chandeliers. Beyond that, the only light in the garden was from a few Japanese lanterns strung out over the pavers.

"Other than some early spring blooms, it doesn't appear the theme continues out here," she said with disappointment, once he offered his arm again.

"Are you cold?"

Violet inhaled softly, surprised he would ask. Perhaps the duke wasn't as self-centered as Amelia made him out to be. "Not at all, Your Grace. It's a lovely night," she said.

"Weston," he gently corrected her.

She dipped her head. "Weston."

He led her along the pavers, their pace slowing the farther away from the house they walked. "Perhaps there's a treasure box out here," she said in a quiet voice, well aware there were others out in the gardens when she heard soft murmurs coming from behind hedgerows.

"Perhaps," he replied. "I'd rather not look for it, though."

"Oh?" She turned and regarded him with an expression of curiosity.

"Not when I already have one standing in front of me."

Violet glanced first to her left and then to her right before she swallowed. She covered her mouth with a hand as she attempted to suppress a giggle. "Are you referring to... to *me*?" she asked in a whisper.

He nodded. "You cannot be too surprised, my lady," he said.

"Well, I've certainly never been referred to as a treasure before," she reasoned.

"What about a tropical flower?" he asked, his fingers reaching up to touch the silk hibiscus in her hair. "You're certainly as gorgeous as one."

Violet inhaled softly. "Not that, either," she whispered, her thoughts suddenly a jumble. After how quickly their time in the ballroom had seemed to happen, everything outside seemed to move at a snail's pace. Even so, her mind was having trouble keeping up with his words. "I am?" Her eyes rounded when she felt a heat in her breasts that seemed to radiate from the very center of her body. Felt the damp at the top of her thighs.

Heard her pulse hammering in her ears. "Weston," she said on a breath.

"If I was stranded on a tropical island, I think I would want for nothing if I found you there."

Barely aware his hand had moved to the side of her neck, Violet gave into his gentle pull and raised her face to his. A moment later, and his lips touched hers in a soft, brief kiss.

Violet inhaled softly. "You'd starve," she whispered, the sound barely audible.

He shook his head. "Making love to you would sustain me for the rest of my days," he said before once again capturing her lips with his. This time, the kiss went on longer, Violet understanding what to do to return it.

She didn't know when it happened, but her hands moved to his shoulders, her chest pressed to his in an attempt to quell the desire that had her nipples puckering behind her stays. For a moment, she thought to beg him to touch her there, to push down her bodice and take her breast in his hand. Into his mouth.

The mere thought of his lips nibbling her nipple had all sorts of unfamiliar sensations coursing through her. All sorts of wicked thoughts racing through her mind.

This wasn't supposed to be happening like this. She wasn't supposed to welcome his lips on hers. She wasn't supposed to allow his tongue to separate her lips so that he might deepen the kiss. She wasn't supposed to welcome the tip of his tongue as it touched hers.

If only he would hold onto her. Place a hand at her

waist to help keep her steady. Her knees felt as if they were turning to jelly, probably because she had drunk the champagne too quickly.

She was sure she hadn't put voice to any of her thoughts, so she was shocked when his other hand moved to the side of her body, sliding up so his thumb stroked the shape of her bodice to the edge of its neckline.

Lifting a hand from his shoulder to place it against the side of his head, she speared her fingers through his dark hair before pulling his head down closer when she finally had to break off the kiss to take a much needed breath.

Accepting her overt invitation, his lips moved to the space below her collar bones, his tongue tracing the slight ridge out to her shoulder and then down along her neckline.

Afraid she might moan too loudly, she placed her mouth against the top of his head and shivered as his tongue and lips continued their trek along the lace.

"Does this tickle?" he whispered, humor sounding in his voice.

"In the very best way," she murmured dreamily.

He raised his head and regarded her with a curious expression. "I would continue but—"

"Oh!" All at once, reason seemed to prevail, and embarrassment had her releasing her hold on him. "And I wouldn't object, but for the fact that you probably already think me fast," she countered, her eyes widening in alarm.

She had allowed the duke to have his way with her. His thumb was still stroking one breast, the nubbin of her nipple probably poking through her stays to make itself evident.

"No," he said in a whisper. "Never." When her gaze dropped to his wandering hand, he suddenly pulled it away. "Oh, pardon," he added, a brow furrowing. "I... I've never done that before."

Violet's eyes rounded. "I've never had it done to me before," she replied, deciding it best she set him straight lest he believe she was fast. "Although I... I didn't mind, truly," she whispered, unable to control the quaver in her voice.

He placed his forehead against hers, so she was forced to regard him through her upper lashes.

"Who must I ask for permission to court you?"

She blinked several times. "You wish to court *me*?" This wasn't supposed to be happening. Not yet. And then only to increase her brother's chances at securing Amelia's hand in marriage.

He chuckled softly. "I do. You have bewitched me, Lady Violet."

"I... I didn't mean to," she replied, stunned to discover she might have meant it.

This was not exactly working out as she had planned, but it was working. Merely a bit more quickly than she expected. If Weston truly felt enough regard for her to wish to court her, he might be persuaded to give his permission for Amelia to wed her brother. Amelia and Philip's future together would be assured.

Could Violet abide a lifetime with Alfred, Duke of Weston? Put up with his pompous airs and sullen manner for the rest of her life? Play at being a happy wife?

Well, she might be able to if he continued to kiss her as he'd been doing.

She was pulled from her brief reverie when he chuckled softly. "Of course you didn't mean to, which is why you are so good at it," he countered. "So... do I seek out Duchess Katherine? Or is there someone else I should speak with?"

About to answer, Violet gave a start at the sound of a snapping twig. They both turned in unison to see Michael and Helena making their way in their direction.

Neither the marquess nor the duchess seemed to have noticed them, though, the two gazing at one another as if they were the only two people in the entire world.

Alfred was the first to react, his arm wrapping around the back of Violet's waist so he could pull her through a small opening in the hedgerow. The widest part of her bell skirt prevented her from passing completely through, and she gasped.

"I've got this," Alfred whispered, quickly bending down to capture a wad of her gown and petticoats in his arms. He compressed them until they were free of the branches and then he moved them away from the opening.

Violet ended up in his arms as he stood with his back to the hedgerow. "Thank you," she whispered, angling her head around his shoulders. Given the density of the foliage, she was sure they weren't visible from the other side.

Not that her father would notice them. The way his attention had been on the Duchess of Weston, he seemed to only have eyes for her. He had been gazing at her as if he was trying to memorize every detail of her.

The same way Alfred was gazing at her.

Violet couldn't help how her breath shuddered. How the flutterbies in her stomach sent the most pleasant sensations coursing through her body.

He held a finger to his lips, his head tilted as if he was listening.

Violet did the same, recognizing her father's voice. She hadn't expected him to say anything—she was fairly sure he intended to do with the duchess what Alfred had been doing to her—so her brow furrowed when she heard mere snippets of his words.

"You cannot be surprised... it's our turn... make me happy... marry... the rest of our lives."

Glancing up, she noticed Alfred's changing expression. A grimace. A wince.

Was that anger?

Or disappointment?

There was a long moment of almost silence, the only sound the faint strains of music from the ballroom.

If the duchess said anything in response, Violet didn't hear it. She couldn't. Not over the pounding of the pulse in her ears, which had begun the moment she had spotted her father.

She gave a start when she noticed Alfred gazing down at her. "What?" she whispered.

He nodded toward the end of the hedgerow, where it connected to another hedgerow that might have lined the back of the property.

Violet nodded her understanding and stepped out of his hold. They quietly made their way until once again there were pavers under their feet.

"Could you hear what she said?" Violet asked, once they were out of earshot and were illuminated by one of the Japanese lanterns bobbing in the slight breeze.

"No," he replied, his expression suddenly dark.

"Could you hear what *he* said?"

Alfred scoffed. "Enough of it. He proposed marriage," he said, his manner once again that of the duke she had come to know through his sister.

They were nearly to the ballroom doors when Violet asked, "Do you object to the duchess marrying him?"

Pausing before he opened the door, the duke seemed to think on his answer before giving his head a shake. "I don't know."

Violet furrowed a brow. "Don't you wish to see your mother happy?"

He gave a start. "What makes you think she'll be happy married to Lord Fenwick?" he countered.

Inhaling softly, Violet allowed a shrug. "He obviously loves her. He's waited for her a very long time," she replied.

Furrowing his brows, Alfred regarded her with a curious expression before he was forced to open the door

—another couple was making their way towards them from inside the ballroom. "I'll find you when it's time for our dance," he said, ushering her through the door and to one of the potted palms.

Violet gave him a wobbly grin as she reached up and plucked a leaf from his hair. "I'll be right here," she replied.

A moment later, and the duke had disappeared in the crush.

CHAPTER 19
A WALK IN THE GARDENS

*M*eanwhile, out in the gardens

"You keep staring at me," Helena accused, her own gaze returning to watch Michael when she was sure of her footing on the garden pavers.

"I cannot help myself," he replied. "You're still so damned gorgeous. Excuse my French."

She tittered softly. "Says the man who is still more handsome than he has any right to be despite three *decades*."

Michael winced. "You needn't make it sound as if a century has passed," he countered. "Although there have been times when it felt as if we'd been apart that long."

Helena dipped her head. "I admit to feeling heartsick for a very long time after what happened," she admitted. "And then, once Alfred was born, things changed." She kept her gaze on Michael, not surprised to see his expression of hurt.

"There was someone else to love?" he guessed.

"Something like that. It was that or continue to be miserable," she said.

They walked in silence for a time until the light from the overhead Japanese lanterns no longer illuminated their steps. Ahead, a series of hedgerows promised privacy from the other couples who were wandering about the gardens.

"It's not too late for us, though," Michael said, hope sounding in his voice.

"I'm not the same young woman you remember from back then," she warned.

"And I am not the same man I was."

Despite the rustle of something in the hedgerow straight ahead—Helena was sure she had seen the dark shape of a couple kissing only a moment ago—Michael never took his eyes off her, even when he paused and turned to face her.

"Will you do me the honor of finally becoming my wife? My marchioness?"

Helena couldn't help her sudden intake of breath. Couldn't help the sense of excitement coupled with concern she had felt after their short conversation over breakfast. He had hinted then he would be proposing, but she hadn't been prepared for him to do it this evening.

"You cannot be surprised," he said when she didn't offer an answer. He took her gloved hand in his and slipped a ring on her fourth finger. Despite the silk fabric, the ring was merely snug.

"And yet I am," she finally replied, her eyes wide at

seeing the ruby solitaire on a gold setting. She lifted her hand to examine the jewel more closely. "It's beautiful," she breathed. "When...?"

"Today. I went with Philip when he went to pick up the one he had specially made for Lady Amelia."

Helena's reaction showed her confusion. "How can you be sure? About us, I mean?"

"It's our turn, my love," he said, pulling her into his arms. "Make me happy. I promise I'll make you happy."

"I might faint for the second time today," she murmured.

"Does the thought of marrying me cause you that much distress?" he asked in alarm.

"No, of course not. It's just so sudden. I think I should like a night to consider it."

She saw his look of hurt and leaned forward to kiss him. "Which gives you the entire night to convince me," she said, arching a dark brow suggestively.

Michael's eyes widened in shock. "Am I taking you to Weston Hall or Fenwick House?"

She tittered. "Weston Hall," she replied. "But that does bring up an interesting matter."

"Where we'll live, you mean?"

Nodding, she said, "I'm not aware of a dowager cottage—"

"I'll buy us something here in Town, or we can live at Fenwick Park for the rest of our lives," he said. "At least... after you're done with London," he amended.

She grinned and settled into his hold. "You drive a hard bargain, Fenwick."

"Whatever it takes to make you happy, my love."

On the way back to the ballroom, Michael felt as if he was walking on air. After thirty years, he and Helena would finally be together. They would spend the night in the same bed, making love and holding one another until dawn.

He had not a care in the world.

His gaze swept the gardens, taking in the early spring flowers and the Japanese lanterns bobbing in the gentle breeze. The gibbous moon rising in the east. The young couple up ahead.

Michael stutter stepped.

"What is it?" Helena asked, slowing her steps.

Blinking, he scoffed and gave his head a shake. "For a moment, I thought that young lady up ahead was my daughter," he said.

"Lady Violet, you mean?" Helena suddenly stopped in her tracks.

"What is it?"

She scoffed and squinted. "For a moment, I thought that young man with her was my son, but..." She shook her head. "He's probably left the ball by now. He rarely stays very long."

About to agree, Michael placed a hand over the one she had on his arm. "What if it is him?"

Helena tittered. "I assure you. I would be the first to know if Alfred was courting anyone," she claimed. "Now, will you take me around these lovely gardens before we depart? I shouldn't want to offend Constance, and I surely will if we leave too early."

"Another turn about the gardens it is, my love," Michael said, glad for an excuse to remain out of doors. Cool his ardor for a time.

Once they were inside, he would have to find his son and daughter and make his excuses. He had every intention of spending the rest of the night alone with Helena.

CHAPTER 20
GOOD NEWS

eanwhile, at the end of ballroom near the French doors

"Where have you been?" Amelia asked, breathless as she joined Violet under the potted palm.

Lost in thought, Violet gasped upon seeing her best friend. "I could ask *you* the same thing," she countered, one of her blonde brows arching in a tease. "I saw you and Philip go into the gardens."

"Well, of course we did," Amelia confirmed, her barely contained excitement making her practically bounce on the balls of her feet.

Violet giggled. "Did my brother already propose marriage?" she asked in surprise. Even before she finished her question, Amelia had her left hand held up, although the white glove was still in place. The telltale silhouette of a ring showed through the silk, though. Violet's eyes widened in delight. "Did Weston give his permission?" she asked in a whisper.

Amelia sobered somewhat. "Not yet," she replied, obviously disheartened. "Crawford will try for an appointment with my brother on the morrow."

"Have you spoken to your mother?"

Her friend's happy expression faltered even more. "Oh, dear. What have you heard?"

Violet lifted a shoulder. "I think my father and your mother are still in the gardens," she said, angling her head in the direction of the French doors. "I've been keeping watch for their return."

Amelia's face brightened with her huge smile. "Do you suppose Lord Fenwick has already asked her to marry him?"

Not about to admit she had overheard some of her father's proposal, Violet played dumb and said, "I think it was his intention."

Sighing contentedly, Amelia angled her head to one side and said, "Can you imagine? Both Mother and me betrothed on the same day?"

A streak of jealousy had Violet giving a start. Why she would experience the Green Monster at hearing Amelia's announcement, she didn't know. It wasn't as if she wanted to be betrothed. At least, not yet.

Or did she?

"What's wrong?"

Violet was about to answer when Philip appeared at her side.

"Dance with me, Sister. I have news," he said, as if he didn't think Amelia had already told her of his proposal.

"I may have some as well," Violet replied, giving

Amelia a beseeching glance as Philip led her to the end of the line for a longways dance.

"I'm sure Amelia has already told you," he said, turning to face her for the first part of the dance.

"Indeed. You've made her a very happy young lady."

"Did she show you the ring?"

Shaking her head, Violet passed under his arm and hooked her elbow into another man's before turning in a circle to finally once again face Philip. "Only through her glove," she said.

He seemed genuinely disappointed. "I was going to hold onto it, but…" The dance forced him to offer his elbow to the woman on his right, and once again they were separated for a time. "But I decided I wanted her to have it."

"Was Father with you when you bought it?" she asked.

Philip nodded.

"Did he buy a ring, too?"

Her brother chuckled. "How did you know?"

Turning to accept the elbow of the man to her right, she caught sight of her father and the Duchess of Weston entering the ballroom. She couldn't make out their mood given the number of people who passed between them as they danced, but after another whirl on an elbow, her father was suddenly standing behind Philip.

Pausing in the dance, Philip listened intently to the words Michael spoke in his ear and then nodded. "I will," he said, giving his father a nod.

Violet continued dancing, her expression of confusion finally prodding Philip into saying, "I'm to see you and Aunt Katherine home this evening."

"Now?" she asked in alarm.

"No. Later," he said, resuming the dance. "After the supper. Or whenever Aunt Katherine is done playing cards and wishes to leave." This last comment had one of his brows arching, as if it might be the wee hours of the morning before the duchess would willingly leave the card parlor.

In the middle of a turn, Violet spotted her father climbing the steps, the Duchess Helena on his arm.

Surely they were going to spend the evening playing house.

A huge grin split her lips as she finished the dance, curtsying to her brother when the music finished on a flourish. She was about to head for the palm trees when she found she couldn't.

Alfred, Duke of Weston, stood in her way.

CHAPTER 21

A NIGHT OF PASSION LEADS
TO A PROMISE

*M*eanwhile

"What sort of jewelry would you like your gemstones to be made into?" Michael asked as he escorted Helena to the Fenwick town coach.

"Surprise me," Helena replied. Ever since their stroll in the Reading gardens, she felt light. Unfettered.

Happy.

He chuckled as he held her hand while she climbed into the equipage.

Bounding in once her skirts had cleared the opening, Michael joined her on the seat facing the direction of travel. "A parure, perhaps?" he suggested, settling in so he could wrap an arm around the back of her shoulders.

"It will be rather sparsely bejeweled," she teased. "There weren't that many gems in that treasure box."

"There will be far more after I'm done choosing additional jewels for it," he argued.

Helena grinned and settled into his hold. "Tell me about your son."

"Philip?"

"You have others?" she asked in a playful voice.

He guffawed. "No. Of that I'm quite sure," he said, his brows suddenly wrinkling at the realization she might think him so different from when they were younger. "I was merely surprised by the change of subject is all."

"How long has he been secretly courting my daughter?" The query held a hint of suspicion and mayhap some anger. Michael's brows furrowed even more.

"That's a very good question, but I'm afraid I don't know the answer," he admitted. "I can tell you he fell in love with her last Season."

Helena gave a start. "That long?" she asked in surprise.

He nodded. "'Love at first sight', he said. I don't think he did more than dance with her a couple of times at some early balls before..." He broke off.

"Weston died," Helena finished for him.

"Yes. So that's why I'm not sure when they actually started courting."

She gave him a pointed glance.

"In secret," he acknowledged on a sigh. "I can assure you, he will make an honorable husband for Lady Amelia, and I think she knows that, too." He chuckled softly at remembering their conversation earlier that day when he had paid a call at Weston Hall. "Now that I have met her, I can certainly understand what Philip sees in her. I believe she is perfect for him."

Helena's expression conveyed her doubt. "Will he take a mistress?"

"Philip?" he said in disbelief.

"You have others?" she asked again, sighing softly at his expense.

He scoffed and squeezed her hand. "I taught him marriage vows are to be honored, no matter the other conditions," he replied.

"Did *you*?"

He nodded. "I did. Well... except in thought," he admitted, dipping his head.

Helena inhaled softly. "Michael," she whispered. Despite wanting it to sound like an admonishment, her gentle rebuke was instead an acknowledgement of his regard for her.

"I have always loved you, Helena, and I always will," he said.

They stared at one another in the darkness of the coach for a moment. About to pull her onto his lap so he could kiss her senseless, Michael was prevented from doing so when the coach stuttered to a halt.

From the way it suddenly swayed as the driver stepped down, it was apparent they had already made it to Weston Hall.

"Head back to Reading House," Michael instructed his driver when they had both stepped out. "You'll be taking the Duchess of Pendleton and my son and daughter home when they've finally had enough of the ball."

"Very good, guv'nor. Have a good night."

Michael gave his driver a nod. "Don't be cheeky, Parker." When the driver's eyes rounded, he realized the man hadn't meant his words to sound as if he was teasing. "Uh... good night, Parker."

"I think your butler is rather suspicious of me," Michael said as Helena led him up the stairs to the second floor.

"Pritchard is a stuffed shirt," she replied. "Besides, he's paid to be suspicious."

Michael chuckled. "I take it I am the first to have come home with you after an evening's entertainment? Since Weston's death?"

She gave him a quelling glance. "Tonight was my first evening's entertainment since he died."

"You didn't take a... a lover?" he asked in a whisper.

Anger showed on her face and then was gone in an instant. "Of course not," she replied, opening the door to her apartments. "I am a duchess, and I have two children I would like to keep free from scandal."

Feeling profound relief, Michael followed her into the elegant sitting room and turned to close the door. Glad to discover there was a lock, he was about to throw the bolt but asked, "Did you intend to ring for your maid?"

Helena turned and regarded him with an expression of disbelief. "Hardly. But you do know what that means?" She kicked off her slippers and seemed to inaudibly sigh with relief as she scrunched her toes into the Aubusson carpeting.

Michael blinked. "I have the honor of undressing you?"

She angled her head to one side. "And?"

He had to think a moment—rather difficult given his cock had realized what it would be doing soon—before his eyes widened. "Hair pins," he stated. He threw the bolt.

"Lots of them," she affirmed.

"Well, then have a seat, and I'll see if I can't extract all of them."

"You had better. Whatever you don't find may end up stabbing you in your sleep," she warned. "Or me."

"I am aware," he replied, chuckling softly when he noticed her expression—was that jealousy?—in the mirror.

When she was seated at her dressing table, he regarded her reflection in the mirror a moment. "You really are gorgeous. And your coronet makes you appear rather regal." Under the gas lights of the room's chandelier, the tiara she wore glittered even more than it had in the ballroom.

"I'm happy to hear you say it, but I'm going to be turning out the gas lamps before I allow you to undress me," she stated.

"Why?" He began plucking the pins from her coiffure, silently counting them in the event she knew exactly how many had been used by her lady's maid.

"I am not the same as I was, Michael. My body is not the same as you remember. I have ugly lines on my stomach—"

"From having been with child," he remarked, carefully removing the tiara from her coiffure and setting it on the dressing table.

"From Amelia, yes," she said, startled by his comment. "I didn't get them with Alfred."

"Do you hold it against her?" Michael asked, spearing his fingers through her hair in search of more pins. His fingernails scraped her scalp, and he reveled at seeing her reaction in the mirror. He hoped she might display the same expression again later that night when they were in her bed.

"Of course not," she replied, a bit too forcefully. When he reached for her hairbrush and began pulling it slowly through her wavy hair, she added, "Well, maybe."

"I intend to kiss every one of them," he warned, a brow rising with his words. "From one end to the other."

Helena inhaled softly and swallowed. "She was a beautiful baby," she whispered.

"Alfred was not?" he guessed.

She locked eyes with him in the mirror. "I know I shouldn't have thought so, but he was the ugliest little thing. All wrinkled, and he had far more hair than he should have had for something so tiny."

Michael chuckled and continued to brush her hair. "Sounds like Philip."

"Amelia was bald when she was born," she went on. Her eyes were half closed. Either she was deep in thought or she was enjoying what he was doing with her hair.

"Violet's was translucent. More fuzz than it was hair," he countered, grinning at the memory.

"She's a lovely girl," Helena remarked. "I am glad Amelia befriended her."

"As am I," he replied, setting aside the hairbrush in favor of undoing the fastenings at the back of her gown. "Does thirty-two sound about right?"

"Thirty-two?" she repeated in confusion.

He reached for a hairpin and held it up.

"Oh, I... I wasn't paying attention when Johnson did my hair," she replied. Upon seeing his quelling glance, she added, "In my defense, I was thinking about what it was going to be like when I saw you at the ball this evening."

Michael allowed a grin. "Good thoughts, I hope," he murmured, undoing the knot of his cravat.

"Mostly," she hedged. At seeing his look of hurt, she added, "My thoughts of you are never bad."

The length of white silk unfurled from around his neck in a few quick moves, and he sent it fluttering to the floor. "If not me, then... pray tell, what would have you vexed?"

The reflection of her gaze in the mirror left his as she dipped her head. "When you loosen my corset, I'm going to visibly droop," she said on a sigh.

"Do you mean to tell me your rigid backbone is due to your corset?" he teased. He knew she would aim a scolding glance in his direction, so he was ready with a kiss to her temple when she did.

"No. I'm referring to my rising moons setting quite

quickly," she countered, a watery grin suggesting she might cry. "Despite my rigid backbone. I wouldn't blame you if preferred to leave it on me."

Michael couldn't keep a grin from forming, and when she noticed in the mirror, he struggled not to laugh. "If you think for one minute I'm going to leave you even partially dressed this evening, you haven't been listening," he remarked. "I don't care if you have striae or if your breasts are saggy," he said, unbuttoning his top coat. He pulled it off his shoulders and tossed it aside. "I wouldn't care if your skin had pock marks—"

"There might be some of those," she whispered, her eyes rounding at seeing how he undid his waistcoat buttons more quickly than she had ever seen Weston's valet do it.

"—or if it was bright green," he continued, the waistcoat dropping to the floor. "I love you, dammit." Two *thunks* followed his proclamation as his shoes sailed against the molding near the door to her bedchamber. His reflection disappeared when he bent to strip his stockings from his feet.

Helena blinked when he suddenly reappeared and she stared as she watched him undo the fastening of his pantaloons and push them down. "Oh!" was all she could think to say when he was free of everything but his shirt.

He slid his hands beneath her arms and lifted her from the tufted seat, ignoring her gasp of surprise. A moment later, and he had her poppy ball gown down around her ankles, the petticoats soon following. Left in only a chemise, corsets, and stockings, she was about to cross her arms in front of her body when he said, "Don't you dare."

"What?"

"Try to hide from me," he muttered.

"Then you finish undressing first," she countered, her chin lifting. She stepped out of the mound of fabric at her feet and rescued her gown from the heap to drape it over the back of a chair.

He blinked and stared at her a moment before his gaze swept the bedchamber. "How do you turn off the blasted lights?"

For a moment, the room was silent. A bubble of laughter suddenly escaped Helena, despite her attempt to cover her mouth with one hand.

Michael chuckled. "I love it when you laugh."

She quickly sobered. "I'll see to the chandelier," she said, moving to pull one of the chains that hung from a central light.

Leaving only one candle lamp lit on a nightstand, Michael joined Helena at the end of the bed to continue what he had started. He tossed the corset onto the pile of petticoats and was about to lift the chemise from her torso when she stayed his hands.

"Not yet," she whispered. "Please."

Michael stilled his movements and finally nodded. "All right." He pulled her hard against the front of his body, and when her mouth opened in shock, his lips claimed hers.

He tried hard to keep his kiss soft—he didn't wish to bruise her lips or to frighten her with his need of her—but thirty years of wanting made it hard to control his desire. He deepened the kiss when he felt one of her hands move to his shoulder. He pulled away for a moment when he felt her rigid spine give way. "I have missed you," he whispered before he trailed his lips along her jawline and reveled in how she gave into his hold.

When he moved one arm to the back of her waist, her soft body seemed to mold against his, her curves filling his voids. Hard and impatient, his manhood pressed into her soft belly.

Moving one of his hands to mold a globe of her bottom, he lifted it and slid his hand along the back of her thigh until her bent knee was at his thigh. Sliding his hand between their bodies, his middle finger speared the dark curls at the apex of her thighs.

She jerked in his hold when his questing finger was replaced with the palm of his hand. She mewled when he pressed his palm harder against her swollen woman-hood. She clung to him as he moved his hand in a circular motion, rubbing her until her ambrosia coated his palm. When she tightened her hold on him, he knew she was close to her release.

He thought about stopping. Thought about leaving her on the precipice. Thought about how much better it might be if she experienced her orgasm when he was buried deep inside her.

Instead, he increased the pressure on her womanhood and whispered, "Come for me," as he tightened his hold on her.

Her breath hitched as her entire body seemed to spasm against his. Her quiet cry filled the room until she pressed her mouth to his shoulder.

He gave her no chance to recover. No chance to catch her breath before he had her on the bed. He followed on his hands and knees, stripping his shirt from his body and the chemise from hers. Sliding his hands beneath the globes of her bottom, he lifted and had her legs spread for him in an instant. A second later, and he had his cock nudging at her entrance.

There was a moment when he thought he should slow down. Take a breath. Kiss her body as he had promised. In the golden light from the single candle lamp, he marveled at how young she appeared, her skin rosy from his ministrations and her dark wavy hair spilling over her pillow

"Hurry," she whispered, one of her hands clutching his bicep.

His body knew what to do before he did, for before he had a chance to form a coherent response, he was buried deep inside her. Deeper when her knees lifted higher to cradle his thighs, and her hands gripped the sides of his torso.

He had thought to kiss her nipples. Suckle them for a time and kiss his way down the front of her body before he gave into his carnal cravings. He supposed there would be time for that later. There would have to be, for his body had already begun the rhythmic thrusting and retreating that would soon have him experiencing a pleasure so intense, he would nearly pass out.

Beneath him, he felt her chest rise, her nipples grazing his heated skin as he thrust into her over and over. When he saw how she looked at him, her eyes dark with desire and a barely-there smile touching her lips, it was nearly his undoing.

When she moved her hands down his torso to grip his buttocks and pull him harder into her, it was his undoing. He ceased his thrusting, cursed softly, and struggled to keep his upper body from crushing hers as a spasm of pure pleasure took him from the here and now.

CHAPTER 22
A DUKE MAKES AN ADMISSION

*M*eanwhile, *back in the ballroom at Reading House*

"Weston," Violet said, dipping her head. She gave Alfred a tentative grin as she tried to assess his mood. For a brief moment, she had thought him angry.

Had he seen his mother and her father take their leave? He certainly hadn't seemed happy about the prospect of his mother marrying her father.

Or had he discovered she was Philip's sister?

"I came to claim our first dance," Alfred said, his manner more pleasant than his expression suggested.

Violet's eyes widened. She hadn't even noticed which dances he had claimed on her card. "Of course. I apologize I wasn't where I said I would be."

He offered his arm. "Crawford might have had the courtesy to escort you back there when this dance ended," he countered, his head jerking in the direction of where her brother had been a moment earlier. "But you're easy enough to find in this crowd."

Violet felt heat suffuse her face. "Crawford seems rather preoccupied this evening," she offered, her own attention distracted at seeing how the middle of the ballroom cleared so an oval was left for the dance. Couples had already begun pairing up for a waltz.

"In what way?" he asked, taking her gloved hand in his as he placed his other at the side of her waist.

Heat from his hand penetrated the fabric of her gown, and Violet inhaled sharply at the sensation. "He's... he's in love," she said with a shrug of one shoulder.

The first few notes of the music had already begun, but Alfred stood rooted to the ballroom floor. "With you?" he asked, his eyes blazing.

Violet blinked. "No, of course not," she replied, almost admitting he was her brother.

The relief she saw in his eyes had her inhaling softly. "Weston," she whispered, well aware they needed to move or a collision would be imminent.

Alfred gave a start and set them in motion. "If not you, then who?" he asked, once they were safely spaced between two other couples in the circle of dancers. Given the number of dancers, another, larger oval had formed around them.

"Before I answer that, will you tell me why it is he vexes you so?" she asked.

The query had his expression once again darkening.

"An old argument is all," he replied. "We were in university at the time. I'm a bit older, and I..." He seemed about to admit something before he added, "It's nothing, really."

Violet angled her head to one side, which worked perfectly with the dance as he twirled her under his arm and recaptured her waist with his other hand. When she was once again facing him, she said, "And yet you are still bothered by him."

Alfred displayed a grimace. "It's not him, exactly. It's..." He shook his head. "It has more to do with his father."

Had she been able to stop, Violet would have, but the momentum of the waltz kept her in motion as did the duke's strong lead. "Lord Fenwick?" she whispered, her brows furrowing. "Has the marquess done something? Besides propose marriage to your mother, I mean?" For a moment, she thought Alfred might have seen the duchess and her father make their retreat from the ballroom.

Wincing, Alfred looked to his left and then to his right before he said, "I learned a long time ago from one of my grandfathers that Fenwick wished to court my mother. I think they had been secretly courting long before he asked permission," he explained.

Knowing the duke's assumption was correct, Violet said, "Go on."

"Well, my grandfather had already betrothed my mother to Harcourt Sheppard," Alfred said.

"Your father," Violet stated, not making it a question. From the odd expression that crossed Alfred's face, she once again relied on him to carry them through the next moves of the dance. "Before he inherited the dukedom. Am I right?" she asked.

Alfred's brows furrowed, as if he was struggling to find the right response. "Is he, though?"

Violet gave a start. "What do you mean?" She stared at him until the dance had her turning under his arm. When she was once again facing him, she understood his meaning. "You don't think Weston was your father?" Her eyes suddenly rounded in shock. "You think... you think *Fenwick* is your father?"

He didn't immediately respond, his gaze directed everywhere but at her. "Is it so hard to believe?" he countered, finally locking eyes with her.

For a moment, Violet thought he was playing her. She stared at him, her gaze taking in his facial features. The color of his eyes. The shape of his nose. The arch of his brows. The outline of his jaw. The shape of his lips. The color of his hair.

Nothing of his appearance would suggest he was related to her father or to her brother or to her.

"Yes," she finally replied. "You look nothing like him. Or Crawford, for that matter," she argued.

Instead of looking relieved at hearing her words, Alfred displayed a grimace. "Not even a little?"

Violet blinked. She blinked again upon replaying the query in her head. "Do you... do you *wish* you were Fenwick's son?" she asked in a whisper.

He shook his head. "I shouldn't have said anything," he announced, his gaze once again sweeping the ballroom and the other dancers around them. "Forget I ever brought up the topic."

"Weston," she said on a sigh. "Surely we can sort this. You must know your birthdate. Your mother and father's wedding date—"

"Don't you think I do?"

Violet's eyes once again rounded. "And?" For a moment, she thought she might be dizzy, and not just from having danced in circles for so long.

When the music suddenly ended, Alfred brought them to an abrupt halt. With her bell skirt still moving about her legs, she could barely remain standing. She left her hand on his shoulder and gripped it in an attempt to remain upright.

"Apologies," he said, keeping her hand in his another moment. "I shouldn't have told you."

Violet stared at him for several seconds, well aware the couples around them were moving to join the crush of onlookers as more couples were lining up for a long-ways dance. "Please, Weston, may we talk longer?"

He furrowed a brow before he quickly glanced around again. "Of course." With her hand still on his, he merely turned and led her toward the French doors. "Perhaps we can find a bench on which to sit."

The air was cool when they stepped out onto the pavers, chillier than it had been when they were out earlier that evening. Violet welcomed it, though, inhaling deeply in an effort to catch her breath and clear her head.

"What did you discover?" she asked, fearing his answer. From what her brother had told her, she was fairly certain her father and Helena had courted in secret long before he had asked the Duke of Woodleigh for permission to marry her. Perhaps her father had taken her virtue. If they had been intimate, it was possible the duchess had been left with child.

She glanced over again at Alfred before he led her to a stone bench at the edge of the garden. Despite the dim light from the Japanese lanterns, she was certain he bore no resemblance to her father.

He waited until she was seated before he flicked his tails back and sat next to her, his elbows left on his knees. His head dropped, and he scrubbed the side of his face with one hand before he said, "According to *DeBrett's*, Lord Harcourt married my mother in June of 1815. I was born in March 1816."

Violet considered his response, splaying out her gloved fingers as she counted quietly. "Nine months, which is perfectly reasonable," she said. "You were no doubt conceived whilst they were on their wedding trip."

"But what if...?" He sat back on the bench and huffed. "What if Mother was still secretly seeing Fenwick? Right up until she had to marry Lord Harcourt?"

Inhaling to answer, Violet realized she would be admitting not only how she knew, but also the identity of her father. "I do not believe that would have been possible," she began quietly. When he turned to stare at her, she added, "Since Fenwick moved to the country in 1814, and this is the first time he's returned to London."

"How do you know this?"

She swallowed. "Lord Crawford. He was born the

same year as you," she stated. Ignoring how he turned to face her, she added, "Fenwick married his late wife in the autumn of 1814 at the country estate where they lived until..." She felt the telltale lump building in her throat and had to stop to suppress a sob. "Until she died," she managed to get out, hoping he couldn't see how tears had begun to collect in the corners of her eyes. "So, you see, there's really no way Fenwick could be your father."

Alfred continued to stare at her for several seconds, a myriad of emotions crossing his face.

"Did you *want* him to be?" she asked gently. Had that been the real reason her brother and Alfred had fought at university? Because Alfred had claimed they were brothers of different mothers and Philip had taken offense?

The duke's attention went to the dark sky above them as he let out a breath. "I think at one time I did," he murmured.

"Had you met him? Fenwick, I mean?"

He shook his head, his gaze still on the heavens. "No. But Crawford... we used to be friends. He spoke so highly of his father. It used to anger me when we were at school. Angered me more when I learned my mother had favored Fenwick at one time." He turned to face Violet again. "I was so jealous of Crawford."

"But why?" she asked.

He scoffed. "My father was..." He allowed the sentence to trail off. "Forgive me. I shouldn't be speaking ill of the dead, and I fear if I continue, I shall say words not meant for feminine ears."

"I would not mind," she replied. "Truly."

Her encouragement seemed to break a dam within him. "He was a cruel and pompous arse," he said in a hoarse whisper.

"Your father was?" she asked quietly.

"Indeed. And when I learned he died, I rejoiced. I was glad until…" He stopped and briefly glanced away.

"Until what?" she prompted.

"I realized he had made me exactly like him. Pompous. Arrogant. Unwilling to—"

"Weston," Violet scolded in a whisper.

"—Accept criticism or offers of help. It's a wonder one of my middle names isn't 'Stubborn'."

Unsure of what to do or say, Violet continued to watch him, expecting he would say more. When he didn't, she leaned over and kissed him on the cheek.

He glanced over at her, obviously surprised by her act of affection. "So you can imagine why I wished Harcourt Sheppard wasn't my father."

Violet nodded her understanding. "You are not the only one who has ever wished for a different family, but…" She stopped when she realized what she was about to say. If they married, he could think of her father as his, in a manner of speaking.

That is, if he could ever forgive her for not admitting her relationship to the Marquess of Fenwick.

"But what?" he prompted.

She straightened on the bench. "Now that you know this… about your father… about the way you are. Do you realize you don't *have* to be like him? At least, if you don't choose to?"

He stared at her a moment. "You mean, I wouldn't have to be a pompous, arrogant arse if I didn't wish to be?" he asked rhetorically. When he noticed her enthusiastic nod, he scoffed softly. "I... I suppose I could try," he admitted.

"I think you've already managed somewhat," she said.

"What do you mean?"

She lifted a shoulder. "You haven't been pompous or arrogant the entire time I've been with you this evening."

Chuckling softly, Alfred dipped his head. "It's easy with you," he said quietly. His eyes suddenly rounded. "Oh, dear. How long have we been out here?"

Violet gasped softly. From the number of couples who were strolling through the gardens, it was obvious the longways dance had ended. Those who were overheated had sought refuge out of doors. "At least twenty minutes," she murmured.

"Come. Let's get back inside before your aunt misses you," he said, quickly coming to his feet. He turned and offered a hand.

Standing, Violet placed a hand on his arm. "Thank you," she said.

"It is I who should be thanking you," he countered.

"I meant... for trusting me," she murmured.

Alfred dared a glance around them before he lowered his lips to her forehead and kissed her. "I might say the same of you."

He was quiet until they reached the French doors. "I'll come find you when it's time for the second waltz."

She nodded and stepped in, not surprised when the duke remained outside.

Straight ahead, her brother stood with a hand on his hip and an expression of anger on his face.

"What's wrong?" she asked as she hurried to face him.

"I've been looking all over for you," he replied. "Where have you been?"

"I was in the gardens. It grew terribly warm in here at the end of the waltz," she replied.

Glancing over her shoulder, she was fairly sure the Duke of Weston was watching her from just inside the door.

She could only imagine what he was thinking.

He thinks I'm playing him for a fool.

CHAPTER 23
TALK OF THE FUTURE

*M*eanwhile, in Helena's bedchamber

Caught somewhere between consciousness and sleep, a warm body at her back and a heavy arm draped over her waist, Helena took a deep breath.

A familiar scent wafted around her, one from a long time ago. With its hints of citrus and amber, it brought back memories from her come-out and the heady days of early courtship. Stolen moments during balls and secret meetings in Hyde Park. Exciting times at *soirées* and in secluded gardens.

The first time she had ever been with a man.

"Do you suppose we could stay here like this for the rest of our lives?"

A grin formed at hearing the words again. She hadn't thought of this memory in a very long time.

When the body moved at her back, she came awake in an instant. She glanced down to discover a hand cupping her breast, and the sensation of something hard nudging the back of one thigh.

Michael.

"What have you done to me?" she asked in a hoarse whisper, her entire body in a strange state between languid lethargy and sexual excitement.

A chuckle erupted from Michael as he raised himself onto an elbow and leaned over to kiss her cheek. "I could ask the same of you, my love," he teased. His lips moved to her bare shoulder, where he left a trail of tickling kisses.

He gently blew air where he had left the kisses and chuckled again when her shoulder shivered in response.

Helena slowly rolled onto her back, which forced him to back up on the bed. The tangle of bed linens suddenly disappeared from atop her, and she let out a cry of protest.

"As I recall, I did not give these beauties any attention earlier this evening," Michael said before his mouth descended onto one of her breasts.

Torn between putting voice to a protest and pushing him off of her or simply enjoying the moment, Helena relaxed into the bed and purred. She placed a hand at the side of his head and smoothed it over his hair, her fingertips spearing it to scrape his scalp.

It was her turn to chuckle when she felt his head shiver. "Aren't you supposed to be an old man?" she teased, inhaling sharply when his teeth and tongue captured a nipple and nibbled it.

"Am I? I certainly don't feel old. Not right now," he said before resuming his ministrations.

"Well, you certainly haven't forgotten how to make love to me," she remarked.

He lifted his head from her breast and blew on it. "I never will," he vowed. "Even when I'm a hundred years old."

She giggled. "I rather doubt you're going to want some old wrinkled hag in your bed when you're a hundred years old."

His head bobbed up and his brows furrowed. "Watch how you describe yourself, my love. I'll not tolerate it," he countered. "Besides, you'll only be ninety-seven."

Helena inhaled sharply, both from hearing his words and from what a wandering hand was doing between her thighs. "I rather doubt I'm still going to be alive when I'm ninety-seven," she said in protest.

"You'd better be, if I'm going to be a hundred."

"Michael," she said suddenly, when his thumb pressed her swollen womanhood and sent an especially sharp sensation of pleasure shooting through her abdomen.

"I could stop if you'd prefer," he said, moving his lips to her other breast.

"Don't you dare," she countered, tittering quietly. When his kisses moved farther down her body, she gasped. "Michael," she quietly scolded, realizing he was trailing his lips along her striae.

"What?" he said when he moved from one silvery line to the next.

"You're tickling me," she murmured. Although there was no hint of censure in her words, she did push down on his shoulders.

He murmured something unintelligible before he suddenly lifted himself from her body and landed on his back. Although he was completely prone, his manhood stood at attention from its nest of curls.

Realizing he had misread her moves, Helena climbed atop him, her knees on either side of his hips.

"What's this?" he asked in surprise. "Am I to play a pony?"

"If you think for one moment I was done with you..." She steadied herself on her arms as she lifted her hips. "Then you have misjudged the situation," she continued as she impaled herself on his manhood.

Michael's "oof" was combined with a chuckle as she leaned back and stared down at him with a look of triumph. A second later, and she had wrapped an arm in front of her breasts. "Why did you do that?" he asked, his expression of happiness replaced with disappointment.

She leaned forward and flattened her torso against his. "There's still a candle lamp burning," she whispered.

He lifted his head and glanced toward the fireplace. Even if no lamps were lit, there were still a few flames flickering there. "Is that a problem?" he asked. He turned his head in the opposite direction and frowned, as if he was judging the distance to the candle lamp.

She gave him a quelling glance. "You just want to see my breasts bob up and down," she accused.

"You say that as if you think it will be a bad thing," he countered, an expression of guilt already evident.

"I rather doubt they're going to do it quite like you're expecting," she said, grinning at knowing she had guessed correctly.

"If I blow out the flame, will you continue doing what you were about to do?"

His query was accompanied by a slight lift of his hips, and she felt him move deeper inside her. "I can use the snuffer, I think," she said, angling her body so she could reach it with the tips of her fingers while his cock remained firmly inside her. She finally had a hold on the silver wand when she let out a cry of surprise as a sharp dart of pleasure once again emanated from her womanhood. Her attempt at snuffing out the flame failed.

Michael chuckled softly. "If I died right now, I would be a happy man for all eternity," he claimed.

"You had better not die right now," she warned. "Remember, you're supposed to live to be a hundred." Her second attempt at putting out the candle lamp succeeded. Only the golden glow from the fireplace illuminated the bedchamber.

In the aftermath before their eyes adjusted, Helena once again sat atop him. The temptation to make Michael wait for his release was too much, and she teased him by trailing her fingertips through the blonde curls covering his chest and down the middle of his stomach.

Although she was aware of how his hands gripped her hips, Helena didn't realize where his thumbs were until her fingertips had reached the dark curls where their bodies met. When he pressed and rubbed her womanhood, her back arched and her chin lifted and her head fell back as an intense pleasure rolled through her. Her keening cry split the night as he began thrusting into her over and over.

Stretched out as she was, she knew he could see all of her, but she found she didn't care.

When he ceased his movements, she felt the warmth of his sudden release and reveled in hearing his groan of satisfaction.

She couldn't help but giggle when she heard his whispered, "I am most definitely living to be a hundred," as she lowered her body to lay atop his.

CHAPTER 24
AN EXIT BEFORE THE END

*M*eanwhile, back in the Reading ballroom

"Aunt Katherine isn't feeling well, and she wishes to take her leave," Philip said, leading Violet around the perimeter of the ballroom toward the stairs.

"But I've promised the supper dance—"

"As have I," he said, aiming a look of disappointment in her direction. "Have you seen Amelia? I thought she might be with you."

Violet considered how long it had been since she had seen her best friend. "The last I saw of her, she was dancing the waltz with you," she said. "Someone claimed the supper waltz on my card. Won't you give me five minutes to make my excuses? It would be rather rude of me to simply leave without letting him know."

Philip paused in his search for Amelia and finally nodded. "All right, but meet me at the bottom of the stairs—"

"In the entry," she countered, not about to have Alfred see her exiting on the arm of her brother. He was probably already annoyed with having witnessed her speaking with Crawford.

"The entry then. Don't be long, though. Aunt Katherine is probably already up there waiting for us."

Violet nodded her understanding and turned to retrace her steps to the French doors. She found Alfred leaning against a nearby column, apparently deep in thought.

"Your Grace?" she said quietly.

He came out of his stupor and regarded her with a look of surprise. "Weston, please, my lady," he said.

"Weston," she acknowledged. "I came to apologize. It seems I will not be able to dance the second waltz with you after all."

Alfred jerked his head in the direction of the stairs. "Did Crawford tell you to say he had already claimed it?" he asked, anger tingeing his voice. "I saw you walk right to him when you took your leave of me."

Violet's eyes widened. "No. He was merely delivering a message from my aunt, Duchess Katherine. It seems she has taken ill and wishes to leave now, so I must go. She is my chaperone this evening."

Furrowing his brows, the duke stared at her for a moment before he said, "The regard you show for Crawford... are you... are you in love with him?"

Blinking several times, Violet was torn between scoffing or tittering at the duke's expense. She quickly shook her head. "I assure you, Weston, I am not. Not like that," she went on, her face screwing up in a grimace. "Eww."

Even when she gave an involuntary shudder, Alfred still appeared suspicious. "You spoke of him in the gardens as if you are close. Pray tell, how is it you know so much about him?"

The reminder of their earlier conversation had Violet struggling with how to reply. It was far too soon to admit Philip was her brother. Until Philip had secured the duke's permission to marry Lady Amelia, she didn't dare reveal her relationship to him. "He's—"

"There you are, young lady," Katherine said as she stepped up next to Violet and gave Alfred a slight nod. The ostrich feather waved about over her head, sending out a slight cooling breeze in its wake. "Your Grace," she added, shoving a gloved hand in his direction.

"Your Grace," he countered, bowing to brush his lips over the back of her hand.

"Aunt Katherine," Violet said. "I promised His Grace the supper dance, so I came to make my apologies," she explained, hoping the relief she felt at the well-timed interruption didn't show on her face.

"Well, I really must take my leave, and since I promised your father I would see to your welfare, you'll have to come along now." She turned her attention on the duke. "If you possess an ounce of understanding, Weston, you will forgive her, will you not?"

Alfred's eyes rounded. "Of course, Your Grace," he replied. "But you will make it up to me with a supper dance at the next ball?" he asked, turning his attention back to Violet.

She nodded. "Of course I will, Weston," she said, giving him a deep curtsy. "I look forward to it. Do have a good night."

He reached for her hand and gripped it more tightly than usual. "I shall, my lady. Good night."

Violet continued to stare at him until her aunt's urgings had her hurrying with her to the stairs. When they had reached the top, she turned to regard Katherine with worry. "Philip said you were feeling ill."

Katherine waved a dismissive hand. "A mere excuse is all," she said. "Word reached me that you had been seen in the company of Weston, and I thought it best I rescue you from 'His Surliness'," she went on. "Besides, I'm afraid my luck at cards has ended this evening. I am out of money."

Violet's eyes widened. "Completely?"

Katherine scoffed. "Heavens, no. I only bring a small amount with me to these entertainments," she explained. "I play until I'm out, and then I take my leave."

"Well, that's a relief," Violet replied, allowing Philip to help her with her mantle. He had obviously been waiting for them for some time.

"Did you ever find Lady Amelia?"

He nodded. "She said she would dance with her brother if he hadn't claimed the dance with anyone else."

Katherine and Violet exchanged quick glances. "Then

no harm done by leaving early," their aunt said as she allowed a footman to help her with her redingote. "Crawford," she said by way of a hint.

Philip held out his arm for her, and they took their leave of Reading House.

CHAPTER 25
A BARGAIN IS STRUCK

The following morning, in the breakfast parlor at Weston Hall

Deep in thought as he made his way to the sideboard, Alfred barely noticed what he dished onto his plate for that morning's breakfast. From the time Violet had left him the night before, he had been thinking of her.

More than thinking of her.

He had imagined she was still with him when he had made his way to his bedchamber. He had dismissed his valet in favor of imagining her undoing his buttons and removing his clothing. Imagined helping her with the fastenings of the gorgeous pale blue gown she had worn. Imagined pulling the silk flower and pins from her hair. Imagined watching her blonde hair fall past her bare shoulders as he pushed her gown down her body.

By the time he had settled onto his bed, his body had

become so heated, his manhood so hard, he had welcomed the cool bed linens.

He had imagined kissing her as they had been doing in the gardens. Kissing her entire body. Taking his member in hand, he had imagined making love to her, at first slowly. When her soft cries had her begging for more, he had quickened his movements and experienced a release he had not allowed himself in a very long time.

Awakening with a grin on his face, his morning tumescence had him doing it all over again—which was probably why he felt lighter than he had in a very long time. Lighter and, dare he admit, happy?

"Are you going to eat all of those eggs?"

Alfred gave a start at hearing his sister's query. "Uh..." He glanced down at his plate to discover he had dished out seven coddled eggs and most of the rashers of bacon. "No. Of course not," he said, scooping several back into the serving dish. He was glad the plate hid the silhouette of his hardened manhood.

"Are you all right?"

He moved to take a seat at the table, but before he did so, he pulled out a chair for Amelia and waited for her to sit.

She stared at him, her eyes round. "Have you gone mad?"

"What?"

Scoffing, Amelia said, "You never hold my chair for me," she said, her gaze darting to the footman who usually did.

"About time I did so, though, don't you think?" he countered, tucking into his meal. When the footman set a cup of coffee before him, he said, "Thank you."

Amelia stared at him. "Who are you, and what have you done with my brother?" she asked. When he glanced up at her with a look of confusion, she added. "Never mind. I prefer you over him. You can stay."

Alfred quirked his lip. "Did you enjoy the ball?"

She displayed a look of suspicion before saying, "Most of it. And you? You hardly said a word in the coach on the way home."

He lifted a forkful of egg to his lips. "I was thinking."

"About?"

He screwed up his face in a grimace, not sure he wanted to share his thoughts with Amelia. He had wanted to speak with their mother, but her early exit from the ball and apparent absence from Weston Hall— she hadn't greeted them upon their arrival—had him thinking the Marquess of Fenwick had taken her to his house.

For some reason, the thought of her with Fenwick didn't bother him as much this morning as it had the night before.

"Courtship," he finally stated, his attention on his plate.

Amelia inhaled softly. "Mine or... or yours?"

Alfred glanced up. "Does someone wish to court you?"

She angled her head to one side and scoffed. "You

needn't make it sound as if you're surprised someone wants to... to marry me," she scolded.

"I didn't mean to," he countered. "I just... I hadn't thought you were... old enough, I suppose," he stuttered.

"Alfred," she said as she rolled her eyes. "This is my second Season—"

"You hardly had one last year."

"—and there *is* someone who I would very much like to marry. That is, if you would give your permission for him to court me."

His fork was halfway to his mouth when he paused and stared at her. He set it on his plate and sat back. "If I give you permission to marry who you wish to marry, then you must help me," he said.

Amelia blinked, not expecting him to bargain with her. "Help you with what?"

"With whom I wish to... to court," he stammered, changing the word from 'marry' at the last second.

Blinking several times, Amelia slumped back in her chair. "You say that as if you think I know whoever it is you wish to court."

"Well, that's because you do."

Amelia's dark brows rose with her surprise. "Go on."

"Lady Violet. I wish to court Lady Violet."

Staring at him as if he'd grown another head, Amelia shook hers. "*My* friend, Violet?"

Alfred displayed a look of confusion for a moment. "Is there more than one?" he countered. "Of course. your friend. I only know of the one Violet."

"Are you *mad?* You're playing me for a fool, aren't you?" she asked, crossing her arms. "Making a funny?"

"I am not," he insisted, his breakfast forgotten.

"Describe her," she ordered, lifting her chin as if she were daring him.

Alfred scoffed. "Blonde hair, blue eyes. She wore the palest of blue gowns at the ball last night, and she had a silk flower in her hair, like the one you wore." He pointed to one of his collar bones. "She has a beauty mark here," he added. "And one here." He pointed to his upper chest.

Amelia's eyes rounded. "That's rather specific."

He directed his gaze to the side. "And a little dimple right here when she smiles," he said, pushing his index finger into the base of his cheek. "Makes her look rather adorable."

Her mouth dropping open in shock, Amelia stared at Alfred for a moment before she said, "I cannot believe you even notice such details on a woman."

He shrugged. "How could I not?" he countered. "I find her captivating and rather clever."

Amelia blinked again as her gaze dropped to her breakfast plate. Hands on her hips, she asked again, "Where is my brother, and what have you done with him?"

It was Alfred's turn to roll his eyes. "If you're not going to help me, then we won't have a bargain," he warned.

Inhaling sharply, Amelia dropped her arms to her sides. "I'm supposed to... to what? Talk her into agreeing to be courted by you?"

"Exactly."

"But... why is it you even think she might be interested in courtship with you?"

Alfred couldn't help the look of hurt that crossed his face. "We spent time together at the *soirée*. We rode horses in the park. We danced together. We would have danced both waltzes last night had her aunt not taken ill," he ticked off on his fingers. "And I... I may have stolen a kiss or two in the gardens."

Amelia gasped and then angled her head first to the left and then to the right, examining his cheeks for tell-tales signs of a strike. "She didn't slap you?" she asked in disbelief.

"Amelia," he huffed. "She... she returned the kiss, in fact. Even slipped her fingers through my hair." The way his head seemed to quiver suggested he was experiencing the same sensations he had felt at the time he was kissed.

"Eww," his sister replied with a grimace, a hand going to cover her mouth. "I cannot believe Lady Violet would do such a thing," she whispered.

"Because you don't think her capable? Or because you don't think she would do it with *me*?"

The sound of annoyance in his voice had Amelia realizing she had to agree to his terms or lose her chance at gaining permission for her own betrothal. "Because I didn't realize she was speaking of *you* when she said she had developed a tendré for someone of our acquaintance."

Alfred's eyes widened. "She said that?"

Amelia nodded. "Oh, Alfred. She didn't say your name, so I didn't know." Her eyes once again rounded as she forced a smile. "Do you realize what this means?"

A look of suspicion crossed his features. "What?"

"If you end up married to Lady Violet, she'll be my *sister*," she said, her grin becoming more real. She stood from her chair and hurried to wrap her arms around his neck and kiss him on the cheek. "Oh, Alfred. You have my support," she said.

"Thank you," he said. "Truly."

Amelia nodded. "I still want to know what you've done with my brother, though," she murmured.

He gave her a quelling glance. "You should be more concerned about our mother," he said, waving toward the door. "I fear Fenwick may have whisked her off to who-knows-where last night. We may never see her again."

"Her Grace is in her apartments, Your Grace," Pritchard said, the butler having entered the breakfast parlor from the butler's pantry at the very moment Alfred mentioned the duchess. "Breakfast and chocolate were delivered to her room earlier this morning."

Alfred regarded the servant with a look of surprise. "Oh. Well. That is a relief, I suppose."

For a moment, Amelia displayed a look of disappointment, and her brother noticed. "What is it?"

"Would it have been so bad if Fenwick *had* taken her home?" Amelia asked. "Anyone with two eyes can see they're *desperately* in love with one another."

Although his first reaction would have been to argue

her claim, Alfred quelled it. After his discussion with Violet the night before, he had come to realize there was little to no chance Michael, Marquess of Fenwick, was his father. As for how she knew so much about the man, he didn't know.

But he was determined to find out.

CHAPTER 26
HOW THE BREEZE
REALLY BLEW

*M*eanwhile, *in the breakfast parlor at Fenwick House*

Violet stood before the sideboard in the breakfast parlor and stared at the array of offerings. A footman had set a ham in the middle, a few slices still giving off steam. The basket of rolls smelled divine. The yellow yokes on the plate of eggs looked as if a dozen eyes were staring at her.

"If you can't decide, might you allow me to step in?"

Giving a start, Violet looked up to discover her brother aiming a teasing grin in her direction. "I didn't hear you come in," she said, stepping aside.

"That was obvious." He scooped several eggs onto his plate and snagged a slice of ham with the serving fork. "Is everything all right? We can have cook make something else if this isn't to your liking."

"Oh, that's not it," she said, finally helping herself to

some ham and a bread roll. "I was... merely lost in thought."

"That was obvious," he repeated, nodding to the footman who placed a cup of coffee on the table and held a chair for Violet. "You were terribly quiet in the coach on the way home last night. Did something happen at the ball?" he asked before taking a sip of coffee.

Violet felt her face grow warm. "No."

He arched a brow and chuckled. "You're blushing." His eyes suddenly rounded, and he set the cup on the table. "Violet Cummings, what *have* you done?" he asked, excitement in his voice.

"Nothing," she claimed. When he continued to stare at her, she covered her face with her hands. "Oh, Philip, I can't decide if it's awful or wonderful."

Not expecting that sort of response, he scoffed. "Met someone, did you?" he guessed before his attention went to his eggs.

Two fingers spread apart so she could peek between them. "I already knew him," she whispered. "Which is why it could be awful."

Intrigued by this bit of news, Philip glanced up at her and then sat back in his chair. "Anyone I know?"

She dropped her hands to her lap and nodded.

"Did I introduce you?"

She shook her head.

"Are you going to tell me who? Or am I supposed to guess from the... oh, twenty or more young bucks it could be?"

She straightened in her chair. "Will you please tell

me *exactly* what caused you and Weston to fight when you were at university?"

Obviously not expecting the query, Philip sat back and regarded her with an expression of surprise. "I told you—"

"Did you fight him because he claimed our father was his father?"

Philip's gaze darted to the side. "Uh..., he may have mentioned something to that effect, but I told him it was impossible. Why are you asking?"

"Did he really throw the first punch that day?"

Blinking, Philip leaned forward and pushed his plate to the side. For a moment, it seemed as if he wasn't going to answer her question, so when he finally spoke, Violet gave a start at hearing his claim.

"We were friends once."

"*What*?" The memory of Alfred having said the same thing the night before came back to her in a flash.

"The very best. Almost the entire time we were at Eton and the first year of university," he claimed.

"You are speaking of Weston?" she asked quietly.

He nodded. "Before he inherited, of course. He wasn't a pompous arse back then," Philip added, rolling his eyes.

"So... what happened?"

"For some reason, he sorted that he was conceived before his mother married Weston. He never actually met Father, but Alfred was convinced our father and his mother had been secret lovers. I think because..."

"He didn't like his own father," Violet said in a whisper.

"Something like that," Philip said. "Father and I always got along. Maybe he was jealous," he murmured. "He is somewhat older than me, and now that we know Father was in love with Duchess Helena, it's obvious he must have discovered their relationship at some point—"

"The dates don't work, though," Violet said. "He even admitted he had looked at a copy of *DeBrett's*, but he didn't believe what he had read."

Philip appeared lost in thought for a moment. "Learning the truth of the matter angered him, I think. He really wanted Father to be his father, and not because he wanted the Fenwick marquessate. He was going to inherit a dukedom, after all."

"You would have been his brother."

"Despite the fact that he looks nothing like Father or me," Philip responded. "Anyway, he grew angry with me. That I couldn't agree with his idea had him so frustrated, he started hitting me. I let him," he murmured, his voice growing quieter. "Several times until I'd finally had enough, and I hauled off and hit him. Punched him in the nose." He winced. "He went down like a rock. Blood everywhere."

Violet winced. "Eww. Did you apologize?"

Philip shook his head. "He never did, either. We haven't spoken since. Every time he saw me after that, his nose went up, as if he wanted me to know it had healed. Looks better now than it did before, come to think of it."

"And his arrogance?"

Shaking his head, her brother let out a guffaw. "I think he decided to become his true father's son," he replied. "I only met the man once, but he was... he was an arrogant man. Convinced he was going to live forever. How, I'm not sure, but it certainly didn't work out that way for him."

"And Alfred was forced to inherit before he had any idea of how to be a duke," Violet said.

"Indeed," Philip agreed. His brows suddenly furrowed. "You've spoken to him," he stated, not making it a question.

Violet nodded. "Last night," she admitted.

"That's not the sort of conversation one has during a waltz."

She shook her head before saying, "It was in the gardens."

Philip's eyes widened. "Did he... did he—?"

"He was a perfect gentleman," she claimed, knowing her blush might give her away.

"Has he tried to convince you you're his sister?"

"No," she replied. Her eyes widened. "Gosh, no."

Philip's look of suspicion increased. "He favors you," he said suddenly.

Violet blinked. "Maybe."

"Do you favor him?"

Her brows furrowed as her lips began trembling. "I... I'm not sure. I only meant to... to lead him on... so it might make it possible for you to gain his permission to marry Amelia."

Philip scoffed. "How long has this been going on?"

She directed her gaze to the sideboard. "A few days. Since the night of the *soirée*. He does seem to be growing rather fond of me."

His eyes rounding, Philip scoffed again. "What did you expect to happen?" he asked in alarm. "A marriage proposal?"

"Something like that."

"Were you playing him? Were you going to beg off?"

She nodded. "Something like that. It wouldn't come to that, though. He would have ended it," she reasoned in a whisper.

"Why?"

Violet closed her eyes. "We haven't really been properly introduced, you see."

"You danced the waltz last night. Someone had to have—"

"He doesn't know I'm your sister. He doesn't know I'm Fenwick's daughter."

Philip scoffed twice as he leaned back in his chair and stared at the stuccoed cherubs in one corner of the ceiling. "Well, I suppose if I'm going to gain his permission to marry Amelia, I had best head to Weston Hall before he learns the truth about you," he said.

"Father hasn't yet returned home, which means he's probably still there," she reasoned.

"Or in Doctors' Commons arranging a marriage

license," he countered. He chuckled softly. "I do hope the duchess has agreed to marry him."

Violet grinned. "Me, too."

"Or Amelia and I will be heading to Scotland."

About to say she might join them as a means to escape Weston's wrath, Violet couldn't when Philip took his leave of the breakfast parlor.

Staring at the slice of ham on her plate, Violet decided she best eat some breakfast.

At some point during the day, she would have to face Weston and admit her relationship to Philip, and she didn't want to be doing it on an empty stomach.

CHAPTER 27
A PROPOSAL COMES WITH A CONDITION

*M*eanwhile, *upstairs in Weston Hall*

"I really wish I could remain in bed with you for the rest of my life."

Having drunk her chocolate and eaten a toast point, Helena regarded Michael with a grin. "Well, I hate to be the bearer of bad news, but you cannot," she said, giving him a nudge. "Eat some breakfast."

Michael groaned and sat up, accepting the plate she offered him. "I think we play well together."

"That's because we do," she agreed.

"Well, I like to think I'm playing for keeps. Have you given my proposal any thought?" he asked.

"I have," she replied, brushing a crumb from the corner of her lips. "And I have decided I will marry you—"

"Thank the gods!"

"—but not until after Amelia and Alfred are both settled."

Staring at her as if she had shot him with a dueling pistol, he looked as if he might fall backward in a dead faint. At least he was still on the bed.

"You needn't look so stricken," she gently scolded. "If it's any consolation, I expect we're going to be sharing a bed frequently between now and then. In fact, we'll have to, because I have every intention of having you do to me what you did to me earlier this morning as often as you're able."

The comment seemed to placate him somewhat. "I shall endeavor to do my best, my duchess," he replied. He ate some of his eggs, his attention on the bed linens covering the lower half of his body.

"Have I vexed you terribly?" she asked meekly.

"I was thinking of going to the archbishop's office today," he replied.

She inhaled softly. "So you were looking forward to a quick wedding."

"Tomorrow would not have been soon enough," he replied, his lip quirked. "But I shall be patient and in search of a bride for Weston," he went on. "Perhaps there is a young lady who can be bribed with a good deal of blunt—"

"Michael!" she scolded, threatening him with a pillow.

He chuckled softly before returning his attention to his meal. "I expect my son will try again today to ask Weston for his permission to marry Lady Amelia."

"Then let us hope Alfred's in a good mood after last night's ball," Helena replied. "I hardly saw him."

Michael gave her a pointed glance. "He was in the gardens with someone," he reminded her.

"Probably just to get some air," she countered. She sighed as she leaned back into the pillows. "Constance is going to be so thrilled to learn there was a marriage proposal in her gardens last night," she said, referring to the Marchioness of Reading and hostess of the prior night's ball. "I'm trying to decide when I'm going to tell her."

"You want to right now, don't you?" he accused.

She tittered. "For someone who hasn't spent a day in my company in so long a time, you know me too well," she admitted. "I won't go until later, of course. Besides, it's far too soon to be paying morning calls."

"Ring for your maid, my love. I'm going to dress and pay another call at Ewen and Ewen. That is, if you're amenable to a parure made with amethysts and emeralds?"

"You were supposed to surprise me," she countered, although her words suggested she was happy with the idea. "But this gives me an opportunity to have my modiste make me a violet gown, so there's that."

"You'll look amazing in violet," he murmured, his eyes darkening. "But not as beautiful as in what you're wearing right now."

"But I'm not wearing anything. Other than the bed linens," she argued.

"Exactly." He once again moved to get out of bed, but she stopped him with a touch to his shoulder. "What is it?"

Helena glanced over at him, her eyes rounding. "I have a better idea."

He paused and turned to regard her with a questioning glance. "Oh?"

She huffed. "You can stay for the rest of the morning," she offered.

Settling back onto the bed, he stared at her a time before he said, "Invitation accepted, my love."

A moment later, Helena gave a shriek as he suddenly pulled her onto his body. A second after that, he was kissing her senseless.

It was another hour before she allowed him out of the bed to dress.

CHAPTER 28
AN APOLOGY IS OFFERED

eanwhile, in another part of Weston Hall

As Amelia made her way back up to her bedchamber, she hoped Violet wouldn't instantly unfriend her upon learning of the bargain she had struck with her brother.

Courtship wasn't actually marriage, after all. Violet could always beg off at the last minute. Play the shrinking violet. Claim she was too young to wed.

But what had possessed Violet to spend so much time with her brother at the Reading ball? She had done the same at the Everly's *soirée* as well.

What had Alfred said about riding horses in the park? About spending time in the gardens the night before?

The poor girl didn't need to sacrifice herself on Amelia's account. Especially now that Alfred seemed to harbor serious feelings for the girl. What else could explain why he felt it necessary to bargain with her in the first place?

"She's going to be so angry with me," she murmured.

"I rather doubt anyone could be angry with you, my lady."

Amelia inhaled sharply when she realized who she was about to run into on the stairs. She had glanced up —and up—to discover the Marquess of Fenwick regarding her with an expression of amusement.

"My lord," she said, her face flaming with embarrassment.

"My lady." He stepped aside and down a few more stairs so he was even with her. He took her hand to his lips. "I look forward to having you as a daughter in the near future."

Amelia's eyes rounded. "Thank you, my lord. I suppose this means your pursuit of a duchess has been successful?"

He nodded. "Marchioness, you mean."

She allowed a wobbly grin. "I fear your daughter isn't going to be as happy."

"What's this?" he asked in confusion.

"My brother... Weston... he wishes to court her," she blurted.

Michael gave a start. "We're speaking of my Violet?" he asked.

"You have others?" she asked, her eyes rounding even more.

He chuckled softly. "No. Just the one." He quickly sobered. "What's this about Weston?"

"Something must have happened during their dance together at last night's ball. He's... he's *smitten* with her.

He wishes to *court* her," she said in a hoarse whisper. "She's already spent so much time in his company. As a means to prevent him from learning about Crawford and me," she continued, unaware of his look of alarm at hearing her words.

"Fear not, young lady, I'll return to Fenwick House and see what I can discover directly from her," he said.

"I was thinking of paying a call on her," Amelia said. "Might I join you?"

"Your coach has arrived, my lord," Pritchard announced from the bottom of the stairs.

Michael blinked, about to say that he hadn't ordered one. "I rather imagine it has brought Philip," he said in a voice meant only for Amelia.

She inhaled softly. "He's come to ask for permission to court me," she whispered.

"To marry you," Michael corrected her. He turned his attention to the butler. "Pray tell, is Weston in his study?"

Pritchard blinked. "He is, my lord." A knock at the front door had him giving a short bow before he hurried to open it.

Michael turned to Amelia. "Perhaps we can delay our departure a few minutes?" he suggested. "In the event our presence might be required?"

Amelia nodded vigorously. "Of course, my lord." They descended the stairs and met Philip as he stood waiting to see Weston.

"Father?" he said in surprise. "Amelia?" He rushed to bow and take her hand to his lips.

"Good morning, my love," she said, standing on tiptoes to kiss him on the cheek.

Philip noticeably blushed. "I came to apologize to Weston," he blurted.

"Apologize?" Amelia questioned.

"Apologize?"

The three turned to discover Alfred, Duke of Weston, standing on the threshold of his study, his gaze darting between the three of them.

"Yes, apologize," Philip stated, stepping away from Amelia and his father to approach the duke. "I never should have punched you, despite how many times you hit me," he said, finally stopping a few feet in front of Alfred to bow deeply. "You obviously had your reasons for believing what you did, and until this morning, when my sister asked what had transpired betwixt us, I hadn't considered how much the truth hurt you. Hurt the both of us."

Alfred stared at him for several seconds before his gaze darted to Michael. "Is... is there another reason you've come?"

Philip inhaled and let the breath out in a huff. "I wish to marry your sister, but I'd prefer to do so with your permission."

His brow furrowing in confusion, Alfred directed his attention on his sister. "Amelia?"

"Yes?" she asked, her lower lip trembling. She took a few steps toward her brother, well aware there were now two other people listening in to the conversation. Her mother was standing on the landing at the top of the stairs, her feet frozen in place.

"Is *this* who you were talking about at breakfast this morning?" Alfred asked.

Amelia nodded. "He is," she affirmed. "I love him, Alfred. I have for... for almost a year now."

The duke gave a start. "Well. Then I suppose it's time you be married to him," he said.

Her eyes widening in delight, Amelia rushed to embrace her brother. "Oh, Alfred, thank you," she whispered.

"You remember our bargain?"

Her elation momentarily stilled. "Of course. I'm off to see her now," she whispered.

He gave her a watery grin. "Well, then, see to it while I speak with this bounder about your dowry," he replied.

Amelia giggled and gave Philip a beseeching glance. "I'll see you soon?"

"Sooner," he said, stepping into the study to follow Alfred.

A moment later, and the door closed.

Michael chuckled softly. "Well, that went better than I expected," he murmured. He offered his arm, but noted Amelia's attention was on the stairs. He followed her line of sight and allowed a grin. "How much did you hear?" he asked, as Helena hurried to the bottom of the stairs and into his arms.

"All of it, I think," she said, tears streaming down her face.

"One down, one to go," he said with a smirk.

"Bounder," she accused.

A few feet away, Amelia stood watching them with a look of bewilderment on her face.

CHAPTER 29
A TRUTH MADE EVIDENT

An hour later, at Fenwick House

Michael and Amelia rode to Fenwick House in the town coach, and the marquess immediately sent it back to Weston Hall to retrieve Philip. Although he had invited Helena to join them, he knew she already had plans to pay a call at Reading House that afternoon.

He hoped the negotiations between his son and the duke hadn't hit any snags and that Weston hadn't changed his mind about allowing Amelia to marry Philip.

As for Amelia's claim her brother wished to court Violet, he wasn't sure what to think.

Only a few days ago, the general consensus about Alfred, Duke of Weston, was that no one liked him due to his pompous manner.

Apparently something had changed.

"Browning, have my daughter join us in the library, and bring tea." Given the study was Philip's domain these days, he decided to meet in the library for the relative privacy it offered from eavesdropping servants.

"Yes, my lord," the butler said before hurrying off.

"Would you like me to wait in the front salon whilst you speak with her?" Amelia asked.

"Oh, no, young lady," he replied, waving her to the stairs. "I think it may take the both of us to determine my daughter's thoughts on the matter of your brother."

"Until this morning, I was of the opinion she needn't sacrifice herself on my account," Amelia murmured as they climbed to the first floor. "All this time, I've only thought she was play acting."

Michael paused on the landing. "What happened this morning?"

She gave him a beseeching glance. "My brother told me over breakfast that he had developed a tendré for Lady Violet. That if I wanted to marry the man of my choosing, I would have to help him gain Violet's hand in marriage."

Michael glanced over to see her expression of pain. "I take it you accepted the bargain?"

"I didn't want to, and I didn't know what to say, especially after Alfred told me they had gone riding together in the park—"

"What's this?" Michael asked, stepping aside so she could enter the library first. The thick Aubusson carpeting covering the floor seemed to swallow their words and the sound of their footsteps.

"I was as surprised as you," she said. "She didn't say a word about it to me. But she did spend an inordinate amount of time with him at the Everly *soirée* a few nights ago, and they danced the first waltz last night."

His thoughts going to the Reading House gardens, Michael remembered how his attention had been entirely on Helena. But there had been a couple kissing only a moment before he proposed marriage. "I may have seen them in the gardens," he murmured, his attention on the fireplace. No fire had been set, but the room was warm enough given the sunshine that streamed in from the two windows. "But I had no idea of his regard for her," he added before he inhaled softly. "Perhaps Aunt Katherine knew," he suggested.

Amelia shook her head. "She probably wouldn't have allowed it, sir. She's not at all fond of Weston. Very few are since his return from his Grand Tour."

Michael chuckled as he motioned for her to take a seat in one of the upholstered chairs near the fireplace. "Perhaps he will be a different person after all this," he mused, his attention going to the door. "Ah, here she is," he added, waving for Violet to join them.

"Is everything all right?" Violet asked, her eyes rounding at seeing Amelia. "Oh, dear. What's happened?"

"I bring good news," Amelia said with a brilliant smile. She quickly sobered upon hearing the marquess clearing his throat. "And not so good news."

Violet's gaze darted between the two of them. "Weston gave his permission for you to wed Philip," she stated, her face lighting up with her delight.

"Indeed," Amelia said. "You don't seemed surprised."

"I am not," Violet replied with a shrug. After their discussion in the gardens the night before, she was sure Alfred had changed his opinion of Philip. "So... what's the bad news?"

Michael indicated she should take a seat as Browning entered with the tea tray. "Will you see to serving first?" he asked. "Might make the news a little less bad."

"Of course," Violet replied, leaning forward to prepare the cups. Once the butler had taken his leave, she said, "Now, what's this about bad news?" She handed Amelia a cup of tea and turned to prepare one for her father.

"Has the Duke of Weston been courting you?" Michael asked.

Having taken a sip of tea, Amelia choked and sputtered at hearing his direct query while Violet almost poured too much tea in his cup.

"Apologies. I find it's better not to beat around the bush," he said.

"It's fine, my lord," Amelia replied, lifting a napkin to her lips.

Violet handed him his cup and saucer, but didn't move to make one for herself. "I wouldn't say *courting* exactly," she finally said. "Although he has put voice to words suggesting he would like to. Last night. During the ball."

Michael and Amelia exchanged quick glances. "Oh?"

She nodded. "Did you know that until last night, he harbored the idea that you were his father?"

Michael noted Amelia's expression of surprise at

hearing Violet's query before his gaze settled on his daughter. "Philip may have mentioned it several years ago. After he completed university. Weston is not my son, though, if that's what you're asking."

"I told him he couldn't be," she stated. "I explained you had never returned to London after you left. I recalled the dates of your marriage and that of Philip's birth."

"In other words, you did the math?" he suggested.

Her gaze darted to Amelia. "I did. Was I wrong?"

He shook his head. "Of course not. Perhaps hearing it from Philip wasn't enough. Perhaps your explanation was more... acceptable. More convincing."

"Well, I didn't punch him, if that's what you're implying," she said.

He chuckled as he leaned forward and set his cup and saucer on the low table. "He could have simply refer-enced a copy of *Debrett's*," he murmured.

"Actually, he said he did," Violet said in a meek voice. "Despite never having met you, he really *wanted* to be your son."

Amelia inhaled softly, and Michael straightened in his chair. "Why do you suppose that was?"

Her attention on her tea, Amelia said, "If you had been our father instead Harcourt Sheppard, you wouldn't be asking that question," she claimed.

"Amelia," Violet scolded softly.

"Everyone thinks my brother is a pompous, arro-gant... *arse*, excuse my French—"

"You're excused," Michael murmured.

"—but he's a fraction of how arrogant Father could be. He probably learned it from *his* father, but he truly believed he would live forever. That he was entitled to it. That it was his birthright," she explained. "Had he lived five-hundred years ago, he would have declared himself king of... of whatever England was back then," she stammered. "But Alfred... he didn't use to be like that. Not until he went to university. Ever since his return from his Grand Tour, he's been behaving as if he has to live up to the expectation that he is his father's son," she continued. "He's not like that with me, though," she added. "At least, not usually."

"What do you mean?" Violet asked.

"He's rather pleasant, really. We talk easily. He finally hired a secretary to help with all the papers. But he knows he needs a helpmate, too, and I do believe once he has a wife, he won't be so prone to arrogance."

Michael sighed. "So... when he comes asking permission to court you, Violet, what shall I say?" he asked, his attention on his daughter.

Violet allowed an exaggerated sigh. "He won't," she replied.

"Why ever not? You think he's so arrogant he won't think it necessary to ask me?" he asked in alarm.

"He won't because he doesn't know you're my father."

"*What*?" Michael was halfway out of his chair before he scoffed and settled back into it. "How can that be?"

Amelia gasped as her attention darted about the room. "Oh, dear. This is all my fault," she said as her eyes widened. "I've never introduced you to him," she said softly. "I mean, I did, but not *properly*."

"No one has," Violet said.

"However, I have mentioned to him that Duchess Katherine was your aunt," Amelia claimed.

"You were never properly introduced?" her father repeated slowly. "By anyone else?"

"No," she affirmed, giving Amelia a brief glance.

"He never asked to *be* introduced to you," Amelia said in her own defense. "And I certainly wasn't going to subject you to him if he couldn't behave civilly towards you."

"And I appreciated that," Violet said with a watery grin.

When he noticed Violet's lower lip began trembling, Michael furrowed a brow. "What is it?"

Violet blinked back tears. "When he learns I am Philip's sister... I think he shall be very angry with me." She turned to Amelia. "And with you. He'll think we were keeping it from him... playing him... deliberately. That I was trying to bamboozle him so he would agree to allow Philip to marry you." She paused and let out a *'huff'* as she settled back in her chair. "Which I was." This last was said in a whisper.

Michael angled his head to one side. "So... you *don't* wish to be courted by him?"

Rolling her eyes, Violet sighed as tears streamed down her face. "But I think I do," she whimpered.

Amelia inhaled sharply. "Oh! Then it's all set. Surely

he'll overlook your relationship to Philip, and it will all be fine," she gushed. "You'll be my sister!"

Clearing his throat, Michael turned to Violet and said, "I might be tempted to encourage you to continue your Season in the hopes that some other young man would discover how perfect you would be as his wife, but..." He winced. "If he *is* who you wish to be courted by, then I will of course allow it. You would be a duchess." He arched a brow. "In all honesty, I have a stake in this, too."

Violet furrowed a blonde brow. "What sort of stake?"

"I proposed marriage to Helena last night," he replied. "Again."

Violet sat up, excitement showing on her face.

"And?" she prompted.

"She's given me a provisional yes," he hedged.

"Provisional?" Amelia repeated.

He turned his attention on Amelia. "Your mother won't marry me until you and your brother are settled."

"Oh, dear," Violet murmured softly.

Amelia shook her head. "This will all be fine," she said with a wave of her hand. She took a breath and let it out in a *'whoosh'*.

"How can you say that?" Violet asked in dismay.

"If we must, Philip and I can always elope in Scotland. But if Alfred is the least bit wise, he'll realize he should have asked that you be properly introduced to him. It will be his loss if he plays the fool and doesn't realize you are the perfect duchess for him," she reasoned.

Violet and her father exchanged quick glances.

"So... who's going to introduce us?"

Amelia brightened. "I am," she said. She stood, which had Michael struggling to come to his feet. "Right now."

Violet reluctantly stood and shook out her skirts. "How about in an hour? I'll need a few minutes to change my gown," she said. "And we'll need a means of transportation."

"Take your time. I'll order the other coach be made ready," Michael said. "Since Philip hasn't yet returned from Weston Hall."

Amelia dipped a curtsy when Michael bowed and left the library. She turned to Violet and took her hand in hers. "Come along. Let us see what we can find to make you even more irresistible," she said. "Alfred won't know what's what, and you'll have him eating out of your hand in no time."

Violet rolled her eyes but followed her best friend out of the library.

A half-hour later, they were in the Fenwick traveling coach and on their way to Weston Hall.

CHAPTER 30
A DISASTROUS INTRODUCTION TO A DUKE

half-hour later, Weston Hall

Moving to stand at the Weston House study door, Pritchard straightened and inhaled deeply before he knocked. The 'come' called out by the man on the other side sounded surprisingly calm. Perhaps he was still in the good mood brought about by the Earl of Crawford. The young man had departed only a few minutes earlier, a huge grin lighting his face as he took his leave.

Pritchard gingerly opened the door. "Your Grace, the ladies Amelia and Violet have paid a call and wish a moment of your time."

Alfred pushed back from his desk and stood. He quickly straightened his coats and moved a hand to his throat, feeling for the knot in his cravat. Determining it wasn't hopelessly crushed, he regarded the butler with a pleasant expression. "Send them in," he ordered.

Obviously surprised by Alfred's manner, Pritchard

nodded and made his way to the vestibule. "His Grace will see you now," he said, turning to lead them to the study.

"I know the way, Pritchard," Amelia said, rolling her eyes when only Violet could see.

"Very well," the butler replied, obviously disappointed he wouldn't be paying witness to whatever the girls were about to do. Lady Violet seemed especially nervous while Amelia was behaving in her usual cheerful manner.

He watched the two curtsying before the door shut, and he moved on towards the back of the house.

"*L*adies," Alfred said as he moved to take Violet's gloved hand to his lips. "To what do I owe this most welcome visit?" he asked, holding onto her hand a moment longer than was necessary.

Amelia opened her mouth to respond and quickly closed it, apparently shocked by her brother's behavior.

"Good afternoon, Your Grace," Violet said, deciding calling him 'Weston' wouldn't be appropriate with Amelia present. "I wish to apologize again for having left the ball before our second dance last night."

Alfred allowed a shrug. "Oh, there is no need to apologize, my lady," he said. "I do hope your aunt is feeling better?"

"I'm not yet sure. I'll be paying a call on her when I

leave here," she explained. She turned and lifted her eyebrows as if to prompt Amelia to say something.

"Might you have a moment for us?" Amelia asked.

"Of course. Please... uh, have a seat," he offered, moving to pull another chair in front of his desk.

"Oh, this won't take long," his sister said. "After our discussion over breakfast this morning, it occurred to me that I never *properly* introduced Lady Violet to you."

Alfred's gaze darted from his sister to Violet. "Well, I'm sure that's not exactly correct," he countered. His eyes widened slightly. "You *are* the Duchess of Pendleton's niece, are you not?"

Violet nodded. "Grand niece," she said. "On my father's side."

"Lady Violet Cummings, may I have the honor of introducing you to Alfred, Duke of Weston?" Amelia asked in a voice filled with pride.

"It is my honor," Alfred countered before he suddenly sobered. "Cummings, did you say?"

Amelia continued as if he hadn't spoken. "She is the only daughter of the—"

"The Marquess of Fenwick," he finished, his expression darkening. For a moment, he thought the floor was about to open up beneath him.

"Yes," Amelia affirmed, grinning.

"Crawford's sister," he added, his gaze still squarely on Violet. For the first time, he realized she possessed the same eyes as her brother. The same blonde hair.

How had he missed their resemblance before now?

"Indeed," Amelia said, nodding happily.

"Leave us," he ordered, his attention turning to his sister.

"What?" she responded, her happy countenance turning to one of confusion.

"You heard me. Get out." He punctuated his order with a finger aimed at the door.

Amelia gave Violet a beseeching glance and slowly made her way out of the study. "I'll be right out here when you're finished," she said.

Violet nodded and turned to face the duke. "Your Grace, I wish to—"

"You had every opportunity to tell me of your relationship to Fenwick when we were discussing him last night," he said, his voice straining with his attempt to control his temper.

How could this be happening? He had spent nearly an hour with Crawford going over arrangements for his sister's betrothal to the heir to the Fenwick marquessate, and *nothing* had been said about Violet being his sister.

Worse, he had spent time with her in the Reading House gardens the night before speaking of his belief that the current marquess was really his father.

Not once had she mentioned her relationship to Fenwick.

Not once had she explained how it was she knew wedding dates and birthdates.

No wonder she knew so much about Fenwick. So much about Crawford!

"You've been playing me for a fool," he accused.

"No, Weston, I didn't tell you because I didn't wish for you to know," she blurted.

Taken aback by her admission, Alfred stared at her for several moments. "So... what? Your subterfuge was *deliberate*?"

"It wasn't like that," she argued. "I assure you—"

"What else could it be? You thought to trick me? To... to what? Make a fool of me?"

"No, Weston. It wasn't like that—"

"You will address me as 'Your Grace'," he stated, his eyes blazing.

Violet inhaled sharply as her eyes brightened with unshed tears. "Your Grace, I didn't wish for your good opinion of me to change because of your past differences with my brother," she argued.

"Oh, so you know about the fight we had at university?" he spat out.

"I only learned of it—"

"*Enough*," he said, stomping a booted foot so hard, Violet jumped back in fright.

Her lower lip trembling, she stared at him in disbelief. "Please, Your Grace, do not deprive your sister of the man she loves," she whispered. "Not because of me, please."

His brows furrowing so he appeared as frightening as possible, he straightened. "I will do as I must," he countered. "Take your leave, and never again set foot in Weston Hall."

Violet inhaled sharply as gray surrounded her vision. Sure she was about to faint, she stepped backward and managed a clumsy curtsy before she rushed out the door. Flattening herself against the adjacent wall, she let out the breath she'd been holding and slowly slid down until she was seated on the floor.

From where she had stood eavesdropping on the conversation, Amelia covered her mouth with both hands and rushed to Violet's side. "I'm so sorry," she whispered. "I truly thought everything would be all right." She struggled to lift Violet to her feet.

Tears streamed down her face as Violet quietly sobbed. "Oh, Amelia, it's not your fault," she said. "I'm the one who has made the mistake. I thought I could make it easier for you and Philip to court if I showed an interest in His Grace."

"Your efforts did not go unnoticed," Amelia replied. When the comment had Violet sobbing even harder, she sighed. "What you did for us that morning you went riding in the park, what you did at the Everly *soirée*, and then last night? It was rather generous of you," she said in a quiet voice.

"I only wished to help you and Philip," Violet said as she tried to swallow a sob. "I never expected to fall in love with your brother."

Amelia's eyes rounded as she stared at her best friend. "You've fallen in love with Alfred?" she asked in disbelief.

A sob interrupted Violet's response as she displayed a watery grin. "Rather stupid of me, wasn't it?" she replied, sniffling. Fishing a hanky from her pocket, she dabbed her cheeks.

How could she have ever imagined marriage to Alfred? When it would have required putting up with his pompous, arrogant manner? She wouldn't have been able to endure a lifetime with a man so unlikeable, so indifferent to others. Having to play-act her way through a lifetime with him might have her behaving as he did.

So why had his words cut so deeply? Why did her heart hurt so much?

"I must go. Your brother has forbidden me from ever stepping foot in Weston Hall," she said. "Good day."

Letting out a sound of disbelief, Amelia watched her friend depart and aimed a glare at the door to the study.

"Arrogant arse," she whispered before she marched up the stairs. "I'm telling Mother."

From the other side of the door to the study, Alfred leaned against the wood panel for support. His entire body still shook from the rage he had felt only moments before. He had shared his deepest secrets with a woman whom he was sure had somehow betrayed him.

However in the world could she claim to love him?

CHAPTER 31
TEA FOR TWO AND TWO
FOR TEA

eanwhile, in the parlor at Reading House
"You were positively incandescent at the ball last night," Constance Roderick, Marchioness of Reading, stated as she led Helena into her parlor. A maid followed, pushing a tea cart with all manner of biscuits and a cake.

"As were you," the duchess said, her face displaying the high color of a blush. "One might think Reading had had his way with you before the guests arrived," she teased. Her best friend had frequently hinted her husband was guilty of having the horn.

Constance tittered. "He tried, but I had to put him off until after the last guest left at three o'clock this morning." She rolled her eyes. "I'm always amazed at that man's appetite," she added in a whisper.

"But you're not complaining," Helena remarked.

"Never," the marchioness confirmed, grinning in

delight. "For a man who was a rake when I married him, I have always been surprised he has never employed a mistress."

"He would never," Helena stated. "He is so beholden to you, and he wouldn't have a decent horse racing stable if it weren't for you." The marchioness had taken over Randall Roderick's horse breeding program twenty-five years earlier, producing a dynasty of horses that were frequent winners on the racing circuit.

Constance gave her an assessing glance as she offered her a cup of tea. "Now, you really must tell me what's going on with you and this... Fenwick. Do I have that right? I don't recall ever hearing of him before I joined Duchess Katherine for tea a couple of days ago."

Helena accepted the tea and nodded. "You do." She deliberately held her cup so the ring on her finger was aimed in Constance's direction. She wiggled it, and grinned when the marchioness' eyes widened in wonder.

"Oh!" she exclaimed. "He's already proposed marriage?"

Inhaling to answer, Helena remembered Constance hadn't been living in Mayfair back when she and Michael had secretly courted. "For the second time," she said. "This time in your gardens. He's been waiting for me for thirty years." She tittered when she saw her hostess' expression of shock. "And I suppose I have been waiting for him."

Constance seemed especially pleased to learn *where* the proposal had taken place. "When will you marry?"

Her eyes rounded. "Oh, and what will you have him make with the treasure chest of jewels he discovered last night? He certainly won't be keeping them for himself, I should think."

Helena chuckled as she took a lemon biscuit from the plate Constance offered. "We'll marry as soon as Amelia and Weston are settled," she replied. "And I rather expect an emerald and amethyst parure is in my future. I'll have to have my modiste make me a suitable gown."

Constance sobered after her momentary delight at hearing about the parure. "It could be years before your children are married," she complained.

"It could, but..." She glanced around as if she feared eavesdroppers. "I spoke with Alfred prior to coming here, and he had just concluded the arrangements for Amelia's betrothal. She is marrying Fenwick's son, Philip."

"Lord Crawford," Constance said on a sigh. "Those two will be having the most beautiful children on the planet," she murmured.

Helena giggled. She hadn't even thought about grandchildren when she learned of the betrothal. "It's a relief, really. It seems Amelia and Crawford have been secretly courting for a year," she explained. "And despite the fact that she always has a chaperone, I've thought for some time my daughter was off gambling at cards. For the past few days, I've been so vexed trying to decide which I preferred."

"Crawford, surely," Constance remarked. "I do see Lady Amelia at the bookshop on Tuesdays," she murmured. "Nearly every week."

"In his company?" Helena asked, suspicious.

The marchioness furrowed a brow. "Come to think of it, I have seen him there, too, but not *with* her. He is always very amiable. Much like her," she stated. She turned to pull the plate of cake closer to her. "Has Weston started courting anyone?" she asked, using a large knife to slice the sugar-frosted confection. "I saw him waltzing with... with Lady Violet, was it?"

"Fenwick's daughter," Helena said, an elegant brow arching. "I rather doubt it was anything more than a dance, though. He doesn't seem inclined to court anyone. Duty and whatnot." Although she considered mentioning that she thought she might have seen him in the gardens the night before, she decided in favor of not mentioning it.

"His duty includes seeing to an heir," Constance remarked, placing a slice of cake on a plate and handing it to the duchess.

Helena accepted the plate with a nod. "We have discussed it," she murmured. "He was able to hire a secretary who I think will work out for him. That should free up some of his time. He doesn't get out of his study much, and it's made him quite cross."

Constance turned her attention back to the cake. "A daily ride in the park will help with that," she remarked, preparing a slice of cake for herself. "A bit of time on horseback always makes everyone happier."

Taking a bite of cake, Helena made a purring sound. "I am so hungry," she whispered, arching a suggestive brow.

Tittering in delight, Constance said, "It sounds as if a particular marquess hasn't forgotten how to please his woman."

"He has not," Helena affirmed. "However, living arrangements are going to be a bit awkward until Alfred is settled."

"Whatever you do, don't give up your apartments until you have another home to move into," Constance warned.

"Oh, I won't."

"And Fenwick can do what Torrington did all those years ago."

Helena displayed an expression of confusion before her face lit up. "Oh, yes. He simply moved into Adele's house and took it over, did he not?"

Constance nodded.

"Except, they didn't have grown children living there at the time," Helena reminded her. "And Weston Hall is Alfred's house. It's an entailed property of the dukedom."

"With Lady Amelia marrying Crawford, won't she be the mistress of Fenwick House?"

Helena nodded. "Indeed," she replied. "Fenwick says we can either move into our own townhouse or we can move to his country estate."

"Do you have a preference?"

Angling her head to one side, Helena said, "I recall only a week ago thinking that I wanted to move away from London, so yes, playing house at Fenwick Park would be my preference, I suppose."

Constance inhaled softly. "Country living for you?"

Helena winced. "I'm afraid my time in mourning only reinforced my desire to remove myself from the capital. I think the clean air would do me good. And I would have more opportunities to ride my horse." This last was said to placate her friend, whose expression conveyed her disappointment.

"We'd miss you," she whispered.

"Oh, I would come back on occasion," Helena replied. "For your balls, and to see the grandchildren," she said as a grin split her face.

Tittering, Constance offered her another slice of cake.

"Thank you, but no. I should be going. I rather imagine there's a wedding to plan, and I am curious as to what Crawford might have had to do to gain Weston's permission," she said.

Constance's eyes rounded. "Oh, yes. There was some sort of disagreement between the two of them at university," she remembered. "Did you ever discover what had them coming to blows?"

Helena shook her head. "Alfred never said, and I'm not sure I want to know. Probably just some schoolboy prank gone wrong." She noted how Constance stared at her and added, "You have boys. You know how it is."

The marchioness rolled her eyes and sighed. "You have the right of it," she admitted. She led Helena down to the vestibule. "I am glad you're out of mourning and that you finally have a man worthy of you," she said as her butler saw to helping Helena with her pelisse.

"Thank you. Do pay a call in a day or two. You have experience in weddings, I do not," Helena said before she took her leave of Reading House.

She ordered her driver to take her back to Weston Hall. Given the short distance in Park Lane, it didn't take long. She stepped out of the coach, surprised to see Pritchard holding the door open for her even before the driver could step down from his seat.

"What is it?" she asked, noting his look of fright.

"His Grace. He is... angry, I think. Lady Amelia has been asking for you, I believe because Lady Violet left here in tears only a few moments ago."

"Tears?" she repeated. "Did she and Amelia have a falling out?"

The butler shook his head. "It was Weston, Your Grace. Amelia and Violet went into the study together, both very happy. Amelia came out first, and when Lady Violet emerged, she was quite distraught. Unconsolable."

Helena allowed him to help her with her pelisse and gloves before she made her way to the study. As usual, the door was closed.

Knocking three times, she called out, "Alfred?"

"Go away."

Had it been any of the other days in the past six months, she might have heeded his command, but not on this day. She turned to Pritchard. "Bring tea and brandy. And cake, if there is any."

The butler hurried off as Helena regarded the door with a wince. Determining it wasn't bolted from the other side, she pushed down on the handle and entered the study.

She stopped short.

Papers were strewn about the floor, the ink pot lay on its side on the desk, its contents spreading over the blotter in an expanding black pool, and several items had been knocked off their shelves.

As for Alfred, he wasn't sitting behind the desk but rather in the leather sofa at one end of the study. He was practically doubled-over, his head hanging down almost between his knees.

Moving to rescue whatever was about to be covered with ink on the desk, Helena ignored his sound of protest. She righted the ink pot, did a quick perusal of the rest of the damage, and finally faced her only son.

For a moment, she was tempted to allow anger to get the better of her. Then she noticed how he shook. Tremors had his entire body vibrating.

She approached him and knelt, determined to look him in the eye. "Whatever is wrong?" she asked in a hoarse whisper. "What happened here?"

He didn't seem to hear her at first, his gaze on his mind's eye. When he finally acknowledged her existence, he cleared his throat. "It seems I have been playing a fool," he murmured.

"I can't imagine how," she replied, displaying an expression of confusion.

"Will you tell me the truth if I ask it of you?"

Taken aback, Helena considered the question before

she moved to sit next to him on the sofa. "If I know it, I will."

He struggled to clear his throat before he asked, "Is Fenwick my real father?"

Shocked into momentary silence by the query, Helena had to suppress the urge to scoff. "I sometimes wish he were, but he is not." She wasn't surprised when he turned to regard her with dark eyes, as if he suspected she might be lying. "You are Weston's son," she added.

He scrubbed his face with his hands, but didn't offer a response.

"Did you... did you wish to be?" she asked. "Fenwick's, I mean?"

He shook his head. "I thought I would know for sure when I met him last night," he murmured. "That I would look upon him and recognize some resemblance, no matter how remote."

"Why?"

Glancing over at her, confusion apparent on his face, he asked, "What do you mean?"

She lifted a shoulder. "Why did you wish to be Fenwick's son?"

He audibly sighed. "When I think about it now, it all seems so stupid of me," he whispered, running his fingers through his hair so it was left in spikes.

"But at one time, it must have been very important to you," she reasoned.

He nodded. "Crawford and I used to be the best of friends at school."

"Oh?" If he had ever mentioned it, she couldn't remember. Surely she would have, though, given the identity of Crawford's father. She only knew they had been involved in a row during their last year at university.

"He's a lot like Amelia. Always cheerful. Happy. He never seemed to have a care in the world," Alfred said in a quiet voice.

"They will make a perfect couple, then, won't they?" she responded, not sure what else to say.

"He apologized to me today. I was sure it was only because he wanted Amelia, but his overtures weren't forced. They weren't practiced," he said on a sigh. "He said he would like us to be friends again. Not just brothers by marriage."

"Did you accept his apology?" she asked gently.

Nodding, he said, "I thought of Amelia. If I didn't accept it, and if I didn't agree to their betrothal, she would never forgive me."

"You probably have that right," Helena said softly.

She sensed an undercurrent of something in his manner. Not anger, exactly, but certainly frustration. "Why is it you wanted Fenwick to be your father?"

Alfred leaned back on the sofa, slumping into the cushions. "Crawford's father wrote to him while we were at university. Frequently. I used to read those letters and think what it would be like to have a father so... *interested* in me, in what I was—"

"Weston *was* interested in you, darling—"

"He never wrote to me once," Alfred claimed.

Helena gave a start. "Probably because he knew I did. I always passed along his greetings when I wrote to you."

The reminder seemed to calm him a bit, but she still felt his body trembling where her hand rested on his shoulder.

"He never taught me what to do."

"He thought he was going to live forever," she countered. "A bit arrogant on his part, yes, but that's why he insisted you enjoy a long Grand Tour. So you'd have a chance to see as much of the world as you wanted to," she insisted. When he gave her a look of suspicion, as if he thought it was because Weston didn't want him in London, Helena added, "The Napoleonic Wars prevented him from taking a Grand Tour when he was your age."

"Really?" He scoffed and made an odd sound in his throat. "Did you know Fenwick has already put Crawford in charge of his marquessate? He's been seeing to it for almost a year. Acts as if it's just another class at university."

"I rather imagine the stakes are a bit higher than the marks he might earn in a class," she argued.

"He's had a professor of sorts in his father, though," Alfred countered. "Fenwick taught him what he needed to know."

"While you think you've had to learn how to run a dukedom all on your own," she said for him.

He grunted his agreement. "I feel as if I'll never know how to do it all."

"That's because you won't," she stated, making it sound as if it was nothing of which to be concerned.

When he turned and regarded her in disbelief, she lifted a shoulder. "Why do you think Weston insisted he was going to live forever?" When she noted his questioning expression, she added, "It would take him that long to learn it all."

"Damnation," he muttered.

"You've taken the right step in hiring a secretary. You have a competent solicitor. You already know you can handle the ledgers. The invoices. The payments. Once you're married, you'll have a helpmate to see to the things you needn't worry about." When Alfred rolled his eyes, she was quick to add, "And speaking of marriage, I've accepted Fenwick's offer."

Alfred stared at her, but didn't say anything.

"Which means you'll get your wish in a manner of speaking, since he'll be your stepfather," she said, smiling for the first time since she entered the study. "However, I told him I wasn't going to marry him until you and Amelia were settled."

A groan erupted from her son.

About to rise from the sofa, Helena remembered Pritchard's comments when she returned from Reading House and settled back into the cushion. "Whatever did you say to Lady Violet to make her cry?"

He lifted his face to stare up at the ceiling. "I suppose Amelia told you?" he complained.

"I haven't seen Amelia since this morning."

"Fenwick?" he guessed.

"I haven't seen him since this morning, either," she claimed.

He sighed, the butler's name coming out as a quiet curse. "If I told you it was a misunderstanding, would that be enough?"

She regarded him with suspicion for a moment. "Probably not."

He gave her a quelling glance. "If I told you she was pretending an interest in me to keep me from learning about Amelia and Crawford's courting, would that be enough?"

This had Helena arching her brows. "Play-acting, you mean?" she said softly.

He nodded.

"Perhaps if I hadn't paid witness to the two of you in the gardens last night..." she whispered, letting the sentence trail off.

As she expected, Alfred's face reddened with his embarrassment. "You... you saw us?" he asked in surprise.

"Oh, so it *was* you in the hedgerows," she accused, a grin lighting her face.

"Mother!"

"I was sure I recognized the scent of your cologne," she said as she beamed in delight. She quickly sobered, though. "So I ask you again, whatever did you say to Lady Violet to make her cry?"

Alfred stared at her for a long time before he finally shook his head. "I told her to leave Weston Hall and to never come back."

Not sure what to say to her son, Helena stood from the sofa and made her way to the door. She was about to open it when she turned and said, "You should probably apologize. She's going to be your stepsister someday."

She didn't wait for him to reply before she opened the door to discover Pritchard standing on the other side of it with the tea tray.

Helping herself to a slice of cake, she stepped aside to allow him entry, and made her way to the stairs.

The cake was gone before she reached the landing.

CHAPTER 32
A SHOULDER TO CRY ON

eanwhile, at Fenwick House

Her eyes swollen and red from crying, Violet attempted a cheery attitude when Browning admitted her into the house.

"Your father requested your presence when it's convenient," the butler said as he saw to her gloves and pelisse.

Violet sniffled. "Where can I find him?"

"In the library." Browning's expression changed to one of concern. "Perhaps I should deliver some brandy with the tea?"

Sniffling again, she said, "Cake. Lots of cake," she countered, managing a watery grin before she headed for the stairs.

Barely past the open door to the study, she heard her brother call out to her. Sighing, she paused and retraced her steps.

"I wanted to thank you," Philip said, coming to his

feet. "For what you did for Amelia and me." He was on his way to join her at the door when he suddenly stopped. "Oh, dear God, what's happened?" he asked in alarm.

New tears began falling before Violet could respond, and he was quick to offer a handkerchief.

"Amelia properly introduced me to Weston," she said between sobs. "He was quite angry to learn I was your sister. He thinks I tried to... bamboozle him... that I was playing him for a fool. But I wasn't," she went on. "He has forbidden me from ever stepping into Weston House again."

"Damnation," Philip muttered. He shook his head. "When I left him... he was in the best of moods. Better than he usually was at school," he claimed.

"He was very glad to see me when Amelia and I went into his study, but... oh, Philip." More tears streamed down her face.

"Did you?" he asked, angling his head to one side. "Try to bamboozle him, I mean?"

She nodded and then shook her head in frustration. "Maybe at first," she admitted. "I only wanted to help Amelia," she whispered. "And you."

"What's this?"

The two looked back to see their father standing on the threshold.

"Weston," Philip replied. "When he learned Violet was my sister, he told her she is forbidden from entering Weston Hall," he explained.

Michael pulled his daughter into his arms and

rubbed her back with the flat of one hand. "I'd say it's not worth crying over, but I think there might be more to this than we know about," he said, his attention on his son.

"What do you mean?" Philip asked.

Violet glanced up at her father. She swallowed a sob. "I was right. When Amelia introduced me, he was angry. Frighteningly so."

Michael winced and patted her back. "He'll settle down," he said in a quiet voice.

"He hates me," Violet whimpered.

"He doesn't hate you. In fact..." Michael paused and arched a blonde brow before he chuckled softly. "Don't give it another thought."

"What?" she asked in confusion, only a moment before her brother asked the same question.

"We're going to have dinner together and stay in this evening," he replied, wincing when he remembered he had promised Helena he would be joining her at some point later that night.

"We are?" Philip asked.

"I didn't really wish to go to Brooks's just yet. We can play some billiards and eat cake to celebrate our betrothals," Michael continued. When he glanced down at Violet, he added, "Chin up, my darling daughter. A man is hard pressed to forget his first kiss."

Violet's brows furrowed as she glanced over at her brother.

"Well, it's true for me," Philip admitted with a shrug.

"I rather think it's the same for young ladies, wouldn't you say, Father?"

"Indeed," he replied, his gaze still directed on his daughter.

Violet's face displayed a rosy blush. "You mean I'll be stuck remembering it for the rest of my life?"

Michael chuckled softly. "Ah, so there *is* one to remember, is there?"

She winced. "I'm going up to the library," she stated, extracting herself from her father's hold.

"What's up there?" Philip asked.

"Cake. Lots of cake," she replied, hurrying to the stairs.

The men watched her go and waited until she had disappeared before Philip turned his attention on his father and asked, "Do you know something?"

Giving him a shrug, Michael said, "Maybe." After a paused, he added, "Give it a day, and I'll know for sure."

CHAPTER 33
REALIZATION DAWNS ON
A DUKE

*L**ater that night, Weston Hall dining room*

"Do you suppose he's been drinking brandy all afternoon?" Amelia asked, her attention on the piece of fish barely clinging to her fork.

Helena gave her daughter a quelling glance, her own gaze on her glass of wine. "There wasn't enough for more than a single glass in the decanter Pritchard took into the study earlier this afternoon," she said. "So I rather doubt it."

"Has he come out of the study since...?" Amelia dipped her head. "Since Violet did?"

Helena took a deep breath. "He has not." Her eyes widened. "Oh, dear." She stood from the table and rushed from the dining room.

Amelia watched her go. "Wait for me," she said, pushing away from the table at the same time a footman was attempting to deliver the next course.

Ignoring her daughter's plea, Helena hurried to the

study, bursting in without knocking to discover Alfred still on the sofa where she had left him. He was no longer seated, though, but was sprawled out so his head was at one end and only one leg was up on the sofa. His eyes were hidden by an arm he had draped over them.

"Alfred?"

He moved his arm from in front of his eyes. "What is it?"

Helena took a deep breath of relief. "Dinner is served," she said, moving closer to regard him with worry.

He stared up at her. "I'm not hungry."

Amelia appeared in the doorway. "You will be in the middle of the night, and then it won't be edible," she said, her fists moving to her hips as she let out a '*huff*'.

"I'm not speaking to you," he stated, once again covering his eyes with his arm.

"Don't be like this, Alfred," Helena said softly.

"What? Miserable?" he countered sarcastically. "It has become my status quo," he added on a sigh.

"It doesn't have to be," Helena whispered.

"Especially when there is someone out there who loves you," Amelia added.

Helena inhaled sharply, her attention turning to her daughter. She was about to ask if Violet was who she meant, but Amelia gave her head a quick shake.

"I am not speaking to you," he repeated. "Please, you two. Leave me in peace."

Helena sighed. "Are you *sure* you won't have something to eat? I can have a tray—"

"I ate all the biscuits and all the cake Pritchard brought," he said on an exaggerated sigh. "Trust me when I tell you I am not hungry."

"Perhaps you would be more comfortable in your bed," she suggested.

"Probably," he agreed.

Helena leaned down and placed a kiss on the top of his head. "I love you, darling. Even if you are a stubborn, arrogant man," she said on a long sigh. Without a look back, she straightened and took her leave of the study.

Amelia watched her go.

"Are you still there?" Alfred asked.

"I thought you weren't speaking to me."

"I'm not." There was a pause before he asked, "Did she truly, do you think? Or was it all a ruse to play me? So I'd give Crawford permission to marry you?"

Giving a start, Amelia scoffed. "She did love you, you idiot. Probably still does, even though she shouldn't."

He jerked and struggled to sit up. "Get out," he ordered.

Amelia shoved her arms down her sides, spun on her heel, and marched out of the study, pulling the door closed as she did so. The resulting *slam* startled Alfred, and he cursed softly. Rising from the sofa, he left the study as if in a daze, slowly climbing the stairs.

For several hours, the image of Violet's stunned expression replayed itself in his mind's eye over and over. He knew he had hurt her with his accusation. He had wanted to for those moments after learning she was Crawford's sister.

She had betrayed him, had she not?

She had withheld information from him when he had been so free with his.

He had told her his deepest secret—and in the process, made himself sound like a fool.

So why did his thoughts of her always go to the kiss they had shared in the gardens? To the way her body felt beneath his questing hand? To the way she had spoken with him when they were on the bench. Her words gentle.

Curious.

Not condescending.

Once he was in his bedchamber, he threw the bolt and made his way to the bed. He undressed without thinking about it, not even bothering to ring for his valet. When he was down to his smalls, he was about to remove them when he noticed his arousal.

Scoffing, he climbed onto the bed and lay back. How could his body betray him so?

How could it not?

From the time he had left the ball the night before until his sister had introduced Violet in his study, he had imagined a life with Lady Violet. Imagined her waking him in the mornings with a kiss to his cheek. Imagined her sitting across from him whilst he ate his breakfast. Imagined them admiring a tank of fish in his study as the creatures swam about in circles. Imagined her serving him tea in the late afternoon. Imagined her taking his member in hand as they dressed for dinner, her deft fingers teasing him into a quick and pleasurable release, and him doing the same for her until she cried out his name and clung to him for support, kissing and murmuring words of love and affection.

He hadn't even imagined what might happen over dinner or later, when it was time to retire, when he took his rigid cock in hand and brought himself to a quick release. The sensation wasn't nearly as satisfying as the one he had imagined with Violet. Nothing about his life was as satisfying as what he had imagined with her.

I never expected to fall in love with your brother.

She *had* been pretending. At least at first. He knew that now. But when had her feelings changed?

During the *soirée*? She seemed truly interested in him that evening.

During their ride in the park? If she was false with him, he certainly hadn't detected any falsity in her manner.

At the ball?

He remembered how excited he had been upon seeing her in the crowded ballroom. How she had watched him descend the stairs, her gaze locked onto his.

Perhaps it was when they kissed. Or when they were almost discovered—or were discovered, since his mother seemed to have guessed it was them in the gardens?

Surely it was before they spoke at length about his desire to be Fenwick's son. She would have had every right to be annoyed at hearing his suppositions. Every right to scold him for his beliefs given what she knew.

Instead, she had given him thoughtful responses. Given him every reason he couldn't be Fenwick's son.

Every reason he couldn't be her brother.

He suddenly sat up on the bed, his eyes blinking several times from the gaslight above the bed. The candle lamp on the nightstand had gone out at some point, and a quick glance at the clock on the mantel showed it was past two o'clock.

His heart beating a tattoo in his chest, he struggled to determine what had him waking so suddenly.

Violet.

Her words on the bench. So insistent he couldn't be Fenwick's son. He covered his face with his hands.

If he *had* been Fenwick's son, then she would be his sister. They couldn't be together as he had imagined, and she knew it.

"She loves me," he murmured out loud. He winced when the reminder of what he had said to her came to mind. Winced again upon remembering her look of distress. Groaned at the thought of the tears he had caused.

"I *am* a damned fool," he murmured.

Coming to his feet, he quickly dressed.

CHAPTER 34
GROVELING DOES A
DUKE GOOD

n hour later, Fenwick House

After waking no fewer than three servants with his request for a means of traveling to Fenwick House in the wee hours of the morning, Alfred opted to ride his horse. "I cannot wait for the coach," he told the groom, who had mentioned it would take twenty minutes or more to hitch up the horses. "I'll take Mouse."

The groom had seen to saddling his walker, and while he was doing so, Alfred spent the time reviewing the other horses in the stable. "I don't recognize this one," he said, holding up a lantern. "Or maybe I do," he added, his brows furrowing when he was sure it was Violet's walker, George.

"That would be the Marquess of Fenwick's mount, Your Grace. He rode it here late last night. Like you, he didn't want to bother with a coach to only go a half-mile."

Alfred gave a start. "Fenwick is here? At Weston Hall?"

"Indeed, Your Grace. Seems the duchess was expecting him."

For a moment, Alfred considered heading back into the house. The thought of waking the marquess—or worse, interrupting whatever it was he and his mother were doing in her apartments—had him changing his mind.

He could request an audience with Fenwick once he had determined if there would even be a reason to do so.

The bracing chill in the air helped keep him awake as he rode Mouse south in Park Lane. The ride also allowed him to rehearse what he would say once he was granted entry into Fenwick House.

He didn't want an audience of servants garbed in dressing gowns as he made his intentions known to Violet.

He wanted to speak with her in private.

Securing the reins around the wrought iron fence in front of the Fenwick townhouse, he looked up to discover a light still on in a third-story window.

A light framing the silhouette of someone looking out.

In the dark, he couldn't make out who it was who saw him, but his nervousness grew as he approached the front door. Lifting the boar's head knocker, he pounded it several times, wincing as he imagined who it might awaken.

He was about to pound it against the blue painted door again, but the sound of a bolt being thrown stilled his movements.

The door opened to reveal a butler wearing a night cap. He was wrapped in a dark robe and displayed an expression of fright.

"Pardon my late arrival, but I am the Duke of Weston, and I'm here to... I wish to be taken to Lady Violet," he stammered, holding out a calling card he remembered to fish from his waistcoat pocket at the last minute.

His eyes widening, the butler glanced at the card before he stepped back to open the door wider.

"If you'll wait, Your Grace, I'll see if—"

"I wish to be taken to her right away," he insisted using his most commanding voice. Although he might not have learned anything about running a dukedom from his father, he had certainly learned how to sound like a duke when the circumstances required it.

"Your Grace," the servant acknowledged, lifting a candle lamp from a nearby shelf. "If you'll follow me."

Several gaslit sconces along the main hall's walls were low lit for the night, their flames casting long shadows of the marble busts mounted on caryatids positioned between doors.

The marble floor led to a central stairway, and although he wanted to climb the steps two at a time, Alfred forced himself to follow the butler at his slower pace. "Is Crawford in residence?" he asked in a whisper.

"He is, Your Grace, although he has been abed for several

hours." The butler stopped in front of the only door with a sliver of light spilling from its base. Gingerly knocking, he stepped aside when Alfred motioned with his hand to move.

"Thank you. You're dismissed."

His expression conveying his uncertainty, the butler finally nodded and made his way towards the servants' stairs at the back of the house.

When the door opened, Alfred stood and stared.

*D*ressed in a night rail and a dressing robe, Violet was tempted to call out that she wasn't receiving any callers when Browning's familiar knock sounded at her bedchamber door. When no words followed, though, she grew curious.

Whatever would her father think when he discovered Alfred, Duke of Weston, had paid a call in the middle of the night?

She opened the door a few inches, and when she realized Alfred was alone, she said, "Your Grace." Habit had her dipping a curtsy, although she clutched her dressing gown more tightly around her, which meant her hand wasn't available for him.

Whatever would have Alfred coming to Fenwick House at this time of the night? Having seen the duke's arrival on Mouse from her window only moments earlier —someone riding horseback in Park Lane at almost three o'clock in the morning was enough to have her peeking out her window—she managed to keep an impassive expression on her face as she studied his dark features.

Although she usually found him quite handsome, his eyes seemed deeper set, his face was flushed from the cold, and he seemed unsteady on his feet.

"Your hair is so long," he commented.

Violet blinked. Not sure what to say, she merely stared at him.

"May I come in?"

Realizing it best no other servants see him hovering about in the corridor, she stepped aside. She closed the door when he was fully in the bedchamber, his gaze not on his surroundings but on her.

"I made a terrible mistake earlier today," he blurted. "And I wish to apologize."

Not expecting to hear such words from him, Violet gave a start. "Oh?" was all she could think to say.

"I'm in pursuit of a duchess, you see, and I am not as clever as you," he stated.

Once again, Violet didn't know how to respond to such an odd comment, so she merely stared up at him.

From the haunted look in his eyes, she knew he had struggled with trying to sleep. He was impeccably dressed, however, which had her thinking he might have come from his club.

But on horseback? No gentleman rode a horse to his club. Besides, he didn't smell of cheroot smoke, nor of liquor.

"I didn't sort it until an hour ago," he added before he rolled his eyes. "I can be rather thick at times."

Her mouth about to drop open, Violet forced it to remain shut until she said, "Sort... *what* exactly?"

"Why it was you didn't tell me about Fenwick being your father. Crawford being your brother."

Violet's gaze darted to the side, and she allowed her confusion to show when she realized she was unable to follow his reasoning. Then, all at once, she understood what he was trying to say. "If you *had* known... if we *had* been properly introduced...?"

"Oh, God," he murmured, his eyes rounding. "I wouldn't have spent time with you at the Everly's *soirée*. I wouldn't have joined you for that ride in the park. I... I wouldn't have danced with you, or..." One of his hands went to his forehead. "I wouldn't have taken you to the gardens and kissed you, and fallen in love with you," he finally said, a pained expression crossing his face. "I would have been miserable for the rest of my life."

Violet inhaled softly and allowed a wan grin to show. "If you really had been my brother, I would not have minded, I suppose," she said in a quiet voice.

"But?" he prompted, taking one of her hands to his lips.

Her eyes widened before her grin did. "I much prefer that you are not." Noting his expectant expression, she added, "Well, especially if you've fallen in love with me."

He chuckled and then quickly sobered. "I want nothing more than to hold you. To kiss you. To spend the rest of the night with you, despite the scandal it's likely to cause," he whispered, one of his hands moving to the side of her head. His fingers slid through her blonde waves to the back of her neck, and he pulled her close enough so he could kiss her on the forehead and then on her lips.

At some point in the middle of the kiss, Violet pressed her soft body against the front of his and moaned softly. When he ended the kiss, pulled away, and looked at her as if he was about to ask why, she whispered, "Well, I'm not about to send you away in the middle of the night."

His face split into a brilliant grin. "Oh, good, because I fear I'm about to fall asleep," he warned. "And if I was forced to ride home, I wouldn't be able to stay awake, and I rather doubt Mouse knows the way home."

Violet tried hard to keep a smirk from showing. "Depressed duke discovered sound asleep on horseback, wandering the streets of Mayfair," she teased.

"Something like that," he whispered.

"So... you're here to play house then?"

"Play house?" he repeated.

Violet grinned as she undid the buttons of his top coat and waistcoat and untied his cravat. Once she had the length of silk unwound from around his neck and folded neatly over the back of a chair, she removed his coats and did the same with them.

When Violet moved to clutch the sides of his shirt, Alfred stilled her hands with his own. "That's enough for now," he whispered, pulling her back into his arms. He kissed her again and then led her to the bed. "As much as I want to make love to you, and I do, my love, I think it's best we wait."

Violet seemed torn for a moment but finally shrugged. "Then lie down before you fall down," she said, giving him a nudge on his chest.

He did as she instructed, grinning when she moved to the end of the bed and pulled his boots from his feet. A moment later, the gas light above was extinguished, bed linens covered most of his body, and her soft body, still encased in the night rail, was tucked against the side of his. Wrapping an arm behind her shoulders, he pulled her farther atop him, until her head was in the small of his shoulder and one of her legs was draped over one of his. "This bed is just right," he whispered. "More so because you're in it with me," he added.

Violet purred her response.

"Are you comfortable?"

"I am," she said, using a finger to trace the whorls of dark hair that showed where his shirt was open at the top.

"Good night, my love."

"Good night, Your Grace," she whispered.

"Weston," he murmured. "Better yet, Alfred, if you'd like, or—"

"Fred, when we're in a bed," she murmured on a soft titter.

He chuckled softly. The room was silent for a time before he suddenly gave a start.

"What is it?" she asked, lifting her head from his shoulder.

"I forgot to propose marriage," he said.

She giggled and dropped her head back down. "You can do it in the morning."

He let out a breath of frustration. "I told you I wasn't very clever."

"Go to sleep, Fred."

A moment later, and they were both sound asleep.

CHAPTER 35
A MORNING REVEALS A MOTIVE

*F*ive *hours later, in the duchess' apartments at Weston Hall*

"I do like this bed," Michael murmured, sitting on the edge of it so he could pull on his stockings.

"Would you say that if I wasn't in it?" Helena asked, amusement evident in her voice.

He glanced over to where she sat brushing her dark hair at the dressing table. Only the moment before, he had helped her into a corset, a series of petticoats, and a blue day gown. "You're not in it now," he remarked.

She tittered as she pulled a ribbon from a drawer.

"Come tie my hair into a pony tail so we can go down to breakfast," she said. "I am starving."

"As am I, you minx," he said, taking the length of ribbon from her. "Making love to you is quite exhausting."

"It's mutual, I assure you," she countered, grinning when he leaned down to kiss her on the cheek.

Michael had the blue ribbon wrapped and tied into an even bow in only a moment.

"You did that as if you knew what you were doing," she said in wonder.

"I have a daughter," he reminded her.

"Doesn't she have a lady's maid?"

"She didn't when she was younger," he replied with a grin. He kissed the top of her head. "I just have to pull on my shoes and we can head down." He moved to a chair. "Are you quite sure you're all right with me joining you and your children for breakfast?"

Helena directed a look of surprise at him. "Well, of course. They both know we're to marry," she replied. "You'll be their stepfather very soon."

"You're quite sure Alfred was upset about what happened with Violet?"

Helena furrowed a brow. "He was. Stayed in his study for hours after it happened, and he didn't even join us for dinner."

"And you're sure there wasn't enough liquor in the study for him to get too drunk?"

"There was only enough for one glass," she assured him.

"Good," Michael said, straightening his coats before he offered her his arm.

"What do you mean by that?"

"The more miserable he is, the more likely he will be to do something about it." At seeing her look of confusion, he added, "I've been where he is. I remember it quite well."

"It wasn't your anger or stubbornness that led you to losing me," she reminded him.

"No, but that sense of loss—it hurt. It was painful. Almost unbearably so. Enough so I never wanted to experience it again."

Helena stared at him, remembering that day thirty years ago when they had both learned he couldn't marry her. "I remember it," she whispered. "What do you expect he's going to do, though?"

Michael chuckled as he opened the door for her. "If he hasn't already..." He paused upon seeing Pritchard in the corridor. The butler's attention wasn't on them but rather on an open door to the master suite.

"What is it, Pritchard?" Helena asked as they joined him.

"His Grace, Weston, hasn't returned, ma'am."

Helena exchanged a quick glance with Michael. "Returned?"

"He... he took his leave on a horse. In the middle of the night, Your Grace."

"Did he mention where he was going?" Michael asked, a wan grin appearing after a moment.

"He did not, my lord."

"Do you think he went off to Fenwick House and...?" Helena stopped, her mouth dropping open in shock.

"We could find out," Michael offered. "In fact, would you like to join me for breakfast at Fenwick House this morning? If Lady Amelia is up and about, she can join us, too."

"What's this?" Amelia asked, emerging from her

bedchamber farther down the corridor. Dressed in a day gown nearly the same color as her mother's, her resemblance to Helena was more noticeable than usual.

"We're going to Fenwick House for breakfast," Helena said. "Surprise your betrothed, shall we?"

Amelia giggled. "I certainly wouldn't object," she said. "And it will give Trimble more time with Mrs. Pritchard for her reading lesson," she added.

"Philip won't object, either," Michael said as he offered his other arm to her.

"I had the town coach made ready in the event you didn't wish to ride your horse home, my lord," Pritchard offered.

"Good thinking, Pritchard. It seems we're going to need it right now."

The four of them descended the stairs. Before they made it past the door to the breakfast parlor, Helena stopped and ducked in to grab a basket of breakfast rolls from the sideboard. Upon noticing her daughter's widened eyes, she said, "I'm starving, dear."

"As am I," Amelia replied, helping herself to one of the rolls.

The three took their leave of Weston Hall, a rather relieved Pritchard watching them go.

CHAPTER 36
CAUGHT IN THE ACT OF...
WHAT?

A half-hour later

Hidden behind that morning's issue of *The Times*, Philip was unaware of who stood on the breakfast parlor's threshold until she said, "Good morning, my love."

The newspaper dropped so quickly, it nearly took his plate with it. "Amelia," he said, quickly coming to his feet. He was about to ask what had her appearing at Fenwick House so early in the day when his father escorted the Duchess of Weston into the room.

"I've invited the entire family to join us for breakfast," Michael said as he held a chair for Helena.

"Future family, he means," Helena said as Philip saw to a chair for Amelia. A footman was quick to bring tea and coffee.

"I haven't yet seen Violet this morning," Philip murmured, his attention going to the door. "Does the entire future family include Weston?"

"It does, but I need to run upstairs and extend the invitation personally," his father said. He bent and kissed the duchess on her cheek before he headed for the door.

"Wait for me," she said, her skirts whirling about as she stood to follow him. "I'm going with you."

The two disappeared from the room as quickly as they had appeared.

Philip blinked, his gaze finally turning to Amelia. "What was that all about?"

She tittered, bursting with excitement over what she had been told in the coach on the way to the house. "My brother. He is *miserable* because he's in love with Violet, but he took exception to her being your sister, you see, and he thinks she deliberately withheld the information from him, but he didn't realize that if he *had* known she was related to you, he might not have had the opportunity to meet her, and therefore, he wouldn't have fallen in love with her."

Philip blinked again. "Oh." His brows furrowed. "Weston is upstairs?"

Amelia inhaled to answer and then scoffed. "Well, he had better be," she said, stirring a lump of sugar into her tea. "His horse is tied up to your fence out front."

It was Philip's turn to scoff. "I've been down here for nearly an hour. When—?"

"The middle of the night," she said in delight. "And the fact that he's *here* means Violet didn't send him away. Which means they have spent *half the night* together. Probably in the same bed. Isn't that *wonderful?*"

Not quite sure he agreed with her assessment, Philip

suddenly wished he had joined his father and the duchess. By now, they would have made it to the second floor and were about to discover if indeed his sister was in bed with Weston. "I suppose," he finally responded.

"This means we have a few minutes alone, if you'd like to have your way with me."

Philip was up and out of his chair in an instant, moving to pull her up and out of her chair. "God, I'm going to love being married to you," he said before he kissed her quite thoroughly.

"You're not going to do anything to harm him, I hope," Helena said as she and Michael climbed the stairs.

"Of course not," he replied. "He's going to be my stepson at the very least."

"And your son-in-law," she reminded him. "So... just a tongue lashing then?"

Michael paused at the top of the stairs and regarded her with a curious expression. "Why?"

She scoffed. "Well, surely he deserves to be *scolded*," she insisted.

"You're welcome to do that if you think it's necessary," he replied. When he noticed her troubled expression, he paused. "What is it?"

"Is it even legal?" she asked. "For your son to marry my daughter and my son to marry your daughter means...they'll be brothers and sisters."

Michael's brows drew together. "It's true. It wouldn't

be legal for in-laws to be marrying in-laws," he whispered. "So if this is going to work, they both have to marry at the same time."

Helena's eyes widened. "Oh," she murmured. "I suppose that can be arranged," she added, struggling to keep up with him when he resumed his trek to Violet's bedchamber. She nearly collided with him when he stopped in front of the door and she huffed. "If you're not going to hit him, or call him out, then why are we even up here?"

"So he can ask my permission to marry my daughter," he replied. "I wasn't here at the house when he arrived, remember?"

He was about to knock, but her hand intercepted his fist. "What if they're...?" Her eyes rounded, as if she was trying to hint at something. "Playing at being married?"

"They won't be," he stated. "I raised my daughter better than that."

Helena blinked, a look of guilt crossing her face. "Although I'd like to believe I raised my son better than that... I'm not really sure if he would be the *perfect gentleman* in a situation like this," she whispered hoarsely.

He gave her a quelling glance and was once again about to knock on the door when it suddenly opened.

"Hello, Your Grace, Hello, Father," Violet said in a quiet voice. She was dressed in a bright jonquil day gown, her hair already done up in a bun atop her head.

"'Morning. Is Weston with you?" Michael asked.

Violet backed up enough so her visitors could see the

bed. Alfred, snoring softly, was sound asleep. "He showed up at three o'clock this morning. Put voice to all sorts of explanations. Apologized profusely, and…" She shrugged. "Well, he fell asleep." She turned to the duchess. "I cannot decide if I should be happy or vexed."

"Happy, darling. Trust me on this," Helena whispered.

"Did he by chance propose marriage before he passed out?" Michael asked in a whisper.

"He mentioned he had forgotten to do so before he fell asleep, which has me thinking—"

"I will be doing so this morning," Alfred said in a groggy voice. "After I ask Lord Fenwick for his permission, of course." He sat up, his eyes widening at seeing who was at the door. "Mother? Lord Fenwick?"

"Alfred James Alexander George Sheppard," Helena said, her fists going to her hips.

"Oh, dear. I'm apparently in lots of trouble, my love," he murmured, his gaze going to Violet.

She giggled. "However could you tell?"

"My mother only addresses me with all my names when I am," he said, his attention still on Violet. "By the way, you look especially lovely this morning. Yellow is a good color on you."

"Thank you, Fred," she whispered, moving to kiss him on the head. "As much as I know you require more sleep, I think it best we get you dressed now. I do believe we're to join them downstairs for breakfast."

He reached up and kissed her. "Oh, if we must. Will you tie my cravat, my love?"

"I will," she assured him.

"Good God. They're already acting as if they're an old married couple," Michael said in a whisper only meant for Helena. From the glare Violet sent in his direction, he knew she had overheard him.

"That's because they are in love," Helena whispered. Her eyes rounded when the duke moved to get out of the bed, and she quickly turned away. While she hid her face with a hand pressed to the side of her face, Michael chuckled. "It's all right, my sweet. He's fully clothed," he said, as Alfred's stocking'd feet and pantaloon-covered legs appeared from beneath the bed linens. His shirt, although slightly rumpled, was open at the neckline to reveal a dusting of dark hair.

"He is?" Helena turned to stare as Violet expertly wrapped his cravat around his neck several times, evening the pleats as she did so. Then she tied the ends into a perfect mail coach knot. "I take it she used to do yours?"

"She did," Michael acknowledged. "When Thaddeus was unavailable. She can also fasten buttons faster than he can," he added, watching as Violet did so with the duke's waistcoat and top coat.

"Did she shave you, too?"

"Oh, God, no," Michael replied.

Helena tittered as she turned her attention back on her son. "How much did you have to grovel to convince this poor girl you were in love with her?"

Alfred turned his attention on his mother. "Not as

much as I should have had to," he replied. His gaze went to Violet. "Which is how I knew she loved me."

Violet tittered. "You were barely coherent, so I thought it best I give you the benefit of the doubt. Otherwise, you wouldn't still be here," she said, running a comb through his spiked hair until he was presentable. "Depressed duke discovered sound asleep on horseback, wandering the streets of Mayfair," she teased.

He chuckled. "Thank you, my love."

"You're welcome."

Michael wrapped an arm around Helena's waist and pulled her closer. "Should I give him my permission?" he asked.

Her eyes widening in delight, Helena said, "You had better." She suddenly sobered.

"What is it?" he asked.

"We left Amelia and Philip alone in the breakfast parlor," she said with worry.

Michael displayed a look of offense. "I raised my son to know better than to take advantage of a situation," he claimed. "Surely you raised your daughter the same?"

Her gaze darting to the side, Helena merely gave him a look of guilt.

The two headed down the stairs as fast as they could.

Five years later, Fenwick Park, Shropshire

"I absolutely adore this sunshine," Amelia said as she lay back on a blanket spread over the recently clipped lawn behind the Fenwick Park country house. The remains of a picnic luncheon were scattered about, and two empty wine bottles poked out from an open basket. A baby was sound asleep nearby, a thumb tucked into his mouth.

"I adore all these spring flowers," Violet said from where she sat on another blanket, one arm holding an infant girl while her four-year-old boy chased a flutterby. "Always did when I was growing up here."

"I adore hosting you," Helena said from where she lounged in a dark green day gown beneath an umbrella. A pair of emerald and amethyst earbobs decorated her earlobes, and a bracelet of the same gemstones was wrapped around one wrist. "All my sons and daughters and grandchildren under one roof. I wish you could all just move here so we would never have to travel to London."

"You'd miss it if you didn't go for at least part of the Season, Mother," Amelia commented.

"True," Helena admitted. "I do like seeing my friends, but the only time they're in Town these days is for the Season, so it works out, I suppose."

"I so appreciated your invitation to join you all this fortnight," Katherine, Duchess of Pendleton, said from where she sat holding a toddler. The oldest daughter of Philip and Amelia, Helen was sound asleep in her lap, apparently exhausted from her play with her cousins. "This is not the best time to be in Bath or in London, and Pendleton absolutely adores a good house party."

"Speaking of the duke, what's become of our men, do you suppose?" Amelia asked, lifting her head from the blanket to look around for any sign of them. They had been involved in a spirited game of croquet, but the mallets, now abandoned, were lined up near the last wicket.

"Either they're playing billiards, or they are sound asleep," Helena replied, grinning when the four-year-old boy slumped against her skirts and announced he was exhausted. "My money would be on sleep." She watched as the heir to the Weston dukedom slowly tipped to one side and was soon snoring softly in the grass. "Lord Bertram is finally asleep."

"You all know what that means," Katherine said, moving to stand despite the sleeping girl in her arms.

The other three women turned to stare at her. "What?" they asked in unison.

"We have a foursome. It's time to play cards," she said, motioning to the table a footman had set up nearby. "I promise I won't take all your pin money."

Knowing better than to try and beg off when it came to the duchess and her card games, the women all giggled as they struggled to stand and make their way to the card table. A footman had delivered a tray of lemonade and glasses and saw to setting them out for the ladies.

The reminder of cards had Helena grinning.

"What is it, Mother?" Amelia asked.

"To think, the entire time you were being secretly courted by Philip, I thought you were gambling at cards in a reading room," Helena remarked as Amelia took a seat at the table.

She scoffed. "I was never playing cards," she argued. "I was... playing coy with Crawford at the bookshop," she teased. A round of titters followed her claim before she indicated Katherine. "As I recall, it was Aunt Katherine who was playing cards while my brother was secretly courting Violet in his pursuit of a duchess," she complained. "Playing house with her in the gardens during the Reading ball." Her brows waggled with her words, and Violet scoffed.

"Playing with my heart, if you must know," she said, her color high, and not because of the afternoon sun.

"That's because I thought your father was going to be your chaperone that evening," Katherine said in her own defense. She shuffled the cards, turning her attention to Helena. "How was I to know Fenwick was playing house in the gardens with you?" she added with an arched brow.

The younger duchess blushed. "We weren't playing in the gardens," she argued. "We were playing in my bed…" She paused as three pairs of eyes widened and stared at her. "We were playing for keeps," she finished with a prim grim. "Now, it's my turn to deal, is it not?"

Katherine passed her the deck of cards. "What is it they say? You can't win if you don't play."

"Well, we're all winners now," Violet claimed.

"Oh?" Helena replied as she dealt the cards for whist.

"I think she means we all won our husband's hearts, Mother," Amelia said.

Helena nodded her agreement. "And they've won ours," she murmured.

CHAPTER 38
AUTHOR NOTES

*G*as lighting in 1844?

In 1792, William Murdoch, a Scottish inventor, equipped his home in Redruth, Cornwall with pipes that delivered coal gas to lamps, giving birth to "gas lighting". The coal gas combined with oxygen in the air to produce carbon dioxide, water vapor, heat and light. Although most homes in England didn't have gas lighting until the 1880s, Murdoch saw to gas lighting for the exterior and interior of the Manchester commissioner of police and the outside of James Watt's and Matthew Boulton's famous Soho Foundry steam engine works in Birmingham in 1797. Thirteen street lamps in Pall Mall followed in 1807, and by 1825, 215 miles of London's streets were lit by over 40,000 gas lights. Those who could afford to have their houses plumbed for gas did so, and soon the homes of the well-to-do enjoyed light at the turn of a dial or the pull of a chain.

In-laws marrying in-laws? Wasn't that illegal?

Actually, it was in England, at least after the Marriage Act of 1835. If a marriage had occurred prior to 1835, the marriage was not void, but it was voidable (should someone complain about it, the church's courts might annul the marriage). So how would the characters in this book get around such a rule in 1844? Marry at exactly the same time!

*Y*our Invitation!

Do you crave historical romance filled with passion and red hot chemistry?

Come join me and my author friends in the Facebook group, Historical Harlots, for exclusive giveaways, chats with amazing HistRom authors, raunchy shenanigans, and more!

https://www.facebook.com/groups/2102138599813601

ABOUT THE AUTHOR

A self-described nerd and lover of science, Linda Rae spent many years as a published technical writer specializing in 3D graphics workstations, software and 3D animation (her movie credits include SHREK and SHREK 2). Mythology, immortality, and ancient Greece have been lifelong interests.

A fan of action-adventure movies, she can frequently be found at the local cinema. Although she no longer has any tropical fish, she does follow the San Jose Sharks. She makes her home in Cody, Wyoming.

For more information:
www.lindaraesande.com
Sign up for Linda Rae's newsletter:
Regency Romance with a Twist
For articles on research and travels, read Linda's Rae blog:
Regency Romance with a Twist